My nose felt like a mashed potato sandwich, and now he was kicking the salami out of what was left of me. I tried to protest, but he didn't seem interested. Just as well, I couldn't get any sounds out of my battered head, nor could I squeeze a word in between the torrents of his curses.

He must have tired of thrashing me for I woke, apparently not too much later, to find the card table chair moved over beside my prostrate remains and the bruiser bodyguard of the late Madame Anna Poritzky Claddington seated thereon, his chin on his hand, his elbow on his thigh, Thinker-like. I didn't dream he had the apparatus for any rational thought, or we might not be in these relative positions. But he seemed to be studying me as though trying to place a particularly pesky mosquito.

When I opened my eyes, he grunted. "You're the lawyer's kid," he said. "What you sneaking 'round here for? Liable to get yourself hurt."

────────────── ★ ──────────────

"...another witty, engaging whodunit."

— Booklist

Forthcoming from Worldwide Mystery by
DAVID CHAMPION

EASY COME, EASY GO
TO DIE FOR

david ch

she d
for he

W♦RLDWIDE®

TORONTO • NEW YORK • LONDON
AMSTERDAM • PARIS • SYDNEY • HAMBURG
STOCKHOLM • ATHENS • TOKYO • MILAN
MADRID • WARSAW • BUDAPEST • AUCKLAND

SHE DIED FOR HER SINS

A Worldwide Mystery/January 2008

First published by Allen A. Knoll, Publishers.

ISBN-13: 978-0-373-26623-4
ISBN-10: 0-373-26623-5

Printed in U.S.A.

she died
for her sins

ONE

I TOOK THE CALL. Airhead, the secretary, knew better than to put preliminary calls through to Bomber. In his view the world's leading trial lawyer should not be bothered with details. Calling was the public defender assigned to defend one Inocencio Espinal in the Fourth of July murder of billionairess Anna Poritzky Claddington.

"The kid wants Bomber," he said. "I told him to work hard and save his money and maybe some day he could afford the best."

"Didn't he take your advice?"

"Oh, he's a piece of work. A little communist. Thinks he's entitled—his birthright as a human being. I told him that's not the system here, and it didn't work so hot in Russia. I further told him if the situation had been reversed, Bomber would be defending the doyen heiress of Chicago. Well, I made the call. I told him he was dreaming."

"I'm very much afraid he is," I said, "but I'll pass on your call to Bomber."

"Oh," he said just before I hung up, "there's one thing more."

"What's that?"

"I think he's innocent," he said, "not that that matters much. He gives you a pain where you can't reach it, nobody can stand him, but I don't think he shot her."

"Then I expect you'll get him off."

"Ha!" he said. "The evidence isn't defendant friendly."

"Okay, I'll talk to Bomber. If he's interested you can lay it all on him."

I went to the street corner to pick up the paper. There it was in screaming headlines (for a local Angelton, CA paper, it was screaming. It would have been understated for a tabloid).

HEIRESS MURDERED IN
BEACHFRONT MANSION
JULY 4 KILLING ROCKS COMMUNITY

Such was the hardening of our citizenry that it had to be noted the community could only get upset over certain murders. This was a doozie. The story was so bizarre I wouldn't have believed it if the background of the victim and her special mansion had not been common knowledge in Angelton, CA for decades.

A pretty young eastern European woman lands a wealthy husband in Chicago. He is old enough to be her grandfather, great grandfather in some cultures, but neither seemed to mind that. There wasn't time anyway, as he didn't live long enough after the marriage to be disappointed. Just long enough to get his estate in order and see that Anna Poritzky Claddington got the whole shootin' match. Some suspected foul play in his demise—though it wasn't all that untimely— he was eighty-six—she forty-one. She was also an aspiring amateur actress. Some said the grief she displayed at his death was her finest performance.

I think the lion's share of the corpus of the estate came from the corpses of animals old Claddington had slaughtered and packed for sale throughout this great carnivorous world of ours.

There was some fuss when old Claddington went to glory. Some distant relatives who had never seen the old man made some predictable noises about the significance of blood, but they were never covered in the blood of the lamb like old Claddington had been in the early days of his enterprise.

He may have been the inspiration for the cigarette ad showing a ninety-plus year old doddering gent at his wedding. His bride is a twenty-five year old blond bombshell. The caption: *They say she's after my money—like I care*.

But then things got loco, as the defendant would say. Anna got more eccentric by the day. Some said she was already "round the bend" when they married. I can see Claddington saying: Like I care. There isn't that much trick in winning a man. Anna Poritzky was a quick study in that regard. No one ever heard Mr. Claddington complain about her in their marriage of just under four years. Anna was heard to say she could have gotten a college degree in that time. She got a bigger payoff on this graduation instead.

So how did Anna Poritzky Claddington wind up murdered in Angelton, CA—in a mansion on the ocean's edge, two thousand miles from her home?

Rufus Claddington bought the forlorn thirty-five acre parcel on the ocean in Angelton sight unseen. In the early 1920s he got the thirty-five acres for less than a city lot in Chicago—and he had the kind of money if he'd made a mistake he wouldn't miss it.

Travel from Chicago to the Pacific Ocean was no piece of cake in the twenties—but Claddington had his own railroad car, which took the sting out of the trip. His first wife Eleanor and he fell in love with the site at first sight. It took them short of two years to build their dream mansion there.

When it was finished, Rufus and Eleanor Claddington came west every winter to take the sun and sea air of Angelton, until Eleanor died in 1961 at the age of 76. Rufus mourned her for four years until he met Anna Poritzky at a charity event at the Palmer House Hotel next to the El in Chicago. She was showing a scandalous amount of bosom for 1965. She told him such tales of love at first sight they would have stopped a senile buffalo in its tracks. After all, she was an aspiring actress. They were married in a fortnight. "Why wait?" she'd said, "Neither of us is getting any younger." He was eighty-two, she thirty-seven.

He'd only mentioned the California house casually and always with a starry look in his eye. She understood it had been a love nest for Rufus and his first wife, Eleanor. After she died, he never went back. A caretaker kept it from going to rack and ruin, though it had been badly neglected.

When Rufus died, Anna surveyed all his holdings and began asking questions about the Angelton house. When she determined the state of the California estate through photographs and telephone conversations with the caretaker, she decided something had to be done. She sent one of Rufus's trusted functionaries out with instructions to bring the place to Claddington standards and to hire a respectable staff and tell them to keep it squeaky clean—lawns and plants mani-cured (her word) and fresh cut flowers put in the foyer daily. They were to understand she might drop in to surprise them at any time and they had to be ready—on pain of losing their jobs.

For thirty-two years, two generations of staff acceded to her wishes and she never once darkened the door. Until July 4, 2001. Then she came, surprising one and all. She was a spry seventy-two. She had never remarried. What was the point? She was so rich. She liked the attention of men, but men themselves had long since started to bore her.

Then while the fireworks were popping in the Angelton sky over the ocean—she had a primo view—someone popped her. The police theory of communist against capitalist seemed a little thin to me. Inocencio Espinal, the accused, had appar-ently just met her that day. He was twenty-three years old, without any traceable crime on his clean record. Not even a parking ticket.

The thing that might have appealed to Bomber about the case was notoriety. He would never publicly admit to seeking publicity, but in my time with him I have developed my suspicions. And too, it would give him another battle to match wits with Webster Arlington Grainger III: the Weller County DA, county seat: Angelton, CA. We've had cases all over the country: Pennsylvania, New Jersey, North Carolina, you name it, but there is something sweet about a win right at home. Bomber knows he gets Web's goat and he loves to do it.

Webster Arlington Grainger III was as old money as the III behind his name advertises.

Bomber was definitely new money—the kind of guy the Graingers wouldn't let in the country club. I don't think that was ever far from Bomber's mind.

There was, of course, the possibility that the court wouldn't appoint him. But if Bomber let it be known he was available and the young Inocencio said he wanted him, I thought it could easily be arranged.

Webster Arlington Grainger III would scream bloody murder, of course, he was very vain about his won-lost record.

I collected my thoughts and my notes and knocked on his door—not too softly, not too loudly, but just right, the way he liked it.

TWO

"COME IN, COME IN!" Bomber said with his patented impatience. He always felt his time was extremely valuable—even when it wasn't.

I was surprised to see him seated at his desk amid his floor-to-ceiling celebrity photos lovingly signed to the great Bombinski—reading the Angelton paper and all the gory, aforementioned details.

"You r-reading the Claddington st-story?"

"Yeah," he said. "Imagine—in little Angelton."

"I g-got a call from the p-public defender."

"Yeah, what's he want?"

"The accused," I said pointing to the paper, "w-wants you."

"Does, eh?" he said, going back to his paper. He didn't seem surprised, so I suppose Bonnie, the aforementioned airhead secretary, told him about the call. I waited.

"What do you know about it?" he asked.

"Only what I r-read in the p-papers."

Bomber still caused me to stutter. No one else did, but no one else was like Bomber.

"What the public defender say?"

"Said the kid was a c-communist and n-nobody liked him—and he thought he w-was innocent."

"Bum rap, eh?"

I shrugged.

"Any theories?"

I shook my head.

"You think this…" he consulted the paper before him "…this Anna Whats-her-name was nuts or crazy like a fox?"

I shook my head and tightened my lips to keep the stammering words from coming out.

"Shall we find out?"

"Up to you."

"Yes, of course it's up to me," he said, not looking up—I could suppose he was doing that to seem less scary to me—minimize the stutter. The thought of him considering my feelings only aggravated my malady. "I'm just asking for your opinion."

"He h-h-has n-no m-money," I blurted, pointing at the paper.

"Ah, yes, lucre," he said, rubbing his chin and letting his hand drift to his neck where his fingers massaged it, pulling the skin back in sort of a do-it-yourself facelift. "Afraid your check won't clear?"

That startled me. If my piddly check wouldn't clear the enterprise would be at rock bottom and we'd all be living in his Chinese red Bentley motor car—a tad under three hundred grand, retail. I shook my head.

"Only thinking of me, eh? Well I think there's enough in the smokehouse to see us through the winter. Pro bono you know, the backbone of the legal profession."

That elicited from me a circumspect laugh. Pro Bomber was more like it. He didn't do a lot of free work on low profile cases—no chasing the country to find some innocent, penniless sap accused of hit and run.

He looked straight at me and said, "I know what you're thinking. You're thinking I only do pro bono in cases liable to garner notoriety." He paused to check out his celebrity walls as if to see if one might be missing. "No need to apologize for it. Keeping your name before the public eye is no disgrace. What good's it do being the best if no one knows about it? In this game you're only as good as your last victory."

"This might not be a v-victory," I said.

"Might not," he said, "with some run-of-the-mill lawyer. No. I like the smell of this one. Something about it—too pat. Communist, eh? They still exist? Is he Chinese?"

"Mexican," I said.

"Yess," he hissed softly, "Espinal isn't too Chinese a name, is it? Not Cuban either. So where do these Mexican communists turn for inspiration?"

"C-Castro."

"So he pops a flamboyant capitalist. Why? To bring glory to the cause? Make Castro Oil sit up and take notice? Southern California's version of Lee Harvey Oswald? Could be. He said he was innocent too, I recall. Ah, don't they all."

"He's guilty, you w-want t-to get him off?"

"Depends."

"On what?"

"Motive, history, rationale, result to mankind. Whole bushel of things."

"You mean if he did m-man-k-kind a service, it'd b-be okay?"

"In some circumstances. Murdering Hitler for example."

"Hitler? S-She's H-Hitler?"

"No, no, my boy. Not that I'm aware of anyway, I'm just giving you examples. But, as I said, the whole thing seems too pat. Why don't you talk to the lad—this budding Karl Marx, or Joe Stalin as the case may be. Get a feel for it. No commitments, of course. Just gathering information for consideration. Oh, and on your way out tell Bonnie I want to see her, will you?"

He must have known that irked me. I liked to keep my social intercourse with Bonnie V. Doone at a minimum. She

had this way of demeaning me, masked with overt, over-
board cheerfulness.

"Oh, hi, Cuddles," she said when I passed through
Bomber's door and approached her desk.

"He wants to see you," I intoned, deadpan.

"Sure thing, Sweet Meat. And you have a lovely day while
you're at it."

THREE

THE LOCKUP IN ANGELTON was unaccustomed to housing violent criminals. Angelton was a peaceful place on the ocean, the ideal only recently spoiled by the occasional violent act—a man offing his wife for infidelity—young bucks blowing away their ex-girlfriends and/or their suitors, a couple of kids hiring a hit on their rich parents.

I'm afraid Inocencio's appearance was not conducive to romancing a jury. I know it is politically incorrect to generalize from appearances, but the accused murderer Inocencio Espinal, *looked* like a murderer. The first impressions may not be the best ones, but they are often the most memorable. To put it bluntly, he looked like he had just picked himself up after a barroom brawl. His hair was disheveled, not so much from a lack of combing as from deliberately combing it to make it look disheveled. His eyes like coals on fire tore right through you and left everything they touched singed. Other than that he was short and slightly built and walked with a macho attitude, even in handcuffs.

The first thing he said was, "You not the Bomber."

Something about the way he said it blocked my customary tact, and it wasn't his heavily accented English. "That's very observant of you," I said. "Go to the head of the class."

"I want the Bomber," Inocencio said like a kid wailing for his mama.

"And I'm here to see if Bomber wants you."

"I am framed," he said. "Now is a trick. Who are you?"

"I'm Tod Hanson, Bomber's flunky, and, incidentally, his son. Anyone who wants Bomber, and believe me, you aren't the only one, has to go through me. Movie stars, supermodels, mountain men, politicians, celebrities—and you." I shrugged, "Just the way it is, Inocencio."

"You say Señor Espinal."

"Sure thing, Señor," I said, unable to keep that touch of derision out of my voice.

Sitting across from the accused in the lockup was always an unsettling experience. I was out, he was in. If nothing else, that put me in the driver's seat. In the case of Señor Espinal that only exacerbated the resentment. Of course there was always a touch of subliminal fear that there would be a snafu and I wouldn't get out.

"I no talk to you."

"So you are better than…" and I ticked off the big names Bomber had represented. It didn't move him.

"No," he said, "equal!"

I stared at him awhile—he stared back. There was more animosity in *his* stare. I was beginning to think if I had a couple more minutes with him, I'd be ready to frame him too.

"Okay," I said, "it's up to you. I can promise you, the best attorney in the country, perhaps the world, is not going to come crawling to a dirty little communist to represent him for nothing."

He started to lunge at me, but the restraining hand of a guard appeared on his shoulder and he sank back. "You want to tell me your story, I'll pass it on to Bomber."

"I see a trick."

"No you don't," I snapped. Not my nature, there was just something impossible about him. "You think Bomber would waste his time—my time—if he weren't considering the case?"

"Why no?"

"Because he doesn't operate that way. Every two-bit criminal wants Bomber, hardly any get him. I'm sorry to tell you, this time you play it his way or take a public defender."

"I lose—is no time to learn my name."

"Ah yes. government lawyers versus capitalist pigs. I notice the jam you're in, you are turning to the capitalist pig."

He didn't like me. That was easy enough to tell. But it was also easy for him to tell I was speaking logic. Not so easy to swallow, though, given as he was to macho swagger. "So it comes down to this, comrade, do you want to bend your precious principles with a shot at the best trial lawyer there is, or do you want to make do with someone who won't have time to learn your name?"

"I…"

"That's not a real question—everyone knows your name."

"Come the revolution we all be equal. We all have Bomber."

"Wrong again. There will only be more public defenders. If you think a guy like Bomber could work for the government, you know less about Bomber than I thought."

He pouted and seeing Inocencio pout was a sight to behold. He got this long, horrid face, and his breathing accelerated like a monkey in heat. I let him cool down.

"So—while I'm here, don't you want to lay it on me on the chance Bomber will be swayed? He won't be unless you tell me your tale—that I can promise you."

Now he was seething. I let him. I figured I owed it to Bomber to give the kid every opportunity—to vindicate himself, or to hang himself. He seemed bent on doing the latter.

He shook his head, "Capitalist system works against me," he said.

"Okay," I said, "brood about that. I'll tell Bomber if he won't come to see you, you want to forget it." I stood up.

"Good luck, comrade," I said with a grim smile. I turned to let the guard unlock the door. I did it slowly, waiting for the word I knew would come.

"Stop!" he said. I turned.

"Decided to play it Bomber's way?" I asked, "until the revolution?"

"No *me gusta* unsmart man."

"Then maybe Bomber is not for you."

He grunted at excruciating length. "What you want to know?"

"Your story from the beginning. Far back as you can remember."

"Mexico," he said—"small place cerca…close to Guadalajara. Nineteen niños. I am eight or nine."

"How's that?"

"My old brother, Leo, he teaches me to drive. Rich man in big car on my side of road. I have to turn quick—we go down a hill—my brother he is killed. That makes me eight."

"How old were you?"

"Twelve."

"A little young to drive isn't it? That legal in Mexico?"

"Is no trouble. There were no cops on the road."

"Ah, but there are, aren't there? You can't escape the cops."

"No."

"That what started your police prejudice?"

"Everywhere I go I see injustice. People with better garbage than we have to eat. This is not a fair world."

"Amen to that, brother. So how does shooting your boss bring justice?"

"I don't shoot nobody."

"Who did?"

"I see nothing. I watch, how you say?…fireworks. I don't hear nothing. First I know about anything, two guys jump me and throw me to the ground."

"You have a gun?"

"No."

"That didn't bother them?"

"They say I throw it in the ocean."

"Why do you think they picked on you?"

"They don't like my ideas for us to all be the same. They like slaves for this *estupida* woman who is rich. She has a huge house and many workers but she never see it. Loco! Every one of us working for her has more smart than her. She have the money."

"I suppose you didn't keep those ideas to yourself?"

"I'm not a liar. I say like I think."

"Did you express those thoughts when they hired you?"

"I'm not *estupido*."

"How did you get the job?"

"My cousin works here. He go back to Mexico for his family. He gets me the job."

"How long have you been there?"

"Only nine months. I work somewhere else before that for six years. Hector is there seven years and never see the Señora. It is my luck—I'm there not even a year and she comes out and someone kills her."

"Who?"

He shook his head. "I don't *know*."

"Someone who worked for her?"

He shook his head. "Everybody like her. Paid good and work easy."

"Do you include yourself in everybody who thought she was a saint?"

He looked at me as though I had kicked him in the solar plexus while he was asleep. "Not me," he said. "She is a capitalist pig. Too much money."

"I thought you said she paid good wages."

"She good to slaves. The slaves say so. But her money next to what she pays…poof!" He blew a sound over pyramided fingers.

"Did you have any conversation with Señora, Señor?"

"She sees me she says I am look strong. Then she ask if I so strong as I look."

"Very nice," I said, "what did you say?"

"I say yes," he preened proudly.

"What were your duties?"

"Keeping the garden up—in case she ever come back."

"By the way, where did you get your name? Innocence—"

"Inocencio. My mother name all boys for popes. She was very religious crazy. In communism we know—Marx said it—religion is a drug to keep the poor from killing the rich. All the world is for the rich. Poor Mexican families praise churches, name niños Leo, Pius, Pablo, Juan, Inocencio, like that."

"All right, let's focus on July fourth—the night of the murder. Who was at the house?"

"I was," he said. For a guy who believed in equality he had a quaint way of putting himself first. "The Señora, Anna—"

"Did you call her Anna to her face?"

"She no better than me. Me they call *Inocencio*."

"Who else?"

"Secretary, Netta, her lawyer, Señor Tushman. They come from Chicago, and her chauffeur, a black man she call Peter. There is Dick, works for Tushman, and me, the gardener— Carlos the house hombre, and Larry the boss. We could do without him. Anna have this grande hombre for her body-guard—maybe her *novio*."

"Okay, where were you all when she got shot?"

"Anna was in back on the grass to be watching fireworks. In the sky up the beach it was a good place to see. Others they were around Anna, but that lawyer's amigo was inside."

"Like an entourage?" I said. "So how far are you from Anna?"

"Like twenty-five or thirty feet."

"See any guns?"

He paused just a second too long. "No," he said.

"Okay, any messages for Bomber before I go?"

"I didn't do nothing, I be, how you say? Framed up."

I didn't much care whether Bomber took the case or not, but if he did, I hoped my exposure to Comrade Espinal would be kept to a minimum.

FOUR

ATTORNEY MORELY TUSHMAN was nothing if not fastidious. Pearl cuff links, monogrammed silk shirts, impeccable tailoring, perfectly creased trousers to his pinstripe suit. His up-to-date maroon silk tie with scrambled blue patterns looked like it had been tied for an upscale necktie advertisement. Not only was he perfectly tonsorial, but his person was scrubbed and polished to a fare-thee-well, and one look told you you were in the presence of a man who was never short of breath and never broke into a sweat. I called him the victim of the perfectly controlled life—a glass of wine with dinner, no more, very few fats and sugars, no smoking, and probably some light exercise. But I'd bet the ranch he never wrote any music or indulged in pastimes the rest of us would consider fun.

He called on Bomber after calling to request an audience—the day I interviewed Inocencio in jail. His quick knowledge of my jailhouse interview showed us what important sources he had in our provincial coastal community, truly dazzling for an outsider. Attorney Tushman sat facing Bomber across his disheveled desk. I was on the side wall in my usual place out of harm's way and backed by Bomber's celebrity photo testimonials. Modesty was not in Bomber's arsenal. Modesty was a quality reserved for old money. Towering ego was Bomber's weakness. But it was also part of his charm—if charm was indeed a word you could use to describe my father. I'd call him a curmudgeon if I weren't so weary of overpraising him. Oh, I don't mean to suggest he was without charm in some circumstances. Like in the presence of young, pretty women, where his ham-handed attempts at some mysteriously based *savoir faire* always made me cringe. I mean look who he hired—Bonnie Doone, old sweet meat herself.

Morely Tushman was such a perfect human specimen, I expected Bomber to skin him alive. Instead Bomber was courteous, and his mood was congenial.

Morely Tushman began, "I'm Morely Tushman, counsel for the late Madame Anna Poritzky Claddington. As you may know I accompanied her at her insistence to California for her first—and as it turned out—only visit. I have been her attorney for most of my professional life, having begun in a venerable Chicago firm where I soon became a partner."

Bomber nodded with an inquisitive eye that said, get to the point of your visit. To Tushman's credit, he sensed that.

"Well," he said, "this is a terrible thing that's happened to Madame."

I could hear Bomber's thoughts—death is a terrible thing. Calling murder terrible is an understatement.

"And I did love Madame. She was eccentric, that's a given, but she could be endearing, and she did so much for so many people, I'd just hate to have the victim become the criminal as so often happens in these cases."

"You have reason to believe that could happen?"

"No, certainly not. It's just—I would hate to have the case turn on her. Your possible involvement does concern me. What should be a small town tragedy will be a national story if you get involved. I would beseech you, Bomber, to consider distancing yourself from this hopeless cause."

"I'm sure, Counselor," Bomber said, "you wouldn't want the wrong person convicted of any crime."

"Certainly not," he said, "but with all due respect, I was there. I saw it happen. Inocencio shot her."

"But why would he do that?"

He looked at Bomber as though a screw had slipped loose. "Why? For his political beliefs. Whatever. You can't refute so many eyewitnesses. Look, I know about right to counsel and all that, and I'm not arguing the boy's right to *some* counsel. But *you?*" He shook his head. "I'm just afraid with your notoriety the case will become a circus—no, no, I'm not disparaging your work, but you will admit to a certain flamboyance—"

"In defense of my clients, of course."

"Yes, of course, nonetheless it is there. I'm just afraid the result might be to ridicule Madame—"

"Madame? Why do you keep calling her Madame?"

"Well, sir," he shifted in his seat, the toes of his shining black wing-tipped shoes rising and falling, "she preferred it."

"She did, huh? Damn silly pretension, wouldn't you say?"

If you could improve on Attorney Tushman's perfect posture, he did, or maybe it was just his attitude that stiffened. "It's what she wanted, and it was a harmless indulgence."

"So you indulged her?"

"We all did."

"Was there any basis in her background to call her Madame?"

"Well, she was European."

"European?"

"Yes sir."

"Royalty?"

"Oh, no, sir. Very humble beginnings."

Bomber registered the information in his memory bank. I knew he'd do something with it later.

I must give credit to Bomber beyond the obvious. He didn't have a need to make debating points in his office. For instance he could easily have said "Eyewitnesses? Surely as an attorney you realize all the wrongs committed in the name of eyewitnesses! Eyewitnesses are notoriously unreliable—emotions wanting to believe something, mistaken identity, psychological factors." But he didn't say boo. And as I think about it, the eyewitness doubts can hardly be buttressed in this case because we were told there were so many of them.

"I trust District Attorney Grainger put you up to this?"

"Oh, no," he answered, too quickly, as though the D.A. had impressed him with the need to keep his name out of it. "Your name came up, that's all," Tushman said, a little ruffled. "I think the district attorney said you might be involved—he volunteered it—with some trepidation I might add, and though I have not personally seen you in action, I have heard enough to know he's not just whistling Dixie. So I just thought I'd come to see you—it's a pleasure for me to meet you—something to tell my grandchildren about—if I had any." Tushman was using the flattery approach. You couldn't go wrong using that on Bomber.

"Do you think we could assemble all the principals in place so I can get a better idea?" Bomber asked Tushman.

"I don't think we could do that."

"Could alter my decision to take the case."

Morely Tushman eyed Bomber warily. "I'll see what I can do," he said.

"Oh, by the way," Bomber asked as though an afterthought—"Do you have any word on the murder weapon?"

"Everyone saw Inocencio throw it in the ocean."

"So someone retrieved it?"

"Ah, no…with all the excitement no one thought to…"

"So they dredged the ocean?"

"I…think that is in the works."

"Well, you tell D.A. Web if he waits long enough the weapon will surely walk into his office—"

Morely Tushman didn't think that was funny.

Bomber stood abruptly and leaned across his desk to shake

it would take me over ten years to save that much money, assuming I found a way to zero out my living expenses.

He parked in the lot of the jail which was at the base of the mountain where it starts to turn seriously upward.

When we met the prisoner inside the room set aside for lawyer conferences, I realized how seriously I had over-estimated the good sense of this guy who needs to convince Bomber he is a worthy cause. In spite of my earlier en-treaties, this is the way he opened the conversation:

"I tell you right now, I don't compromise my belief to get you for a lawyer. I do not becoming capitalist."

"You know the difference between principles and preju-dices?" Bomber asked. "What part of your anatomy houses a brain, if any? Social graces? Ever heard of 'em? Let me tell you something, kid, you want to beat this rap or not? I can tell you how to drive the last nail in your coffin of conviction, and this is mouthing off and making everybody hate you. Guilty, likeable guys often get off. O.J. Simpson's a good example. Not guilty guys who are despised often get nailed."

"That is not right."

"Well, thank *you,* Dr. Einstein. I couldn't agree with you more. But you want to catch on how to make it through this vale of tears with a minimum hassle you make nice."

"I will not be what I am not."

"Why not? What you are is no great shakes. It's not as though you were going to your death stoutly insisting the earth is round, rotates on its axis around the sun. That might be worth dying for. But just being a horse's ass for the sake of being a horse's ass?" Bomber threw out his arms, palms up.

"Capitalism is like flat earth. Communism *is* the earth going around the sun."

"That more important to you than staying out of jail?"

"Do not give up what you believe," the kid actually

sounded like he was lecturing Bomber. It was kind of fun. Then he drove it home, "you do not give up what you believe."

"Perhaps not," Bomber said, "but I'm not being accused of a murder I know I didn't commit."

The kid looked at Bomber with a sudden new respect. He actually said he didn't commit the crime, did he believe it? "How do you know I don't do it?" he said with a quiet hopefulness, yet not fully able to accept the good news.

"Just a hunch," Bomber said. "Based on my quick assessment of you from what Tod told me and meeting you—you don't have any baloney in you. You may be a horse's ass, but *sans* baloney. Don't get cocky. My hunches are far from a guarantee of success. If I can impart the hunches to the jury and make them their own, we might have something. No jury will swallow any hunch about a guy they don't like. So why don't you tell me what happened, Kid?"

"Don't call me Kid," he said sharply.

Bomber glared at him. "You're a slow learner, aren't you?"

"No," he said with a chip on his shoulder.

"Well, see if you can grasp this lesson. If I am to represent you, I am in charge. You don't tell me what to do in any fashion, on any subject. I want to call you Kid, Kid is what I call you, Kid. If I want to tell the jury you're a scumbag, that's what I tell 'em. Any sass from you and as your generation says, you're history. You catch onto that—Kid?"

Now it was the kid's turn to stare. "You cannot make fun of me," he said.

"Oh, no? Watch me," Bomber said. "So tell me what happened out there on the Fourth of July. And misleading me will hurt you far more than it will help you."

"I don't know what is happening. I watch fireworks and suddenly two guys throw me on ground. I yell, 'Hey!' and kick and punch, but they push me down."

"Where were you standing? Where was the victim?"

"I am standing away. They together near…the *Madame*," he pronounced this last with an inflection in a falsetto voice. He continued in the same voice—"'Call her Madame,' that lawyer say—not *The* Madame because that sound like a puta boss." He shook his head in wondrous disgust. "Is enough to turn Rush Limbaugh to communist."

"You worked for the Madame nine months, correct?" Bomber agreed it was amusingly pretentious to call the eastern European peasant *Madame*.

"Yeah."

"What did you think of your employer?"

"Loca. She is crazy. The money she wastes on that house could feed half of Russia."

"Given to hyperbole, are we?" Bomber asked, but I don't think Inocencio understood.

"How did you get along with your coworkers?" Bomber asked.

"The slaves? I don't like them and they don't like me," he said.

"Your prejudices are showing again," Bomber said. "Too bad we can't spring you and make you a poster boy for altruism. Unhappily you didn't practice what you preached, so we can kiss goodbye any benefit we could have gotten were you anything more than a blowhard."

Inocencio glared at Bomber. Bomber glared back for a few moments, then stood up—Inocencio's eyes darted around the room. He was scared. "So, you take my case?" he asked, his eyes unstoppable.

"Not impossible," Bomber said, "I've got a few more questions to ask of others first—but by all means if you can't brook the uncertainty, get yourself another boy—no hard feelings—" Bomber tightened his stare: "None at all."

When we got back to the office, Bomber told Bonnie Doone to track down Lawyer Tushman and put him through when she did.

I hoped that was something she could handle.

SIX

MORELY TUSHMAN, attorney-at-law, chief counsel for the late
Anna Poritzky Claddington—Madame Anna Poritzky Claddington, if you please, agreed to Bomber's request for a reenactment of the crime scene.

We all gathered at Madame Anna Poritzky Claddington's
Angelton house, and very nice digs they were indeed. The
main house was decorated in quiet good taste of a southwest
shucks-we're-just-cowboys flavor—rich cowboys. It was the
handiwork of the late Mr. Claddington's first wife. The scene
of the crime—the backyard—was simple and impeccable.
Inocencio must have been good at his job. The backyard was
a tiny percent of the grounds in Inocencio's care. The sprawl-
ing acreage began at the street and rose up a hill overlooking
the beach. It butted up against public sand on the east, not too
far from a group of volleyball nets. The sand beach was flat.
The Claddington property rose from the flatness like a
pregnant belly and was an easy visual demarcation of public
to private property. Landscaping on the hill was an orderly
menagerie of tall pine trees, eucalyptus and palms mainly,
plus lower growing flowering shrubs: oleander, hibiscus, cal-
leandra, and bougainvillea. This eclectic planting gave the
public face of the property a random yet orderly appearance.
It was a nice blend into the cemetery farther east, which was
ringed with pines. I was told pines were not endemic to
Angelton and were planted by those who suffered a nostalgia
for the eastern landscape.

The grass behind the house ran on a little beyond both sides of the house giving the feel of a yard limited by the boundaries of neighbors. But there were no boundaries anywhere near the house—the nearest being the Pacific Ocean out back. There was a terra cotta tile patio behind the house, then the grass began and went to where the property dropped off to the Pacific Ocean.

It was enough of a fall out back so anyone walking beyond the water's edge could not see the house. The steepness of the drop formed a natural barrier to casual intruders, though Bomber noted there really was nothing keeping a determined killer out. At the edge of the grass above the water was an iron railing and fence, but it was only three feet high. The depth of the grass from patio to railing was perhaps forty feet.

The whole contingent was there. The secretary, Netta, a prudish looking woman who had kissed her libido goodbye sometime ago; a sweet and gentle black chauffeur, Peter; a gorilla bodyguard, Harley; Dick, the young-looking middle-aged blonde gofer for Morely Tushman; and we had Larry and Carlos, Inocencio's coworkers on the scene to round out the dramatis personae.

I was elected to play Anna's part, and it was a creepy feeling sitting there on the chaise with my legs up, looking up the beach to where the fireworks had been on July fourth.

Bomber tried to interview the Chicago bunch but Lawyer Tushman cut him off. "Sorry, Bomber, we agreed to a reenactment, that's all. No questions."

It became quickly apparent Morely Tushman was circling the wagons.

"Surely you have nothing to hide," Bomber said, needling him needlessly.

"You know better than that, Counselor. We certainly have nothing to hide, but that wouldn't prevent some misstatement or some innocent comment that a clever counselor such as yourself could twist seventeen ways to Sunday in court. All right," he said with a command clap of his hands, "places everyone."

Bomber had secured the permission of the court to have Inocencio brought to the scene. The D.A. sent a representative from his staff to observe. I got the feeling Webster Arlington Grainger III wanted to minimize his contact with Bomber, who so often outrageously embarrassed him. Besides that he had opposed what he termed a "charade," but irregular as it was, Bomber-in the service of truth and justice—got a judge to go along with him. The deputy sheriff brought Inocencio to the backyard, the prisoner in handcuffs and hobbling in leg irons.

Chairs were placed beside the chaise, and one by one the Chicago contingent took their places. The foot of the chaise lounge was up to the railing with the Madame being far enough back to see over it. On either side of her feet—up at the railing—were the bodyguard, and chauffeur to her left, Morely Tushman to her right. Just behind Morely Tushman was Netta, Anna's secretary. It seems Dick was suffering from an unnamed malady and spent the Fourth on the living room couch under a blanket.

I could see from my position on the lounge that Inocencio had a clear shot at my head, which was where Anna got it.

"I think Inocencio was closer," Tushman said. Inocencio said he was not. Carlos and Larry were in the house preparing refreshments, but Carlos said he saw Inocencio standing just about where he was.

"All right," Bomber said, taking command. "Does anyone see any discrepancy from what you remember—your position, or anyone else's?"

"We do not," Morely Tushman answered quickly.

"I appreciate your desire to answer for everyone, but per-

ceptions do change from person to person, and I'd like to poll
the troops, if you don't mind."

"I mind," Tushman said, "I'll do it for you—" he turned to
address the seated troops. "Anyone remember anything different in the positions of July fourth?"

"Oh my," Bomber said. "How delicately put."

"I don't think anyone here has any doubts."

"Then let me ask them."

Morely Tushman shook his head. "Not our deal. Now are
you going to take his case?"

Bomber smiled. "I was about to abandon it, but you just
changed my mind."

Tushman turned scarlet. "Me?"

"Your tireless stonewalling makes me think you have
something to hide."

"That's ridiculous."

"Perhaps," Bomber said. "That's just one more question for
a jury."

Attorney Morely Tushman was not a happy man when he
tromped out of the backyard and into the house to set up his
garrison there. Before the deputy took Inocencio back to the
lockup, Bomber asked him, "How sure are you of where you
were when the boys jumped on you?"

"Sure," he said, irked that his word had been questioned.
"But what matter does it make? I don't shoot her from thirty
feet—I don't shoot her from twenty feet."

"And when did you find out someone shot her?"

"The first I know anything is when those guys they jump
on me."

"When did you throw your gun over the railing?"

"I didn't have a gun." He shook his head vehemently.

"All right. Do you still want me to represent you?"

"Yes!" he shouted as though Bomber were hard of hearing.

"Have you thought how you would pay me?"

Inocencio was as stunned as though he had been hit between the eyes with a sledgehammer. "Pay?" he frowned. "The court pays…no?"

"The court will pay the public defender—as under any respectable communist system. I am an unreconstructed capitalist operating under a famously successful capitalist system."

"But that makes no sense," Inocencio said. "I have no money. The state should supply me with an attorney."

"And they will, just not with me."

"I don't give up my principles," he insisted.

"And I won't compromise mine," Bomber said. "So you may think about it for the rest of the day—and understand, I don't need your case *or* your money. My principles dictate when I work, I am paid by the beneficiary of my toil."

"Why don't you do for the good of the people? *Por bueno?*" Inocencio asked with a smirk.

"Pro bono?" Bomber said. "I don't say I haven't worked for nothing in my time—in the service of a noble cause. But you don't fill that bill."

"But how do I get money? In *jail* for God sake. I don't have no money—no capitalist pig possessions—"

Bomber shook his head and clicked his tongue. "That's too bad," he said. "When people get things for nothing they appreciate them less. Especially punk kids like you." Bomber seemed to deliberately irk the lad, and he took the bait. I realized this was my signal to swing into my "good cop" routine. I walked with Inocencio as he was being led back to the Deputy's car.

"Inocencio," I said, "you might look at it this way—if he doesn't get you off, you won't be able to pay him anything anyway. Your means of livelihood will have disappeared into the jail with you. If he does get you off, it should be worth something to you. If it isn't, I'll have to agree with Bomber that he shouldn't take your case. So why don't you suggest you pay a part of your income after acquittal? What do you make an hour now?"

"Ten dollars."

"So give him a dollar of it—offer him fifty cents, settle for a dollar."

"You think they take me back? Madame is dead—we all going to be out of work. With newspaper make me look like a killer, no work for me."

"No job, no pay—no victory, no pay. It's better than a contingency agreement. Think about it."

He looked confused. "Think…?"

"Yeah. Or do you want me to make the offer for you?"

He shrugged. I could see the wheels grinding. It had to make sense to him, he was just coagitating about the damage it would do to his precious principles if he agreed. Finally it was principles be damned—"Okay," he said, "five percent."

I smiled—Inocencio was so unlikable he was likable.

Bomber was waiting for me in his Chinese red Bentley, drumming his fingers on the leather steering wheel. I slid into the passenger seat and told him what we'd worked out.

He smiled. "Let's see," he said, "twenty bucks a week—a grand a year at full employment. Not enough to gas up the Bentley, but better than a kick in the pants. We win the case, I'll look into retirement, so you better write a lot of music."

That was Bomber—making fun of my avocation—writing modern classical music. I had followed my star for a number of years, but as Bomber pointed out it was a lot of fun, good food for the soul, but it didn't put any bread on the table. So I went to law school—at his expense—and he was never more generous with me than while I was in law school. My graduation marked my transition from royalty to indentured servitude. My paybacks for all those tuition fees was in the form of the niggardly salary he paid me. But on the rare occasion

I am honest with myself, I realize I wouldn't take twice the money to work for some average law firm.

As we pulled away from the curb in the car, Bomber began singing softly, "Chicago, Chicago, what a wonderful town…"

SEVEN

BONNIE DOONE GOT ALL the names and addresses of most of the principals which only went to prove Morely Tushman couldn't be all bad.

Bomber was right, Chicago *is* a wonderful town. I checked into one of those too-tall hotels near the posh Gold Coast centrally located between the penthouse mansion overlooking the lake which had housed the Madame herself, and which for some years was Netta Forsley's home, and the almost downtown office of Attorney Morely Tushman in the John Hancock building. A taxi driver told me the John Hancock was so tall it swayed in the wind. I didn't like being in tall buildings that swayed in the wind. That takes the adage "go with the flow" to more of an extreme than I'm comfy with. Otherwise I could take or leave these heights, as long as I am not called upon to step out on a balcony that gives you the feeling you are pasted to the side of a building thirty stories up and at any moment the glue could come lose.

Chicago is the windy city, after all. And it was blowing pretty good as I made my way across the sidewalks on the lake from my tall hotel to the late Madame's penthouse—too high above Lake Michigan.

The doorman had been forewarned of my impending assault. He was dressed as a Mummer's Day Parade band leader, or one of those Banana Republic dictators with gold braids everywhere. I hoped they wouldn't get in the way of his opening doors. Here was truly a man who could open doors for you. It was a little considered talent, being genial to the right people and stern to the wrong and having the perspicacity to know the difference. Netta had warned him so he only maintained the stern demeanor until I announced my name. He saluted me, if you can imagine, and I mused briefly that this could be a variation on the old theme the butler done it. The doorman done it? It would have been a long shot in more ways than one. Some two thousand miles long. The drum major pushed some intercom-buttons and into a telephone handset announced my presence, I was duly sent up in a special express elevator that stopped only at the penthouse—at which point I was to insert the special magnetic card he loaned me with severe instructions to return it on my leave-taking. I decided I would wait until I left and had dutifully surrendered my elevator card to ask Major Domo about the Madame.

Dour was, I decided, the word for Netta Forsley. When she wasn't gloomy. "Come in, Mr. Hanson," she said with a British lilt, "will you have a cup of tea?"

"Oh, my," I said, "very well, yes, I suppose that would be nice," trying to imitate the continental consideration.

When she left the room I gave the place a quick once over—without pulling out drawers or lifting the Aubusson carpets. The place looked like an antique shop. I don't know much about antiques and I doubt if I could tell real from fake, but this stuff looked pretty legit to me—there was just so awful much of it—like she had foreclosed on an antique shop and brought home all the stock. Where there should have been one table there were six; one chair, eight. But the view of the lake was lovely, and outside on her generous deck were dozens of wind resistant plants and a small army of concrete dwarfs. Netta returned with the tea and saw me looking outside.

"Aren't they the ugliest things you've ever seen?" she asked.

"Well, they're unusual," I said, not wishing to commit to the wrong answer.

"I can't stand them," she said. "Madame got them because someone told her they would bring her luck—ward off evil spirits or some such rot. Well, we had a time getting those up here I can tell you. But the Madame would have them and when she set her mind to something there was no stopping her. She was very superstitious was *the* Madame." Hadn't she heard Morely Tushman's edict about not calling her *the* Madame? Perhaps Netta used it deliberately in protest of Tushman's authority, or as an expression of her independence.

"Would you like to sit? If you can find a space," she said. "Madame foreclosed on an antique shop she'd underwritten. Some falling out with the owner."

"Oh?"

"Yes, the Madame was like that. You were a hero one day and she would give you all this money and carte blanche to do anything you wanted, and the next day she'd become disenchanted and want it all back."

"Weren't there any agreements?"

"Sure—all in writing. All legal—didn't Morely Tushman see to it himself?"

"So what happened?"

"Oh, I suspect Alton Wagner missed a payment on Madame's loan. She was a stickler that way. But if she had been satisfied she might have overlooked it."

"Where was the shop?"

"Here," Netta said, "downtown."

"Nice?"

"Oh, my, the nicest. Madame wouldn't associate herself with anything that wasn't up-market."

"So how did she become disenchanted?"

"I wouldn't know, I'm not privy to those details. Some personal slight," she said, "it usually was."

"Where can I find this Alton?"

"Why he's gone to California, I'm told."

"You know where?" I asked. "It's a big state."

"It is that, but I'm afraid I can't help you. Madame was just so glad to be rid of him, nobody pressed for details."

"Would Morely Tushman know?"

"I suspect he might. His fingers were in every pie."

"How do you find Attorney Tushman—?"

A thin smile crossed her face. It was almost painful to look at. "I could say in the phonebook," she said, and the smile broadened just a tad.

"What's your opinion of him?" I said trying to dispel mis-understanding.

"Well, I suppose he's all right," she said. "for what he is. He's a *lawyer,* don't you know? And there's a reason we have all those lawyer jokes."

"Did he treat the Madame all right, would you say?"

"Well I *suppose so,*" she said *con brio.* "She wouldn't have kept him on otherwise. It was always 'Yes Madame' this, and 'Yes Madame' that. Her every wish was his command."

I suspect she was going a little heavy on the protesting so I asked, "How did he treat you?"

She didn't answer right away. There was a nice bit of pursing her lips and letting her eyes wander about. "Well," she said at last, "aside from the fact he is throwing me out of here, I couldn't complain."

"You mean he wants you to move soon?"

She nodded. "Yes. I devoted thirty-two years of my life to Madame and I'm not good enough to stay on even until they find a buyer."

"No!"

"He's given me two weeks."

"Two weeks!" I was getting worked up for her. "Where will you go?"

"Oh, I'll find a place. The Madame *was* generous with the money. I'll be getting a nice inheritance. All the same it makes me feel tawdry. Like I'm soiling the place—"

I decided relief from her self-pity was called for. "Can you tell me what kind of person the Madame was?"

Netta looked around the room as though in search for hidden cameras, then hunched over in confidence. "She was awfully stuck on herself. And I don't mean she didn't warrant that. In her time she was one of the most beautiful women in the world, and she had the attentions of the most powerful men in the world—she had them at her feet, I tell you." She paused as if weighing her next words. "In a world where a woman was judged by how many important men she could get, Madame had to be near the top."

Was Netta jealous? I wondered. How could she not be?

"But I fear that spoiled her—and it did not serve her well in later life when the good Lord saw fit to cut her beauty down to size; and a good thing. She was hard to take sometimes as it was, I can't imagine what she would have been like if she were still beautiful with men falling all over her."

"She didn't treat you well?"

Netta had a way of stiffening her spine in an accent of disapproval. "One day she was fine, the next a shrew. I don't know how poor Mr. Claddington took it all those years. I hired on as a temporary secretary, but Madame begged me to stay when I wanted to move on. Well I soon saw how helpless she was. And she made it worth my while financially. I know a lot of people didn't like her but I got to like her myself—I just didn't pay any attention to her moods. But I don't know why anyone would want to kill her. So that's all I have to say. I'll leave you to your important work."

"Who arranged the seating in Angelton—for the fireworks?"

"I don't know as it was arranged. I was always to be closest to the Madame, perhaps Mr. Tushman told the others where to sit. He's the only one besides Madame who could."

"Did you see the bodyguard and chauffeur leap on Inocencio?"

"After it happened, yes. My attention was drawn to the Madame who as I say I thought suffered a heart attack or some such."

"How long was it between when you saw something was wrong with the Madame and when you noticed the two men on my client?"

"How long? I really couldn't say. Memory in times of excitement is not too reliable. I don't think it was long," she said. "I'd say a matter of seconds more than a matter of minutes."

"Well, Mrs. Forsley," I said.

"Oh, it's Miss," she said. "*Miss* Forsley. I never married. Not that I didn't have my opportunities."

"I'm sure you did," I said soothingly. "What can you tell me about Madame's other acquaintances? Personal friends— business entanglements. Any other antique operations anywhere?"

"The Madame didn't confide financial arrangements in me," she said pursing those penurious lips. "All I can say is she could be very generous at the outset of meeting someone, then want absolute control. This didn't always go down well and fights would ensue."

"So there were other business deals?"

"Oh, yes, I'd be safe in saying so. I remember some of

Madame's pet schemes. She was going to launch a cosmetics line, but it didn't sell—there were other forays into the business world—none of them successful. I don't know why she couldn't be happy with her husband's great wealth, she always wanted to be off doing something of her own."

"Friends? Enemies?"

"Oh, certainly—often they were the same people—love-hate relationships, you know."

"Any names come to mind?"

"Well, there's the old actress who runs the Chicago Theater Company—why can't I ever remember her name—old age, I guess. It'll come to me. The Madame was some angel to those people, I'll say. Why I believe she kept them afloat single handedly. She left them a tidy sum in her will, I will say."

"How much?"

"Five million if I'm not mistaken."

"Whew—" I said, whistling softly. "Any chance Madame threatened to take her out of the will?"

"Every chance. Madame did that all the time."

"Maybe there was something about this time that made the actress fear she'd really do it." We'd just had a case that involved a will—*Too Rich and Too Thin* I called it in my accounting—so I was especially cognizant of the influence of bequests.

"Oh, why can't I think of her name? She was rather well known in her time. Stella Mars!" she said clapping her hands once. "I knew I'd get it. Hard to dredge things up at my age I can tell you."

"At my age, too," I said hoping not to sound too patronizing. "Are you sure everyone was in their place at her side when she was shot?"

"Well, I can't swear to it—the fireworks were surely distracting; but you'd think we would have been aware if someone moved to that position, then came back after the shot. But, if you ask me for my opinion, there's your killer under your nose. An angry communist."

I shook my head. "Doesn't make sense."

Suddenly Netta's body twitched, as though a thought had just occurred to rack her. "Surely *I'm* not a suspect," she said un-surely.

I lifted an eyebrow like it wasn't an easy task. "At this point we don't rule out anybody—or that it could have been a combined effort. So the more help you can give me, the quicker I can clear you."

"Well...I *never!* I devoted my *life* to her."

"And weren't you getting a little tired of it?"

"She could be trying, that's true," she said, "but murder, Mr. Hanson?" she shook her head. "I can't even imagine it."

Nor could I, but I didn't say so. Netta was from all accounts, sitting on the wrong side of Madame Anna Poritzky Claddington to be the perpetrator. And I didn't see her having the cunning to smuggle someone in there without the others knowing. Someone to shoot her employer. So unless they were *all* in on it...

"Did anything unusual happen in the week or two before she died? Any consternation? Any arguments, conflicts with anybody?"

Netta shook her head while pursing her lips. The lip pursing with Netta was almost a tic. It was the old-maid school teacher's signal of disapproval. "Conflict was just business as usual around here, and I don't remember anything that stood out."

"Did she keep a diary? Any letters? An appointment calendar?"

"No diary that I know of. I have stacks of letters. Madame

was not one to throw anything out—especially if it put her in a good light—as for the appointment calendar, I was just looking at it before you came. I can't find anything unusual there."

"May I see it?" I asked.

"Certainly," she said, rising. "And I'll get the letters."

EIGHT

WHEN NETTA CAME BACK into the living room, with her arms overflowing with letters and an appointment calendar, I could see the murder was finally registering on her face. The ramifications of her mistress suddenly being snatched from her, not the least of which was her notice to skedaddle.

As Netta approached I saw the letters in the box were tied in bundles with different color ribbons—each denoting a different suitor I guessed.

When she dumped the contents on the main desk in the room, I went over to sift through them.

It was illuminating to see the widely different styles in the letters—each man his own man so to speak. One was matter-of-fact, businesslike, another flowery, and another purple. One thing was certain, these guys were all ga ga over the good Madame.

I spent almost two hours with the letters while Netta was packing boxes to move, but I didn't see a sign of anything suspicious in the letters which dated as far back as sixty years. It did show me what a magnet for men this woman had been. She had not been above a little manipulation, as was evidenced in some "Gosh-no" protests from a couple of the men.

When I finished the letters, I turned to the calendar for the year—giving me about six months before her fateful July fourth trip.

It was a blue leather-bound, almost letter-sized book with

one of those lovely silk ribbons (dark-blue to match the cover) sewn in the binding to mark your page.

July fourth said "fly to Angelton, in a private jet." (Was she bragging for posterity?) It was written in red with stars drawn floating around the words in the generous box provided for the date.

Featured names in June:

30 !!Ronnie Quigley!! Here 5 p.m.
Stella Mars, lunch 12:00
26 Zachary Roseleer 12:30 p.m. *Fleur de Lis*
24 *Otto Underwood* Dinner, Palmer House 7 p.m.
17 Theater Chicago Theater Company 8 p.m.
Another Part of the Forest
13 Meeting with employees Mr. Morely Tushman's office
5 Morely Tushman

May was just as busy, April too. March, February and January were sparser, owing, I supposed, to the unfriendly Chicago winters.

I showed the book to Netta. "Recognize any of these names?"

"Well, certainly. I've looked at it." She took it and began reading. "As I said, Stella Mars is the former actress who is the director of the Chicago Theater Company."

"Friends?"

"Well," she said, pursing her lips, "why don't you ask her? She doesn't live far from here. I can give you her address."

I nodded. "What do you know about Ronnie Quigley?"

"Does something with the Theater Company, that's all I know. A good looking young man, of course. A flatterer. Boosted Madame's ego—for even though she was old, she didn't think of herself out of the romance market. It was embarrassing sometimes the way she shamelessly flirted as though she were a twenty year old."

"Did you know Zachary Roseleer?"

"No."

"He's boxed in in the calendar. Know what that means?"

"Just Madame's way of emphasizing, I guess. Pretty random I'd say from my experience. Like nervous doodling."

"Meaningless?"

"I'd say so, but then, with the Madame, you never did know."

"Otto Underwood I recognize. He's running for president. She went to a dinner, I suppose?"

"That's what it says."

"You mean she could be deceptive with her appointments?"

"Not impossible. Madame was a tricky one sometimes."

"Did Madame go to the theater alone?"

"Usually."

"Ever invite you?"

"Heavens no." She seemed astonished at the suggestion. "I was a lowly secretary."

"Yet she must have appreciated you."

"Well, I suppose she did sometimes."

"What can you tell me about the meeting in Morely Tushman's office with all the employees?"

Her lips tightened, her eyes crinkled and froze in place.

"You'd better ask Mr. Tushman about that. I don't think it is my business to speak to matters of that sort."

I nodded my understanding, then leafed through the other pages of the appointment book. "Any of those other entries noteworthy?"

"I couldn't say. Madame was secretive about her life and even though I was her personal secretary, she didn't share much of herself with me. 'Past is past,' she used to say, 'I don't care a fig for the past. We must live for today.' And she never would say a word about her past."

"Make you at all suspicious?"

"Wasn't my place."

"Even so, you must have been curious?"

"Well, I suppose in the beginning I was—then I just accepted it."

"Ever any hints? Any people show up out of the blue from her past?"

"Well, there are the letters, of course, but I never did see any of those men."

"Ever wonder what they were like?"

"I have normal curiosity," she said with that puckered face that signaled disapproval of the question.

"Any of them still alive?"

"I don't know—as I said, she never talked about her past."

"Might I make copies of the letters and the appointment calendar?"

"I think you'd better consult Attorney Tushman on that. I'm really not in a position to release any documents—or copies." Her eyes rolled to the ceiling, followed by a heavy sigh. "I probably shouldn't have shown you as much as I did."

"Would Morely Tushman know about Madame's past?"

"Why don't you ask him?"

With that invitation to take a powder, I took it.

At the building's front door, I returned the magnetic elevator card to the doorman, wrapped in an undisguised twenty dollar bill—with the number 20 up. I smiled ingratiatingly, he smiled gratefully and put a couple of fingers of his unemployed hand to his cap bill in a salute. "Thank you, sir," he said.

"My pleasure," I said, one of his industry's staples. "I'm sure Madame Claddington would have wanted it."

"Ah, the poor Madame," he said, pulling an appropriately long face. "A real loss."

"Good to you, was she?"

"Oh, yes sir—very nice."

"I guess no one with the exception of Netta, her secretary, was in a better position to see who came and went to the Madame's apartment than you."

"Ah, but I kept my own counsel in these matters. I was not a gossip."

"I'm sure you weren't, and she surely appreciated it," I said, pumping away at his old ego. I saw at a glance I had not been, as feared, too broad. "Now that she's gone in this tragic, untimely manner, you have any theories on why or who?"

"Oh, no sir—I can't even imagine how anyone could be so cruel."

We stared at each other for a few moments, then on a hunch I slipped him another twenty. He lit up and gave me another salute with three fingers this time. I wondered what it would take to get the whole hand, then I decided to go for broke.

"What would it take for a full fingered salute?"

He looked at me quizically, I suppose to feign a nonunderstanding, but he understood.

"The Madame was very special to me," he said in a hushed, reverential voice.

"How special?" I asked, trying to match his "special" voice.

"A hundred…" he said, tentatively. When I didn't flinch he said…"more."

I was glad I had it, and I forked it over and became the proud reception of the full-fingered salute.

"Understand," he said, looking over his shoulder, "my job is to keep everything I see to myself."

"Yes, and admirable, too, while the subject is alive."

"Yes, sir." He paused so long I thought my one hundred and forty bucks had disappeared down the black hole of unanswered prayers.

"I always remember what my father told me about politics," he said.

"Politics?" was he speaking generically?—"What did he say?"

"He said, 'Politics makes strange bedfellows.'"

I grunted. "I think Lincoln or someone said that first."

"Yes, sir."

"Would we be talking…*presidential* politics?"

"That we would, sir."

"I understand Otto Underwood is favored."

"That would be so, sir."

"Especially at this address?"

"In a manner of speaking, sir."

I wanted to know in what manner of speaking, but I didn't want to inhibit him by asking directly.

"Perhaps in the negative manner?" I asked.

"Like the Chicago weather—the Madame was—hot one day, cold the next."

"Asked your opinions did she?"

"You might say that, sir."

"What was your opinion?"

"My opinion, sir, expressed to one of my residents is always their opinion. If I have contrary notions, I keep them to myself."

"What was her opinion? About Otto Underwood?"

"As I said, like the weather. But the very strange thing is, the day she left for the coast she told me she'd made a momentous decision, and she would tell me all about it when she returned."

"And she didn't return."

"No, sir."

"Did you tell anyone about that conversation?"

"Oh, no, sir. I never would—"

"Have any idea if the Madame told anyone else?"

"I've no idea," he said.

I thanked him with a full hand salute and left with his intelligence.

NINE

LAWYER TUSHMAN WAS TIED UP all day, his secretary told me on the phone, and though I was a young man who recognized the brush off when he saw it, I didn't immediately think that was the case. She said she would call my hotel as soon as he saw a break in his schedule and could work me in. She had such a refreshing voice, I didn't disbelieve her.

I made an appointment to see the actress/impresario or was it impessaria? Stella Mars, at her apartment—also overlooking Lake Michigan.

A maid showed me into the home of the director of the Chicago Theater Company, or CTC, as it was abbreviatively and affectionately known. The living room faced the lake— the midwest's Central Park. The twenty-nine miles of lake frontage afforded status to a goodly number of citizens.

Stella Mars's walls were festooned with pictures of herself in various of her triumphal performances, or more like every performance she ever gave—along with publicity stills and theater posters. In the corner, as though looking out over Lake Michigan, was a life-size bronze bust of her; on the tables were other sculptural representations of the grand dame. It was a room—not cozy in its dimensions—lovingly devoted to the lady of the house. It was a white carpet, white furniture kind of place. You wouldn't get dirty there and you'd be afraid to sit down.

I waited on my feet a respectable period of time. She was a *star* after all—and I wondered if she'd ever kept the Madame waiting. It was a question I wouldn't ask her—there were certain pretenses you never breached, unless you were Bomber Hanson, and then you might get away with it because a certain reputation for outrageousness had preceded you.

Finally, after allowing me time enough to read all the tributes on the wall twice, she appeared in a white Shantung floor length dress with a diaphanous covering that astonishingly led to a train. The ensemble matched the furniture so she was at one with her environment.

From the top it was obvious actress Stella Mars was no fan of the erstwhile actress Madame Anna Poritzky Claddington.

"Anna, yes, oh Anna," she said. "She wanted everyone to call her Madame and I did, shamelessly to her face, but that face is out of the picture now, so Anna it is."

"She gave you money, didn't she?" I asked.

"Ah, but up front we had an understanding—her performing days were over. She would *not* buy her way into even a walk-on in *my* company."

Sounded tough, I thought. Easy to be tough when the Madame is dead and gone. "What was the Madame like near the end?"

"She was creepy," the Duse said with a shudder of her frail shoulders. "She had become an old crone with an ego larger than life."

"I guess we all have them."

She stared me down with her "sez-who?" look. "Yes, young man, that is hardly a startling revelation. But in polite society we don't wear our egos on our sleeve as Anna did." I looked on the walls where she displayed her prizes, awards, and pictures of big shots with generously autographed tributes to her, and I thought of Bomber's walls and wondered if anyone had ever given a course in comparative egos.

"The money…?"

Again the glare. "Young man, do you want my honest opinion or some gibberish tempered by the woman's financial largesse?"

"Oh, honesty, of course," I said. "Can you comment on the talk that the Madame was becoming disenchanted with your theater company?"

"Not so. We had disagreements, certainly—Anna was not a hands-off personality, so when she gave you money you had to realize it was encumbered with the proverbial strings."

"And that didn't bother you?"

She shrugged. "Adapt or die has become my motto since I took over this company. Life is short and art is long, they say, but in this business art is only as long as the money holds out. Art is not a profitable business you know. Subsidy transfusions are always required."

"And Madame left you a nice subsidy in her will?"

"She did that," she said.

"Did you know about it?"

"Oh, Anna would never do anything without realizing full credit—in advance, if possible. She did tell me, yes."

"And did she threaten ever to take you out of her will?" I asked the big question, which I thought I knew how she would answer it, but her answer surprised me.

"Oh, all the time," she said. "It was a continual battle with Anna."

"Why?"

"Oh, she wanted her fingers in every aspect of the art: repertoire, casting, scenery, marketing even. She was a control freak."

"Were you?"

"Well," she said in a huff, "I was *in* control." She calmed down. "The ideal patron is one who gives money without asking anything in return. There are a lot of those, of course, and we get one hundred to a thousand or so from them. There is an adage which generally holds true—the more someone gives, the more they want."

"What did Madame want with her testamentary bequest?"

"Just what I told you. She wanted to run the show. She was always throwing her weight around with her money. You don't think she was some kind of altruist do you?" She shook her head. "Anna was power hungry, and the only power she had to wield was her money."

"How did you keep her from pulling her funding?"

"Oh, usually I sent some pretty young man over to flatter her. Tell her how vital her support was to young aspiring actors like he. She fancied herself an actress you know, though she was far from it. Then he might do a little harmless flirting. You see, Anna didn't want to admit she was old and totally undesirable to the opposite sex she had in the past had such good fortune in reducing to putty."

I smiled. It encouraged Stella Mars.

"She got crazier and crazier as time dragged on. She began to talk as though she had been a famous actress, when, in fact, the closest she got to the stage was the front row where she would make her entrance at the last minute carrying a bouquet of flowers which she held throughout the performance as though waiting on the edge of her seat to present them to the star. Instead, at the end of the show she walked out with the flowers herself, as though she had been the star, as though she could have done better, or perhaps because she was so disappointed in the performance she couldn't bear to part with the flowers.

"More than one actress who had heard of Anna's reputation with the flower gambit was unnerved to see Anna sitting in the front row holding her flowers like a critical cudgel.

"One by one her friends abandoned her—some through

death, which Anna never felt was a satisfactory excuse—or from exhaustion. Only her homosexual lawyer remained a constant in her life."

"Do you know him?"

"Well, I should say so. He is CTC's lawyer as well. It was one of Anna's stipulations for her bequest."

"Why?"

"The question of the hour where Anna is concerned, and the answer is invariably power. Maybe it wouldn't have had to have been her lawyer, any lawyer might have done as long as she could control him and by extension us. Then, too, I have a theory that she also wanted to control Attorney Tushman, and if she could tie him up on enough boards and charities, he wouldn't have time to work for anyone other than Anna."

"Know any reason anyone would want to kill Madame Poritzky?"

She shook her head. "I've thought about it a lot. A strange interlude if you ask me. I wonder if someone wasn't aiming at Morely Tushman instead."

"Why would anyone want to shoot him?"

"Oh, I don't know—those lawyers travel in big-time circles. Chicago isn't exactly a crime-free town, you know."

I knew. "Think he has mob clients?"

"Not impossible," she said with a crinkled nose.

"Specifics?"

She shook her head, "No, not me," she said with a shudder.

"You ever feel disposed to get rid of the Madame?"

"Oh, well, yes, of course—get rid of, but not kill. It's a little drastic don't you think?"

"I do," I said. "Someone didn't."

She smiled a smile that carried to the back of the balcony. "Now if you'll run along young man, I'm holding auditions for *The Importance of Being Earnest*."

I wrote my hotel phone number on the back of my card and handed it to her. She took it as though afraid she might contract a deadly disease by touching it. "Call me, please, if you remember anything that might shed light on our case."

"Don't sit by the phone," she said.

TEN

LAWYER MORELY TUSHMAN'S SECRETARY left a message on my hotel voice mail that the good barrister could squeeze me in between 5:45 and 5:55 that afternoon, and I was not about to look that gift horse in the mouth. But ten minutes wouldn't put a dent in the questions I had for him.

Morely's firm was an old one, and his name was not in it. His office had a generous view of the city and a slice of the lake.

I was in the staid offices in the Hancock Tower fifteen minutes early—not so early as to be a boor, but early enough in case he had an unexpected lull.

An intelligent looking young secretary greeted me with dancing eyes and an unprotected smile on her unpainted lips. I always liked girls who didn't paint their faces, who didn't feel any need to artificially enhance the product.

"Mr. Hanson, hello," she said, poking her hand out at me. Surprised, I took it and shook it warmly. It could easily have been my imagination, but I thought she held on to it just a tad longer than a polite but aloof business greeting called for. My heart started to do funny things. Whoa boy, I checked myself, as Bomber might were he on the premises. It isn't rational to fall for every intelligent looking girl without makeup. There are getting to be too many sporting the natural look. But the sparkle in her eyes as they lasered in on mine was too much for a clay-footed boy like me. Immediately I thought of the contrast between this girl whose name she said was Joan

Harding and our own Bonnie Doone, back in Angelton. Bonnie was brassy—if she had played an instrument it would have been a slide trombone with all the connotations the sliding actions suggested. Joan would be a violinist, playing ethereal melodies, sometimes muted, sometimes soaring to the heavens, and lifting me right off my feet.

Her hair seemed bent on being a page boy. It was a vibrant brown, not one of those mousy colors you see so often flee with the bloom of youth.

It wasn't until she released my hand (boo hoo!) that I noticed the small egg-shaped mark on her neck that looked like a brown birth mark. It was the tell-tale "scar" of a violinist. A quick survey of her left hand, now reposing on the desk in front of her offered a hint of clear sailing—no rings on her finger.

"You play the violin?"

"Yes," she said. "Do you?" and as she said it, she looked at my neck which was as clean as a plucked chicken. To forestall the frown of moderate disappointment that was forming on her face, I said—

"I write music."

"Oh?" she said with a hint of suspicion that I might be a heavy metalist—an anathema to a violinist. "What kind?"

"Classical—" I couldn't get the word out fast enough. "Violins…"

Her eyes warmed like a wood fire on a blistering Chicago winter night. "Oh, wow," she said, "I'd love to hear some of it."

"I'd love to play it for you—" I looked around the room. "Is there a piano some place?"

"I have one in my apartment," she said deadpan while my heart headed for Mars. To get myself under control I visualized her six-foot-five inch bronzed, muscle-bound roommate who got his kicks lifting weights. Probably bench pressed Joan to the ceiling. Or worse—*me!*

"Gosh," she blushed, "you came to see Mr. Tushman, didn't you? I shouldn't be detaining you. He's expecting you—looking forward to it—let's talk when you finish."

"Yes," was all I could get out, seeing as how my tongue was balled up in knots at the back of my throat.

I took in her form as I followed her down the short hall to the boss's office. She had a beguilingly slender body with just a little extra width to her hips, befitting a woman in the baby-making stage, who sat at a desk all day and sat playing the violin the rest of the time. Her legs poling out from underneath a white, almost nurse-like skirt, were sturdy, healthy under-pinnings. She moved as though she were oblivious to my invasive stares, but I knew she wasn't. It gave me a momen-tary flush of empathy for women who were forever being ogled. Perhaps if you were attractive, you got used to it.

She knocked lightly on the door, then opened it. I tried to gauge the knock on Bomber's knock meter and decided he would have chastised me with a "Knock like a man, Boy!" Of course if I knocked too loudly he'd grouse "I'm not stone deaf, Boy!"

With a touch of old fashioned manners, Attorney Tushman stood to greet me and shake my hand. He was impeccably turned out as before with mother of pearl cufflinks, a red silk tie with a scrambled pattern, custom made white silk shirt with his initials embroidered on the cuffs (yes, *both* of them). I wouldn't be surprised to find the dark navy suit was also custom made. I was so awed by Tushman's perfect tailoring that I didn't see Joan slip out of the room.

"Sit down, Mr. Hanson," he said seating himself on his high-backed, leather swivel chair. The walls were wainscoted with a green wallpaper above the dark mahogany below. There were engravings of fox hunts with dark green mattes around the room.

"I'm sorry I can't give you more time now, but I am just swamped with work."

I wondered if he had ever said that to the Madame. I thought not, but I only nodded my peon's understanding.

"I do want to help you. I should be most grateful if you find someone else committed the murder—as unlikely as that would seem to those of us who saw it happen—" he threw out his hands in one of those gestures of inexplicable hopelessness. "Perhaps someone put him up to it—but if so, I doubt you'll find him in Chicago."

"In California?" I asked—somewhat incredulously. "She hadn't been in California for some thirty years—isn't it unlikely anyone would even remember her?"

He shrugged. "Perhaps it's just what it seems: a deranged individual acting alone. No nefarious plots, no real good reason—just a nut."

I nodded.

"What can I tell you?" the barrister said with a cocked eyebrow.

"Where to turn the most complete information on people who accompanied Madame Claddington to Angelton? Can you give me a copy of her will?"

He was making notes on his yellow legal pad.

"Give me biographical sketches of her employees; her business associates—tell me what happened between her and the antique dealer. Where can I find him? Any skeletons in her closet? In anybody's?" I threw him a glance to see if he flinched. I didn't say *your* closet, but he caught my drift. But he didn't look up from his yellow legal pad and the black Mont Blanc, seven-hundred-and-fifty-dollar fountain pen, that was moving in proscribed motions making his notes.

"Did she have any political connections, organized crime

acquaintances? Any friends or relatives who were ever communists? Does the name Zachary Roseleer mean anything to you?" I paused for an answer. He looked up with scrunched eyebrows.

"I don't believe it does," he said, "where did you get it?"

"From Madame's appointment calendar."

"How did you get that?" he snapped, an anger which I thought *had* to be uncharacteristic of this controlled lawyer.

"I peeked at it—it was on her desk."

"Young man, you have no right to go snooping in her personal things without my approval."

"Oh, sorry," I said, contrite as a cardinal sinner in the confession booth. I was waiting for the assignment of Hail Marys and Rosaries—I wasn't Catholic, but Morley Tushman was. "Is there any reason you might withhold permission? I was hoping for a copy of her calendar."

"We shall see," he said, "I'll let you know—"

"Zachary Roseleer one of the names you don't want me to see?"

"I didn't say I don't want you to see anything. There are simply certain protocols we follow in Cook County. Being an attorney yourself, I'm sure you can appreciate that."

"Certainly," I said, far from certain.

"As for this Roseleer is it?"

"Yes."

"I don't recognize the name. Perhaps if I saw it in context…"

"Did the Madame see many people you didn't know?"

"Well, she had her own life, certainly. I was simply her attorney."

Something about the way he said that and the way he reacted to my seeing her calendar told me he was a great deal more than her attorney.

"So there could be other names in her datebook that you don't recognize?"

He nodded. "There could be."

"Would you be good enough to check it and annotate the names that appear there?"

He made a note. "That could be a chore. She had an active social life for a woman her age—and I certainly wasn't privy to all of it."

"I'd appreciate anything you could do." I said. "Was there more to her relationship with Stella Mars than meets the eye? What about Netta Forsley? Is there a reason she is being asked to move so quickly?"

He stopped writing and looked me in the eye with the intent to wither me, I'm sure I'd made him edgy. "Mr. Hanson," he said, "Netta Forsley has been and is being well taken care of. It is the duty of an executor of an estate to do everything in a timely manner. Netta Forsley is no longer needed, we gave her a good severance package, and as you will see, she was handsomely provided for in Madame's will. There is a lot of heavy work to be done at the penthouse and Netta can't do it owing to her age and physical condition. Besides that, she had a close relationship with the Madame for many years and her emotions could easily get in the way of an orderly conclusion of Madame's affairs—so I am asking her to move in a reasonable amount of time—she hasn't complained about it, has she?"

"Oh no," I said, knowing I was protecting Netta more than I was being accurate. I was also aware of his excessive protesting which took too much of my precious time and may have borne further scrutiny. "I understand you had a meeting of all Madame's employees in your office. Can you tell me what that was about?"

"Yes, Madame'd put them in her will, and wanted me to go over it with them so they understood."

"That a usual procedure?"

He nodded. "I counseled against it. It's generally not a good idea to reveal bequests. It gets the beneficiaries worked up and Lord knows the Madame could change her mind at any time."

"And did she?"

"Certainly. All the time," he stopped, "but, not after that meeting. That was only a few months before she died."

I nodded eagerly—the sycophant's sycophant.

"I'm sorry, our time is up," he said without looking at his watch. "I will instruct my secretary to give you anything we can. I do want to cooperate. I may have given a different impression when I spoke with Bomber, but that was in the heat of the moment. I am most eager to solve this case and put it behind us. There are bequests in her will, as you will see, to just about everyone. If it should develop that one of the beneficiaries was involved in her death in any way, why he or she—wouldn't be a beneficiary any longer." He smiled, telegraphing his self-satisfaction at his funny.

"May I call on you again?" I asked when he stood up.

"Certainly," he said, and I wanted to add for him, "as long as it doesn't interfere with my billable hours." "I should have more time in a few days. In the meantime, see what you can do with the information my secretary will give you."

He ushered me out almost without my realizing it. In a jumble of words he seemed to communicate with his lovely secretary, and as soon as he turned to return to his office— like a car turning on a dime—she sprang into action spinning her rolodex like a Las Vegas croupier spinning the roulette wheel. She wrote down names and addresses, then consulted files in her drawer and behind her desk, taking files to a room off to the side that had in it a copy machine.

Her efficiency was as beautiful as she was. In what seemed like minutes, she presented me with a copy of the will, files on each of Madame's employees—files that would have done the FBI proud—the antique dealer's name and last known address, and a copy of the agreement between the dealer and Anna Poritzky Claddington, as well as the letter of dissolution and a copy of the bylaws of the Chicago Theater Company.

There was no mention of Zachary Roseleer.

Then I noticed another omission: Dick, the guy who seemed to be a gofer for Morely Tushman, I asked the secretary—she frowned, excused herself, and cantered into Morely Tushman's office. Her face on her return told the story.

"He is a personal friend of Mr. Tushman's," she said. "He has no connection with Mrs. Claddington. He went along for the ride, and it was the first time he met the Madame."

How nice, I thought. It was the first time Inocencio met her too, and he's in jail for her murder.

Then it occurred to me there was no information on Morely Tushman himself. I thought at least a client list might come in handy, but I considered it the better part of valor to let Bomber pursue that one.

Joan's efficiency endeared me to her more. I knew I wanted to see her again, but I hadn't had time to formulate an approach. I always rehearsed my spiel to gain favor with a woman. Since the time I was a freshman in college and had this wild crush on a blond coed named Carole who had bought books from me while I was working in the student bookstore. I wanted to ask her to a dance. It was five weeks in advance and I thought that plenty of time. But though I'd rehearsed and memorized my lines, I was so nervous I was trembling. I'd found her schedule in the file outside the bookstore and lay in wait before her 9 o'clock class in *Man and Civilization.*

She breezed into the hallway in front of the classroom. At the last minute I stepped in front of her and croaked "Carole—I'm Tod Hanson—would you go to the dance with me on the fifth of next month?"

She looked at me as though one of my oars had disappeared and the other wasn't hitting the water.

"Do I know you?" she said, and this was definitely not as I'd rehearsed it.

"No, but I'd like you to," I said, steeling my resolution that the rehearsed lines—with time devoted to getting the kinks out—were definitely better.

Carole looked away from me—was this disdain on her face?—and marched into the classroom in an expertly executed maneuver of scum-escape.

Now I was suddenly confronted with Joan's smile and a broad wink, and I choked out the word "Lunch?"

I realized if she wanted to be a smart aleck she could have said, "What about it?"

Instead she said, "Love to. When?"

"Tomorrow?"

"Perfect!" she said—and I smiled a sappy smile. "Where?" she said.

"Oh, I don't know the city—why don't you pick?"

"Okay—I'll think about it. Someplace intimate but not suggestive or presumptuous. Nice but not *too* pretentious."

I laughed. She was wonderful. "I wouldn't rule out pretentious," I said, and we both had a good laugh. I was thinking how I would justify to Bomber the cost of a pretentious lunch with Morely Tushman's secretary, when she said, "How about the Orleans over on Michigan near Jackson?"

It sounded good to me. "I'll look forward to it," I said, and we shook hands. That simple, overworked, gesture never felt better.

Her buzzer rang—"Whoops," she said, "the boss is calling. The Orleans—about a quarter to twelve."

"I'll be there," I said, as she scurried down the hall.

ELEVEN

BACK IN MY HOTEL ROOM, I sorted through the information Joan, Attorney Tushman's secretary, had given me. First I read the will.

It was a clumsy document with attachments, a thick trust, codicils, and I could see why a meeting with the beneficiaries was called for. Though that would have more usually been held after the testator's demise, the Madame wanted credit, appreciation and gratitude while she was alive to see it.

Morely Tushman was named executor, of course, wills and trusts being the financial plum of the estate biz. He would then appoint his law firm as the estate lawyer, effectively doubling the fees.

The bequests were generous, and, as expected, Netta Forsley was in for one hundred thousand, as was Madame's chauffeur of forty-some years. The theater got their five million with the stipulation the company be renamed the Anna Poritzky Chicago Theater Company. No mention was made of the husband who made the money. There were miscellaneous other charities in for fixed amounts and all other employees at the time of her death were bequeathed ten thousand each. A thoughtful gesture—hardly enough to kill over. This group included our client Inocencio, Larry and Carlos the other two Angelton house workers, and Harley the bodyguard who had apparently been recently hired.

Reading the files of the employees, one word came to mind: sanitized. For instance, Harley worked as a security guard in night clubs when what he actually was was a bouncer. I wondered if in the pursuit of that professional attainment he hadn't served some time as an enforcer of the Chicago crime syndicate, but I was letting my imagination run amok.

Peter the chauffeur was apparently a Christlike figure who devoted his life to the Madame. He was black and beautiful, gentle and patient with her moods. He was closer to the Madame for a longer time than any of the others. Perhaps no one could claim a better reason for killing her—I continually wondered about the bodyguard and chauffeur who pounced on our client. If there was a chance for hanky-panky it must have been there.

I called Bomber with the news of the will.

"Hmm," he said. "Not a bad setup. All the beneficiaries are unsophisticated. I'll bet Tushman doubles the fees and no one says 'Boo!' They get theirs—there aren't any residues to speak of, no percentage of net estate to bother with—the theater gets its five million—and the devil takes the hindmost. It's all calculated to yield handsome fees—why not make some inquires about his firm? What kind of shape is it in financially?"

"Oh," I said, "it looks p-pretty sound."

"How so?"

"N-nice offices—everyone l-looks prosperous."

"That's just the kind of firm to wonder about. Tremendous overhead. Get a couple of clients that don't pay their bills and pow!—bankruptcy."

"C-can you call him—maybe you could ask a few questions—or if you know someone else in Chicago—c-could you c-call them?"

"I do know a Chicago lawyer. You go to see him. Tell him I sent you—" that was Bomber, never do anything I could do half as well. "Abner McNaughton is his name. He'll be in the phonebook there."

"I was hoping you'd call M-Mr. Tushman yourself. I can't get him to t-tell me about himself or h-his friend."

"Friend?"

"Yeah, the Dick person who came along."

"What do you want to know?"

"I'd like a c-client list."

"You probably won't get that. Of course, you realize it looks like he is under suspicion."

"Isn't he?" I chuckled.

Bomber laughed too. "Until we nail someone, every one is under suspicion. What's with the friend?"

"He was in her Angelton entourage—T-Tushman gave me information on all the rest but not on D-Dick Funkhauser."

"*Fun*khauser?"

"Yeah, isn't that s-something?"

"Indeed. What's he say, he didn't know the Madame—first time he met her?"

"C-Correct. I wanted to t-tell him our client hadn't m-met her before either, but I didn't."

"Might have gotten a rise out of him."

"By that t-time I was out of his office so the s-secretary would have gotten the rise."

"Well, keep at 'em, Boy. I'll call him, but I don't expect he'll be any more likely to part with the info for me than he would be for you. Don't give up the ship—and call Abner— he was a Korea buddy—my pilot."

I got back on the phone and made some appointments— covering the Chicago crowd. When I got back to California I would see the antique dealer and the presidential candidate— if he was in town.

Peter Williams was my first meeting. He was tall, stooped, thin, and very black. He had a welcoming smile that embraced you in total. His apartment was modest and hardly in the ritziest section of town, but I got the feeling Peter didn't live in his apartment or in any section of town; he lived within himself.

Inside his small rooms it was apparent no effort had been spent on décor. The furniture, what there was of it, was as serviceable as it had been when he got it handed down from the Madame in one of her forays into redecoration.

"Please be comfortable," he said to me, while shaking my hand warmly. I sat on something I pegged as French Provincial which might have seemed out of place elsewhere, but here in this room so devoid of pretension it seemed content with its mismatched fellows.

Peter's view from his living room was not of Lake Michigan, but of the yellow brick building, slightly taller, across the street.

"Home sweet home," Peter said with a smile. "You'll have to forgive the mess, I'm not much of a housekeeper since my X passed."

"You were divorced?"

"Oh, Lord no, why do you say that?"

"You said ex."

"Oh, I'm sorry, I keep forgetting, folks think of that as an ex-wife. No, no, X was her name—she didn't go by no other. See, she didn't have much schooling and she never learned to read or write her name—so when something in that line was called for she just made her X and somewhere someone started calling her X. She was a good soul," he said, "and I loved her with all my heart. She was one of those persons, Mr. Hanson, that couldn't do enough for you. She made me feel like a king, she did. Not a day passes I don't miss her terribly."

His eyes were misting.

"But you aren't here to talk about my X, may she rest in peace. I loved the Madame too," he said, "—in a different way, of course," he hastened to add lest I get the wrong idea.

"Good to work for, was she?"

"Aces with me," he said. "Oh, I hear tell everybody didn't get on so easy, but I got no complaints. She never talked down to me—I guess you can't relate to that—"

"Oh, yes, I can," I said.

He eyed me with suspicion. "Well…" he said skeptically, "…maybe ever'body has they insecurities. But it's different, you know when she hired me feelings about us negroes was suspicious. She told me people told her I was going to steal her purse. Her car even. When she asked them 'Why he do that?' they'd say just look at him—he's a nigger and that's what they do." He tightened his lips, his eyes were tearing. "I'll never forget all she done for me."

"Now she left you a nice bundle, didn't she?"

"Whoo—ooo, did she ever!"

"What you going to do with it?"

"Ooo—ooo, I don't know. Put it in the bank for my old age," he chuckled. "Least ways I'll be able to afford to *get* a little older."

"No new car?"

"Nah, she give me her car. The Madame had a lot of cars in her day. She give me her favorite—this old Rolls out there." He pointed to the street in back of his apartment. He shook his head at the memory. "Ooo—ooo, the places we went together in that car, umm, um. Got over one-hundred-thousand miles on it an still perks along like it was new."

"Any of those places you took her make you think? Like someone of them would want to kill her?"

He didn't think long. "Nah, she was eccentric okay, there ain't no denying that, but why would anyone want to kill that sweet old lady? I tell you, I don't know what this world is coming to—something like that happen."

"What happened the night of the murder? You jumped on the Mexican gardener, didn't you?"

"Yes—"

"How did that happen?"

"Like I told the police, there was such a commotion, and somebody yelled, 'He shot her, stop him' and Harley and I being the closest, I guess, jumped on him."

"And the gun?"

"He threw it in the ocean."

"You sure?"

He nodded cautiously, his tongue touching his lips.

"Did you see the gun?"

His eyes clouded in thought. "I don't rightly remember I saw it or not. Was dark. Seemed like he throwed something."

I didn't press. It was our first crack in the story and I didn't want to have Peter cement any erroneous opinions in his mind.

"How long did you know Harley—the bodyguard?"

"He was on the job only a couple 'a months. I didn't know him before that."

"Why was he hired?"

"Oh, I 'specs you should ask Mr. Tushman that question. Scuttlebut was the Madame used to feel safe wid me along, but the older I got the less safe she was." He shook his head, "Lord, I'da laid down my life anytime fo' that woman, she know'd that, but she just started fretting here lately that I might get hurt if we ever had any trouble."

"Did you ever—have trouble, I mean?"

"Never! Thirty-four years in her service and I never even got a scratch."

"Any idea why she should suddenly fear 'trouble'?"

"Never did understand it."

Perhaps the Madame knew something Peter didn't. I had a feeling it would be helpful if I could find out.

"Does the name Zachary Roseleer mean anything to you?"

He narrowed his eyes. "No...I...should it?"

"You took Mrs. Claddington to the Fleur de Lis restaurant June twenty-sixth—I assume to meet him for lunch."

"Oh, I never went to lunch. I stayed in the car."

"Did she mention anything about Zachary or the lunch and the reason for it, either before or after?"

"Madame didn't speak to me on familiar terms. She was pleasant to me, but it was all business."

"Can you remember anytime when she might have broken that rule? When she might have told you something about any of her associates—people she met—Stella Mars for instance, or the antique dealer? Otto Underwood the guy running for president? Ronnie Quigley—anyone?"

"No sir," he said with a touch of remorse. "She just wasn't like that."

Hard to imagine a thirty-four year relationship and not a personal word between them. In fact, I didn't believe it. Not that I thought Peter was a liar, but I do think he would stretch or cover the truth in what could have easily been a misguided attempt to protect his employer's memory.

But, I thanked Peter, told him to call me if anything came to mind he had an inkling might help us.

"Yes, sir," he said. "Glad to help if I could—but there's just one thing—"

"What's that?"

He shook his head. "It don't look good for your man—all those folks saying they saw him done it." Peter pursed his lips. "Me…I ain't that sure. Lotta fireworks going on…"

I bade him goodbye. I felt good just having talked to him.

TWELVE

ABNER MCNAUGHTON, attorney-at-law, had a modest suite of offices on La Salle Street in the heart of the financial district. He reasoned, I suppose, if you wanted to make a killing in estates and trusts, you went where the money was.

Chicago was enlightened in the ways of outdoor art as no other North American city. A stone's throw from Mc-Naughton's office artist Roger Brown's colorful mosaic *Flight of Dedalus and Icarus* draped the domed entrance to 120 N. La Salle. The mosaic portrays the mythological father and son escaping King Minos' imprisonment on feather wings.

There was, apparently, a small furor when the mosaic went up. The denizens of the staid financial district felt that "men flying in underwear" did not reflect their corporate policies.

Mr. McNaughton, who had risen to shake my hand, was ruggedly handsome—robust looking.

"Well, gee, Bomber's kid," he said, sitting down and inter-lacing his fingers behind his head. He rocked back on his high-backed swivel chair like he was flying a plane on automatic pilot. "I can see some resemblance in you—he was younger than you when I knew him—but I suspect you favor your mother more—count your blessings. Sit down, sit down. But jeez, it's good to see you and be reminded of those days. They were good times. Your dad was quite a guy. Still is, if what I get from the media is anywhere near correct."

"Well," I said, "you know the media—hype."

"Of course. But I tell you, none of us would have pegged

Bomber for the law," he shook his head, "high powered real estate sales maybe—mainframe computers, huckstering at a carnival perhaps—but I guess his line isn't that far from salesmanship and showmanship. Now me—nobody would be surprised to find me behind a lawyer's desk—estates and trust, nothing high blown and fancy like tort law. Don't have to lick the boots of some hairbrained judge. Not that Bomber is too good at that. Incredible the stuff he does—the cases he's had. Who'd a thunk it? as they say."

"What was he like then?" I asked. "In his early twenties, I guess."

"You kidding? He was eighteen. Fresh out of high school. Could have gotten a college deferment—didn't want it. I was out of college so I couldn't play that song. I tried to sing the ballad of law school but the draft board was tone deaf so I enlisted in the airforce. I quickly took to flying planes, like the proverbial duck to water. I loved it."

"I guess Bomber loved it too."

Abner McNaughton frowned. "I don't know about that," he said. "Bomber always said he joined up for the extra hundred bucks a month hazard pay they gave us." He smiled. "Ticked off a lot of the infantry boys who said crawling on your belly in a fox hole was far more hazardous then flying up in the sky, high, dry, and out of firing range."

"How did he get attracted to being a bombardier?" I asked, "That part of the story has always been murky."

Abner McNaughton was startled. "He didn't tell you?"

"No."

The frown returned. "Perhaps I shouldn't—ah, what the hell, you're an adult." He settled back in his chair as though preparing for winter hibernation. "Derry—that's what we called him then—his name was Derrick you know, and I don't think he liked Derry very much—sounds kind of sissy. Anyway, Derry wanted to be a pilot—the bucks, the glamour, whatever. Only trouble was he didn't have the aptitude for it. I think his mother told him he could do anything he set his mind to, and he believed it. But he was a disaster behind the controls. I won't go into how he conned the brass to give him a shot at it with only his high school diploma under his belt. He'd had a couple of downs and—"

"What's a down?"

"Instructors take you out and rate you—pass or fail. You flunk, we called it a down. Three downs and you're out. In those days, you had to be pretty bad to get a down. Cost a lot of dough to train the kids. Sam didn't want to waste it—but he didn't want inept pilots crashing planes either. That would have been more costly. So Derry has two downs going into an emergency landing session. The instructor cuts the engine and the student had to land the plane in a field. First he has to select the field, commit to it, and circle around and land. Derry did it okay—I mean, the instructors were not about to cut the engine unless they were pretty close to a flat, open field. It was on takeoff he had the trouble. He kicked up the throttle, and just as the plane was lifting off one of the wings dipped and hit the ground. An accident! And an accident is an automatic down. The instructor landed the plane, got out, checked the wing—a small dent was all—and flew it back to the airfield. He went to bat for Derry, saying he did nothing wrong, it was a freak atmospheric thing that caused the wing to dip. They bought it, and Derry stayed in the program. But then came formation flying. I was in his formation and, I'm telling you, he came within inches of my wing with his wing, and I had visions of us all going down in a fiery crash."

"So, that was the end of him?"

"No. Somehow the instructor didn't see it. The real trouble came with the instrument flying. They put a canopy over the cockpit, give you flight patterns and you have to coordinate all these instruments—the clock, the altimeter, the gyroscope, the airspeed, and he just couldn't do it. Well, he was crestfallen, that's all. He washed out. He had to fill his time, so he became a bombardier—and he took to it like the same proverbial duck."

"Because he loved it, or to cover his disappointment?"

Abner McNaughton looked at me with new respect. "That's very perceptive, young man—I always wondered about that myself—all this calling him 'Bomber' baggage—it was a little much for some of us, but we played along. We knew the disappointment he felt—of course, it took some doing on his part. We were so used to calling him Derry, but he'd correct us with something bizarre like 'that's Bomber to his intimates,' or 'my close friends call me Bomber—would you like to be included in those exclusive ranks?' It was sort of funny, but we knew he was serious so it was harmless enough, and it didn't take long until we were all calling him Bomber. It pleased him. I think that is one of the secrets of his success—he stays with something until everyone wants to cry uncle. 'Perseverance pays' said Cal Coolidge, and Bomber persevered in spades."

"Didn't help him make a pilot."

"Well, no, but Jesus, he had no aptitude for it. None! You know about trying to get honey from lemons."

I knew. I felt a little that way in law school.

"Well, I guess you didn't come here to schmooze about your dad," he said. "What can I do for you?"

I explained my mission in Chicago. "Bomber wanted to ask you if you were acquainted with a lawyer named Morely Tushman? And his firm Williams, Belweather, and Stark?"

He nodded thoughtfully—"Heard of them. French cuffs, monogrammed—polished shoes, and bayonet sharp creases in the pants of the impeccable fifteen hundred dollar suits. Always admired men who could fuss about their clothes as much as women do," he said, but I didn't believe him.

"Bomber wanted to know—could they be in any financial trouble—either Williams, Belweather, and Stark, or Morely Tushman himself?"

"Any pressure that would make it to their benefit to have the executor clause in the will kick in?"

"Exactly," I said. "Then, too, he wonders if the firm might have any shady clients—underworld—crime syndicates? Or maybe just unusual clients?"

McNaughton laughed. "So what's Bomber doing sending you here—saving the cost of the phone call? Tell him he coulda called collect."

I shrugged. "That's Bomber," I said.

"Hasn't changed," he said. "Well, tell you what—I'll ask around—I have some sources with noses like gophers. Where can I get in touch with you?"

I gave him my hotel phone number.

My first thought after leaving Abner McNaughton was, where could I find the closest telephone to call my dad? Then I thought how silly, I can certainly wait until I get back to the hotel room.

On my way, I passed the Daley Center Plaza with its modern sculpture by Picasso. No one knows what it is supposed to be—speculations run to animals like baboons and butterflies—but as Picasso himself has said "People who try to explain pictures are usually barking up the wrong tree."

By the time I got back to my hotel my mind was crowded with fragments of melodies for musical sketches I couldn't wait to put on paper. Not surprisingly, they featured the violin in homage to the lovely young lady I just met. A string quartet might do nicely—Joan might even be able to perform it sometime. I already had *beacoup* ideas for the sweetest violin parts I'd ever imagined.

In the hotel room I whipped out my staff paper and began jotting at a furious rate. I'd forgotten all about calling Bomber.

By the time I thought of Bomber again, I thought, why should I? I'll just keep McNaughton's sketch of the young Bomber as my secret. Secrets like that sometimes gave you a feeling of power for knowing something about someone they didn't know you knew. Of course, that power would be diluted in this case because I wouldn't know if Bomber knew that I knew or not. Most likely, he'd put the specifics of his airforce experience out of his mind, being satisfied to trade on the dramatic first mission that was turned back because of an armistice.

Wouldn't Abner McNaughton call him and tell him? Maybe that end of the secret would add to Bomber's power over me.

If Bomber remembered all that McNaughton told me, wouldn't he have told me himself, rather than risk letting me hear it from a stranger? On the other hand, maybe he wanted me to know without having to tell me himself. Maybe the only result would be a stand-off, powerwise, culminating in an unspoken understanding, with no appreciable power residing in either side.

Darn!

THIRTEEN

BEFORE MY LUNCH with Joan Harding, I dropped in to see Harley Holiday, the bodyguard Madame had hired late in her life. I don't know why I wanted to surprise Harley, I guess I didn't peg him for an appointment kind of guy.

My mistake.

Harley Holiday had apparently not made big money on his trade, if his digs were any indication. He lived in a little wooden bungalow on the fringe of Chicago—not the best neighborhood, perhaps, but not the worst either.

In retrospect, the surprise visit was a dumb idea. Especially to one in his line of work.

Nobody answered my knock at the front door. There was a car parked on the front lawn, covering it on one side of the garage driveway—oyster white paint was peeling off the garage door—the trim on the house was an aqua marine look-alike. The car was vintage without the value and might have been better served with a pair of tires to complete the wheels in front.

My second knock also went begging; so, foolishly, I tried the door. It was an instinct thing. I didn't plan to walk into a stranger's house just because the door was not locked. I don't know what got into me, because that's exactly what I did. Then, instead of calling out to Harley—I tiptoed in. I don't know what I expected to find—perhaps I should just confess to the excitement of exploring the unknown. If it turned up any kind of clue, so much the better.

It wasn't much of a place—filthy, dirty gold shag carpeting on the floor of a room virtually devoid of furnishings except for a threadbare couch that was probably found on the street by a slumlord with a sign: FREE COUCH. If I was looking for something, I wasn't going to find it here. So I made my way into the next room—it was the kitchen—where a stool was pulled up to the counter. Dirty dishes and sandwich remnants were strewn all over the counters. No sensitive material likely to be here.

As I made my way in the direction of the bedroom hall, I thought I heard a grunt. It stopped me dead in my tracks. When all was quiet again on the western front, I eased into the short hallway and down the narrow passage in the direction of a greenish glow coming from the bedroom at the end of the hall. I heard no more sounds, so I carefully plodded the few steps to the open door—where I peered in to see a computer screen lit up on a Nintendo game. The door was halfway open, and something told me not to step in any farther, but I couldn't resist taking a peek around the corner to see if I might find something useful here. It was another bleak room with the computer on a card table on the far wall, a mattress on the floor, and a card table folding chair pushed askew in front of the computer. Just as I was about to peek around the door, it slammed on my face, knocking me on my back with blood oozing down my mouth onto the floor. Through blurry eyes with a nose feeling like mincemeat, I saw not a man but a mountain—in my delirium I thought Madame sure knew how to pick them—when I felt his pointy black boot dig into my side, knocking my wind to Mount Rushmore.

My nose felt like a mashed potato sandwich, and now he was kicking the salami out of what was left of me. I tried to protest, but he didn't seem interested. Just as well, I couldn't get any sounds out of my battered head, nor could I squeeze a word in between the torrents of his curses. He had quite a repertoire, and I remember thinking just before I slipped, mercifully, from consciousness that I wondered if Harley Holiday had ever exchanged any of those sentiments with Madame Claddington, or anyone in her bailiwick.

He must have tired of thrashing me for I woke, apparently not too much later, to find the card table chair moved over beside my prostrate remains and the bruiser bodyguard of the late Madame Anna Poritzky Claddington seated thereon, his chin on his hand, his elbow on his thigh, Thinker-like. I didn't dream he had the apparatus for any rational thought, or we might not be in these relative positions. But he seemed to be studying me as though trying to place a particularly pesky mosquito.

When I opened my eyes, he grunted. "You're the lawyer's kid," he said. "What you sneaking 'round here for? Liable to get yourself hurt."

"Apparently," I said, and was sorry I had put into play any part of my battered body.

Harley Holiday had a neck like a fire hydrant and his smarts were in the same league. But I'm sure he served his purpose: no one gave Harley Holiday any guff. He could have crunched your garden-variety mugger between his thumb and forefinger.

In retrospect the surprise visit was a dumb idea. That cannot be said often enough.

Two things came to mind. He could have killed me and didn't—as far as I could tell. He could have skedaddled and escaped responsibility and facing me—perhaps in the hope I would die peacefully to be therefore out of his hair.

But there he was—the Thinker; doing his best at thinking away.

"If you knew who I was," I finally managed, "why didn't you…" the pain was telling me to make my remarks as brief as possible "…say something?"

"Didn't place you, kid. Heard someone prowling my house—hadda protect it. Coulda been dangerous—didn't recognize you right off. I wouldn'ta been so violent. I didn't mean to cause your demise or anything—just protect m'self."

Demise? Did he say *demise?* What a lovely word under the circumstances—under any circumstances, really.

"I hope you don't think I had anything to do with Madame's demise," he said as though the oh-so-remote thought just occurred to him.

"Not before you beat me up," I croaked.

"Hey, I told ya—it's nothing personal. Yuda done the same under the circumstances."

I saved my energy. What good would it do to tell him I didn't have the strength? Then it dawned on me—my lunch date with Tushman's secretary Joan Harding.

"What time is it?" I asked—there was no possibility of me looking at my watch.

He looked at his. "Ten-fifteen; why, you got a date?"

"Strange as that may seem."

"Geez, you're in no shape—let me try to clean you up." He got up and left the room. I tried to pull myself up-my head was pounding like the "Anvil" chorus from *Aida*. My eye was caught by the pool table felt green of the computer's screen, and I remembered the solitaire game. A good sign I thought— I still had about ninety minutes to pull myself together—but the way I felt, ninety days might not do the job.

He returned with a wash cloth and a bowl of water. He sat it on the chair and got to his knees to do the ministrations. I almost left my skin when the cold water hit my face. He was not going to be a gentle nurse.

The sight of my spilled blood oozing from the cloth to the soup bowl full of water did not lift my spirits.

"Have you good as new in no time," he said.

"New?" I said, and was sorry I did—"Ooh," I muttered.

"Maybe," he said, fingering a cut and sending me through the roof. It took a good hour before I was able to sit up and breath without thinking each breath would be my last. I herded my ninety minutes and for some reason (insanity?) I didn't consider calling Joan to cancel.

"I don't have any antiseptic," Harley said—I was grateful for small blessings at that juncture. I could imagine the sting of antiseptic on my open flesh. I stood with great effort and felt woozie. The computer was staring me in the face. Little dancing figures kicking each other in the face.

"Where'd you get the computer?" I asked. He jerked his head in my direction, and I realized I had made another *faux pas*.

I was about to apologize when he said, candidly, "Madame gave it to me—"

"Before or after she died?"

He threw me a barbed look. "You want another nose job? She told me I could have it before she died. I got it after."

"Anything interesting on it?"

"Interesting? I play the games mostly."

"Did Madame use it?"

"No—that's why I got it."

"Netta?"

He shrugged.

I struggled into his bathroom and looked in the mirror. Not pretty. Two dark black eyes, cuts and abrasions as they might say on a coroner's report. Contusions was another word that came to mind. Could I really go to lunch with Joan Harding looking like this? Had I been more sane and less crazy to see her, I would have done the prudent thing. But my physical handicaps were exceeded only by my emotional handicap.

I went to meet the girl I thought would be the love of my life, with the unexpected help of Harley Holiday, who insisted on driving me to what he referred to quaintly as my "assignation." He had a handful of big words, and I loved the way he used them.

When we pulled in front of the restaurant he put a hand on my knee and said, "Any way I could catch a glimpse of the young lady?"

"Oh, geez, Harley—give me a break will you? It's going to be hard enough explaining this hunk of hamburger in a suit without complicating it."

"I could tell her what happened. Don't want her to think you came out of a fair fight looking like that."

"Thanks, Harley, really—but not this time—we hit it off, I might introduce you to her."

"Fair enough," he said, driving my rental car off into the sunshine. It didn't occur to me until much later, that Harley's nice-guy act was a ruse to keep his eye on me.

I took a deep breath and felt the pain as I headed toward the restaurant door. Trepidation was in my bones. I was sure I was making a mistake, but I saw nowhere to turn. Always the chance my condition would work on her sympathy, I supposed.

FOURTEEN

I SAW JUST A SLIVER of the striking brown hair on the back of her head through the collection of chewing heads in the dining room, molars intent on mastication, but it stopped me in my tracks. I suddenly envisioned Joan in all her loveliness and compared the thought of my battered face to her beauty. I couldn't face her. It would ruin any chance I might have. It would be the indelible impression of a loser never to be overcome.

There in the entry to the dining room, frozen in my indecision, ready to abandon all hope before entering that particular hell, I decided to leave a note with a fifty dollar bill with the maitre d'. The note would say I had been detained by a bad accident and I would call her in the p.m.—I had arranged for her lunch to be paid for.

I turned to look for the maitre d' and saw instead a woman enter the restaurant who looked uncannily like my mother. A light bulb exploded in my head. My mother was desperate to have me married. The sloughing off of any opportunity for the merest relationship in that direction would be an affront to her—a sacrilege. I made the immediate decision to abandon my search for the maitre d' and turned to face the music in the dining room—fully expecting to be rebuffed by the pretty secretary. Rebuffed, resented, and rejected. But for Mother, I could do no less. In consideration for putting up with Bomber all those years, if nothing else.

Bite the bullet, they say, I bit and marched into the dining room with my ragged head held as high as the pounding pain would allow. All the while I heard, in my near delirium, Mom's voice—"Go for it, Tod, go for it!"

When Joan saw me approaching the table, she actually started to rise to greet me. Then she quickly scanned my face and fell back as though hit in the solar plexus by a medicine ball.

"What happened?" she asked, her jaw dropping to the demure top of the most alluring dress I'd ever seen. It was off-white silk and did amazing things to that brown glistening hair. There were unopened menus at each of our places.

"I was afraid to let you see me—I turned around in the entry."

"I'm glad you came back," she said, reaching for my hand—and when she lay her hand on the top of mine I was at once glad I came. "What made you come back?"

"My mother, believe it or not."

"Your mother?" she said looking back toward the waiting area. "Is she here?"

"No, she's in California. It was her voice urging me on. She wants me to meet a girl in the worst way."

"Well, you did—lucky for both of us. My mother wouldn't object if I met a suitable man."

"Is there such a thing?"

She did the laughing: I wasn't about to exacerbate my pain. "Not to hear her tell it. She hasn't approved of any of my beaus—"

"Beau—what a quaint and kind of wonderful word."

"Yes, isn't it. It's Mom's word."

"How about your father? Did he approve?"

"Oh, Daddy's wonderful. He'd approve of Jack the Ripper if that's who I wanted. But what *happened* to you?"

"I got worked over—in the line of investigation."

"Who?"

"Madame's bodyguard. Harley Holiday—know him?"

She frowned. "Not personally, thank goodness. I've seen him in Mr. Tushman's office."

"Doing what, may I ask?"

"Meeting with Mr. Tushman. Something about Madame, I suppose. She prevailed on Mr. Tushman to find her a bodyguard—and he did."

"Did he ever! She's dead and he's still protecting her."

"So how did it happen?"

"Stupidity," I said. "*My* stupidity. I went to talk to him at his house. He didn't answer the door—it was open—" I shrugged.

"So he beat you up? He came home and found you rifling his drawers?"

"Not exactly. I was looking for clues. Harley was in the perfect position to have committed the crime then throw the blame on our client."

"I want to help you," she said, looking me over. "What can I do?"

"Call the paramedics?"

She laughed. I loved her laugh. Maybe the most important thing about a woman—her laugh. Joan's was aces. I could do a whole movement of a string quartet based on her laugh.

"I know what you can do for me. Heal me in a jiffy."

"What?"

"Play your violin for me."

"Oh, geez," she said, "that might make you terminal."

"Somehow I doubt that," I said.

"Well, if you insist."

"Great, when?"

"Whenever you feel up to it."

A dilemma, I thought. If I waited until I really felt good, I might be back in Angelton. But did I want to essentially waste the visit because the simple act of moving caused me a low grade misery? "You're on," I said, noncommittally. "Let me see if I can start the mending process overnight."

She smiled and winked at me, and my heart went up in one of those moon rockets.

"Tell me about your mother," she said, "I like her ideas."

"I have a special affinity for her, I guess. Tragedy does that."

"What tragedy?" she asked, shifting her pretty eyebrow inquisitively.

"She lost her only daughter, my sister, to suicide. Sis had a withered arm, the result, it was said, but not in public, from Mom's taking thalidomide on a European holiday—at the suggestion of an ill-informed doctor. Sis despaired of ever getting a man to make the babies mom so dearly wanted, so she drove her sporty car off the pier."

Joan looked like she was about to cry. "Sad," she said. "Do you think she felt pressure to marry and have kids?"

"I don't know—maybe—but maybe she was just so sad she didn't have dates. And she was the most wonderful girl—cheerful, fascinated with everything. Apparently the cheerful was a cover-up for her deep sadness and despair. I guess you can imagine, it hit us pretty hard."

"Gosh, I don't know how anybody'd ever get over something like that."

"Not easily—or quickly. Mom and Dad were in a funk for months—morose for months more. I was beside myself, but I quickly saw that the house and practice had come to a standstill—and though I was just a kid, I was the only one in the house with enough equilibrium to function."

"Good for you."

"Yeah, but I have a confession—"

"What?"

"It's embarrassing," I said.

"Why?"

"Because—my father is this—I don't know—the most imposing figure you ever saw."

"Tall and built like Schwartzennegar?"

I chuckled at that. "Hardly," I said. "He wears elevator shoes and that still doesn't get him to my height. No, he's imposing in his personality. He's an in-your-face kind of guy without actually being in your face—if you know what I mean."

"Not really."

"Bombastic. We have to call him Bomber because he was almost a Bombardier in Korea."

"You call him Bomber?"

"You bet. And he's kind of curmudgeonly, too. Well, maybe you'll meet him. That would be better than any description I can give."

"But what's your confession? That he's bombastic?"

"No, that ever since sis died and I took over in a manner of speaking, I've stuttered in his presence. I don't stammer with anyone else, no matter how intimidating they may be—only Bomber—and he can be nice as pie and I still stutter."

"Hmm," she said, her forehead crunching in thought, "why do you suppose that is?"

"I don't know—all I can figure is I am so embarrassed for him that I, a kid, had to be the strong one when sis died. And he is always…since…so much stronger than I…intimidating…maybe it's tied up with that somehow."

"Amazing," she said, shaking her head.

The waiter was hovering, and when I saw him I realized we hadn't even opened our menus. I could talk to her for hours without knowing five minutes had passed.

"The waiter is swooping down," I said, opening my menu, "feel like ordering?"

"If we have to," she said opening hers, "I'd just as soon talk to you."

"Me too—" Wow, what a warm feeling she gave me. If you believed in chemistry, we were the Du Ponts.

"What are you going to have?" she asked.

"Something soft," I said, "soup, mashed potatoes. Don't think I should chew until I get my jaw wired."

"Seriously?"

"Half—"

"Shall I take you to the doctor? Wouldn't that be a good idea under the circumstances?"

"Maybe I'll take you up on that—and maybe I'll ask you another favor."

The waiter showed up and we ordered. He expressed facial consternation at my order, but I couldn't face explaining it to him.

When he left, Joan said, "What's the favor?"

"Harley Holiday brought me here in my car. I have to pick it up at his place—I could use a ride."

"Sure, glad to," she said. "After work okay?"

"Fine."

"I'll take you to the hospital, then go to work—if that's okay. I'll pick you up when they have you put back together."

"Fair enough."

"And Tod?"

"Yes."

"I want to help you investigate," she said. "Will you let me?"

"What a nice thought," I said. Then pointing to my face, "Me winding up like this is an inconvenience—if it happened to you it would be a major tragedy."

"Does it happen often?"

"Oh, harassment and intimidation are part of the game. It doesn't often do this much damage, but to risk a face as pretty as yours—"

"Oh, how sweet," she said.

The food came and I negotiated the soup between my parted lips with only a few minor mishaps. Joan was having a salad where everything was chopped to a faretheewell, and she seemed to enjoy it.

"Maybe there is something you can do to help, safe and clean."

"What?" she asked. "I do want to help. If someone did this to you there must be more to it than meets the eye."

I wasn't sure—but if that thought would enlist her help I wasn't about to disabuse her of it. "Can you find out Harley Holiday's background? How Morely Tushman happened to hire him and exactly when? And if you can find any information on a guy name Zachary Roseleer, I'd be ever so grateful."

"Do I get it? You want me to rifle my boss's files for the cause?"

"Heavens no. Aren't you the keeper of the files?"

"Maybe."

"So we could call them your files?"

"Maybe—a stretch perhaps, but go ahead."

"So I don't see anything unethical about you checking your files now and again."

She sighed heavily. "And I just *met* you," she said.

FIFTEEN

HOSPITAL EMERGENCY ROOMS should be avoided at all costs. Not only are they laughably named—my visit to the "emergency room" took me just over an hour and a half to be admitted to the inner sanctum and a bed, and another twenty-five minutes until a harried doctor sauntered in, looked at me and asked, "What seems to be the trouble?" So much for emergency.

"You're the doctor," I said. "I had the stuffing beat out of me, and I thought it might be nice if someone in your calling took an inventory of what was left."

"Good thinking," he said, and began unceremoniously poking me.

The good news (and bad news) for the day was Harley Holiday had brought my car back to town and left the keys with the restaurant doorman who recognized me immediately. I didn't immediately realize how he could do that, then I caught on—Harley'd told him to look out for a guy who looked like a freight train had run over him.

The bad news was, of course, I missed the opportunity to drive thirty minutes or so with Joan.

The doctor was frowning as he probed my abdomen. "Nasty business," he said. "I don't even want to think what the other guy looked like," he said with a bemused smile.

"Not a scratch on him," I said.

"Naturally, you're a gentleman."

"Yeah," I said, with dull pain working its way over my carcass.

"Well, I can't find anything here to enhance our revenue, so unless you strenuously object, I'm going to kick you out to make room for someone with real problems. You'll heal in no time—be a little tender for a couple days. A bit of advice for the future: when you see a macho coming toward you, turn the other way."

"Thanks," I said.

When I got to the waiting room, I was delighted to see Joan was waiting for me.

"What a nice surprise!" I said.

"And it's nice to see you on your feet!"

"He wanted to put me in a coffin, but I couldn't afford it."

She smiled and cocked her head that way you do when you think you are being put on but aren't sure. "Oh, bosh," she said. Bosh, she really said "bosh"! Quaint and charming. The profanity that comes out of the mouths of girls my age still astonishes me and makes me uncomfortable. Joan said "bosh"! When you feel yourself falling in love the strangest and simplest things become endearing.

"Come on," she said, "I'm taking you home." I thought she meant my home, but I was pleasantly surprised.

We got into a cute white car made by one of our major World War II Asian enemies, and it soon became apparent what she was doing.

"Oh," I said, "you mean *your* house."

Her eyes twinkled, "Is that all right?"

"Oh, I'd hate to be a burden."

"I thought you were a Hanson." Corny, maybe, but it made me smile.

"How did you get here so fast—don't you have to work?"

"I told Mr. Tushman what happened to you and he was

aghast. He held his head in his hands and just shook it back and forth. 'Harley,' he said over and over—"

"You find anything out about him?"

She shook her head. "No. He got him from an agency. Thought the Madame was paranoid about someone wanting to hurt her, so he got a bodyguard to keep her happy."

"Maybe she knew something," I said. "Turned out it wasn't paranoia after all."

"That's what I said to Mr. Tushman. He said he was sure there was no relation between her fears and what happened."

"I wonder," I said.

"You think there was? What would it be?"

"That's what I have to find out," I said. "How about the Roseleer guy? And…"

"And?"

"I hesitate to ask this—"

"Good," she said, "hesitate away. I've already got so much work I'll forget how to play the violin before I'm finished."

"Don't do that—but…"

"But, huh?"

"Your firm's client list—"

"Oh, geez, you really want to get me fired, don't you?"

"I really don't."

"That may be a little much," she said, frowning. "See what I can do with my own stuff before I put my neck in the noose."

We pulled into an apartment building with underground parking—not on the lake, I was relieved to see, but a lot nicer than I could afford. No doorman, but an elevator.

I am always ill at ease when I am alone with a woman for the first time in her home—or mine for that matter. I don't know exactly why I'm so uncomfortable, all I know is I always think I may have found another venue for stuttering and may at any moment break out in the most embarrassing stammer. I never have—that privilege has always been reserved for Bomber, but I still fear it. The more I like the girl, the more acute the feeling.

Her apartment was as lovely as she was. Craftsman period rip-off furniture, warm colors on the windows and upholstery—an upright piano in the left corner.

"Geez, you have a nice place here. Old Tushman must be a generous boss."

"Pooh," she said, "my father helps me. He got one look at what I could afford on my salary and he decided he wanted to help. I *love* my father."

That was magic to my ears; I'd read that girls who liked their fathers were more amorous.

"Now sit on the couch—put your feet up and I'm going to prepare a feast of crackers and water—you do drink water, don't you?"

"W-water—" Darn! I was so startled I almost slipped into a stutter. "Sure, I drink water."

"Thank goodness," she said, "and you aren't allergic to crackers or anything are you?"

"What kind of crackers?"

"Saltines."

"Not too much salt, I hope," I smiled.

"I can scrape it off."

"Okay."

True to her word, she brought me a saucer of crackers and a glass of water. "Don't say I don't know how to entertain," she said with an engaging, crooked smile.

I took a saltine cracker, chomped on it and said, "I never had a better cracker in my life."

She seemed pleased. "There are more where that came from."

I looked around the room as though crackers might pop out at me from the piano—or her violin case on top of the upright. Then I noticed something.

"You don't have a television?"

"Used to. Gave it to the Salvation Army. Chewing gum for the eyes. I used to sit and watch it all the time. I couldn't turn it off. I was beginning to sprout those knobby roots, and I was afraid if I watched one more night I'd be rooted to the couch for eternity. It was like kicking cocaine, but I did it. Hauled it out of here myself. Ever since, my violin playing has improved two or three percent."

"Wow—that much."

"Well, maybe not. Want a book? A *New Yorker* magazine? I'm going to disappear into the kitchen for three or four hours to see if I can top the crackers. I wouldn't want you to get bored."

"You don't want me in the kitchen with you?"

"I'm afraid you wouldn't be comfortable. You must heal—"

"If you can't stand the heat, stay out of the kitchen?"

"You're welcome to, I suppose—but if you feel like it, why don't you try the piano?"

I liked the idea. I could tell she was not that keen on having me in her kitchen, which was only a small room without a lot of room to navigate.

I moved my aching body over to the piano and sat on the leather, adjustable bench. There was music all over the place. "You must play the piano too," I said.

"Amateur city," she said, "you show me how it should be done."

"What do you like—classical, romantic, baroque?" I leafed through her music—she had everything. "Contemporary?"

"How about something romantic?" she asked.

"Schumann?"

"Love it—" she said, sliding away into the kitchen.

I played from the *Kinderszenen opusiis and Album fur Die Jugend—Opus 68,* and pain shot up my fingers into the upper arms, and I thought I'd have to give up. Then I turned to an easier piece—*Erster verlust,* which you'd think might mean first lust, but it is first loss-and someone told me all great novels were about a great love lost.

Erster verlust came out all right. It is a pretty easy piece, and I was able to pull a little passion out of it.

Traumerei was next—some stretches for fingers, but simple enough. It means Reverie and that's how I played it. Before I knew it, my pain was being pushed out by my piano playing. I was lost in the music, and I thought of playing just for Joan Harding, who was probably so busy in the kitchen she wasn't listening.

Perfect Happiness *(Gluckes Genug)* was next—and it was just what I was feeling in Joan's cozy apartment.

A Tale of Distant Lands, Curious Story, Great Adventure, Almost Too Serious, one by one I found special meaning in the titles, and when I looked up I saw Joan standing beside me. "You play divinely," she said. "But doesn't it hurt?"

"Not if it doesn't hurt you."

She laughed. "We'll save the pain for the fiddle—"

"After dinner?"

"If you're up to it. I'd love it," but she frowned, "calling it dinner may boost your expectations beyond the fare—but it's ready."

There was a table set in an alcove that jutted off from the living room. The tuna salad was simple and simply beautiful arranged on the crinkly, shining lettuce.

"Well," she said, "dig in. The larder was bare, as it usually is. If I have too much food in the house, I blow up like a balloon. Like the TV—no restraint."

"This is wonderful. What are you talking about? I was happy with the crackers."

"Go on," she chided me, "tell the truth—a little peanut butter would have capped it off, wouldn't it?"

"Peanut butter? Speaking of no restraint. How would you put it? Blimp City."

After dinner she got out her violin, plopped some Brahms and Mozart on the piano music rack and said, "Let's warm up on the Mozart—"

I started and when she came in, I was astonished. She had the sweetest tone without the corny, overdone vibrato you so often hear from amateurs. She played like a dream, and I told her so. Whereupon she leaned over and kissed my battered cheek.

"Thank you, kind sir," she said. And we lost ourselves in the Brahms whereupon followed yet another congratulatory kiss, this one more centrally located on the face.

"How are your bruises?" she asked as we came up for air.

"What bruises?"

She purred.

"You made me forget them," I said.

"Want me to massage them—? Gently…?"

"Oh," I said, "oh, would you?"

"I would," she said.

SIXTEEN

PLAYING THE VIOLIN wasn't Joan's only talent. She gave me a massage that made me forget everything.

When we could put it off not a moment longer, she drove me back to the parking lot where Harley Holiday left my car. The tariff was a little stiff, but I paid it without flinching.

I floated back to my hotel, as lightheaded as I'd ever been.

The phone was ringing when I opened my hotel room door. It was Bomber.

"What in the Sam Hill is happening out there, Boy? You on vacation or what?"

"What," I said. I liked to minimize my chatter with Bomber, it cut down on the stammering. I certainly wasn't on vacation—so "what" it was.

"What's going on? I haven't heard a word from you—"

"Takes t-time," I said, angry that one word seemed to be my limit.

"Takes time, huh?" he said. "Isn't that the last refuge of the procrastinator? The question is *what* is taking time?"

I was embarrassed, even though I was only on the phone. I had the irrational fear he was reading my mind and knew everything that went on with pretty Joan Harding.

"Investigating."

"What have you found so far?"

"Ch-checking names on the Madame's c-calendar. Talked to T-Tushman, Netta, and Harley Holiday."

"Who, the bouncer?"

"Yeah."

"Anything there?"

"Maybe, don't know what. R-roughed me up a b-bit."

"Roughed you up did you say? Bad?"

"Pretty bad."

"Hospital?"

"Yeah."

"What'd they say?"

"I was okay— N-need to rest and r-rec-cuperate."

"Well Jesus Jenny, Boy, you all right?"

"Need a few more d-days—maybe a week…or so."

"You want to come home?"

"N-n-no. I'll b-b-be ok-kay."

"Sure?"

"Sure."

"Want me to come out there?"

"No, thanks-n-not necessary."

"Send Bonnie? Just to look after you?"

"NO!" He had sent Bonnie to North Carolina on the tobacco case after I'd suffered some skull damage—reported in *Nobody Roots for Goliath*.

"Since when do you want to stay away from home?"

"This is a tough c-case."

"They're all tough cases," he said. "If it were an easy case the public defender would still have it."

The wit and wisdom of Bomber Hanson…

"Any theories?"

"The way that moose came d-down on me, I'm checking his b-background," I said. "Don't know a Zachary Roseleer, d-do you?"

"No."

"Alden Wagner? He's an antique dealer."

"'Fraid not."

"I'm working on it. And t-trying to get Attorney T-Tushman's client list—"

"Never get that, unless you break in and rifle all his files."

"Maybe do better—"

"Really?" he was impressed. "How?"

"Sources," I said mysteriously.

"Well, good going, Kid. Think that fag attorney is involved?"

Good old Bomber, it's a good thing being politically incorrect was still not a crime. Bomber would be a three time loser. "Don't know yet," I said. "Anything th-there?"

"I talked to that punk pinko again," he said, "what a lost cause he is. Still got a chip on his shoulder the size of a Mack truck. He is such a horse's petutie about everything—he couldn't be guilty. But the bad news is, he's pushing the case. Old Wcb, that hapeless, hopeless DA wants to get us on the boards. Naturally. He thinks he has a slamdunk and the longer we fish around, the shakier his case will become."

I admired Bomber's optimism. "Maybe," I said.

"It will never be stronger than it is now—take my word for it. You'll find something, I know you will."

I grunted at his optimism.

"Well, keep up the good work. Call me if you need anything," and he hung up before I said goodbye.

I was happy. He hadn't given me directions or ordered me home. There were more piano/violin duets in the offing—perhaps the laying on of more hands in the guise of massaging. Paradise!

Under the circumstances, I didn't sleep that badly. It hurt when I turned over, so I tried to minimize that. I was pretty stiff when I got up around nine, so I decided to lie back down.

At ten the phone rang.

"Hi there," it was the cheery, unmistakable voice of Joan

Harding, and my pain took flight the moment I recognized her. "Did you have a reasonable night?"

"Yes," I said, "but now that you called the day is better."

"Listen, I'd love to have lunch with you, but I'm thinking I should be doing some work here—it is so quiet when most of the partners are out of the office—" she paused for it to sink into my head.

"Yes," I said.

"So are you amenable to dinner?"

"Oh, amenable," I said, "yes, amenable. In *extremis*."

"Suppose I drop by the hotel around six. Would I find you there?"

"You bet," I said, "room 812."

"Oh, by the way—" her voice dropped to a whisper, "The Krondike agency has interesting clientele. They're in the book."

"I'll check them out—thanks. See you sixish?"

"Righto, gunner," she said, and I listened to the dial tone a while before I hung up.

I looked up the Krondike folks in the phonebook. Not too far from the hotel. I could walk if I didn't mind the pain. Supposed to be good for you to walk those things out. I'd have been embarrassed to get a taxi for three blocks and change, so I got dressed and hoofed it.

A little stiffness, some soreness and too much discomfort, but I made it. It was a flat brick building in the middle of the block without a lot of fuss made for any of the tenants.

It was on the directory inside that I saw my target:

Krondike Agency
Security Services

I took the elevator to the fourth floor. I went through the door with their name on it—half glass—obscure, like in the old detective movies. My first take was this was not a luxury operation. The personnel looked like fugitives from blue collar jobs. The receptionist was chewing gum. She took a quick look at me and said, "Looks like you should have come here earlier."

"Yeah," I said, "good thinking. You got somebody I could talk to about rectifying that?"

Her frown told me rectifying might not have been one of her down home words. "You know," I said, "so it doesn't happen again."

"Let me see who's available." She picked up the phone and dialed. Her first try was available. She pointed down the hall.

His plastic sign on his desk said he was Elroy Harker, and it was a good thing, to, for I got no other introduction.

Elroy was a burly guy. I could see him riveting bolts on one of Chicago's finer high rises. "Yeah, man," he said on seeing me, "take a load off. Looks like you came to the right place."

"Good. This is rent-a-cop then?" I don't know why that came out of my mouth—it obviously hadn't cleared my brain first.

He frowned. "We don't like to call it that. We deal in security. All kinds. What did you have in mind?"

I pointed to my face, "Help," I said. "What do you recommend?"

"Depends. This unfortunate mishap something liable to happen again—or was the licking administered a one time event—like some hothead in a bar someplace?"

"Let's just say if I needed personal protection, what would you advise?"

"Whatever you want. We have security patrols, bodyguards—we can go day shifts, night, around the clock."

I frowned. "They come with references, I suppose?"

"Certainly," he said.

"Pricey?"

He spread his hands wide. "How much are you worth?" he asked. "It's not cheap. I'd say if you are strapped for cash maybe you want to consider a Rottweiler."

"So what kind of people hire bodyguards?"

"All kinds," he said, "anyone who has any reason to think someone might do that to them." He pointed to my face.

"Where do you get your guys?"

"All over," he said, looking at me in a way that said he didn't appreciate the question.

"What about liability?"

"We're fully insured."

I mean if the guy clips someone *too* good."

"Your safety is paramount. Our operatives use only as much force as is necessary to protect you."

"Yeah? Like what?"

"Depends—steps in—keeps an attacker at bay. This wouldn't have happened to you if one of our boys was on the scene."

I had to smile at that. "What about confidentiality?"

"In spades," he said.

"Where should I turn to get references?"

"Got all you want."

"Yeah? What kind of people?"

"What kind?"

"Yeah—presidents and kings—chauffeurs?"

"Well, we've handled candidates—presidents have the secret service."

"Oh, sure," I said as though I forgot, "but you do candidates, really? Like Otto Underwood then?"

I saw him flinch. "I'm not at liberty to offer you specific names, but yeah-like Otto Underwood."

"Wow!" I said. "Any organized crime?"

"The Mafia?" he asked as though he were speaking to a dummy. "They have in-house security."

"Oh, sure," I said eager to appear a little less stupid. "I meant do you get any of their guys, to, you know, work for you?"

His forehead was creasing, his lips where shielding his grinding teeth. I knew at once I'd overstayed my welcome. "Where did you hear about us, anyway?" he asked.

"Harley Holiday," I said, as though that were the most natural thing in the world. If he had suspicions about that he didn't express them.

"Good man," he said. "Now you take Harley—if he were on your case the other guy would have looked like you do. You'd be clean as a whistle."

"Yeah, I imagine," I said.

"Well, I'm glad old Harley sent you here. Lot of ungrateful guys in this business only too happy to go around the company."

"You mean hire out direct?"

"Exactly."

"No, no—I wouldn't do that," I said, "I mean where's your liability insurance in that case?"

"Exactly," he said.

I thanked him, told him I'd consider using them, stood, and added as an afterthought: "So if I happen to run into Otto Underwood, you think he'd give you the thumbs up?"

He looked at me severely, then broke into a thin smile and gave me two thumbs up—way up.

SEVENTEEN

I STARTED WATCHING THE CLOCK at about five-thirty. I had a distant hope that Joan would surprise me by being early. Sixish it seemed to me could easily encompass a half hour on either side. Every time I heard a sound in the corridor my heart bounced. Each letdown took a little out of me. I didn't dare speculate on what Bomber would say if he knew I thought I was falling in love on the job.

"Again?" is what he would probably say. That would be followed by the standard lecture on the pitfalls of mixing business with romance.

By the time the knock came on my hotel room door, I was almost a basket case. I leaped to open the door, and we fell into each other's arms. When we came up for air, she said, "Good news! I got a pretty good client list—"

"Where is it?"

She pointed to her head.

"You *memorized* it?"

She nodded. "I didn't want to write anything down. So I remembered those that might be important."

"Such as?"

"Are you ready for this?" she asked. "Maybe you better sit down."

"Okay." We went as one to the stuffed chair in the corner. I sat. She sat on my lap.

"Is this okay," she said, "or do you hurt too much?"

"No, no, it's more than okay."

When we were cozy, she held up a mock trumpet, "Tah ta ta tah, ta tah—" she said. "Ladies and Gentlemen, my fellow Americans, I give you the next president of the United States, Otto Underwood!"

"NO!"

"*Au Contraire.* Yes, yes, yes. Yes!"

"Wow! Zachary Roseleer?"

"No."

"The Krondike agency?"

She nodded, enthusiastically.

"Any great secrets from the files?"

She frowned. "Hey, greedy, I only had a day—a lunch hour, really."

"So what did he do for Otto Underwood?"

"I don't know. Not much apparently, but that's the other thing—Mr. Tushman has his own private files—locked. That might—or might not—tell us more."

"You have a key?"

"Course not."

"Know where to find it?"

"No." She shrugged her shoulders. "Maybe a clandestine *Mission Impossible* visit in the middle of the night."

"Hmm," I said, "no piece of cake as they say down at the bakery. Any ideas?"

"I'm thinking."

"Sure is good of you to help out like this," I said. "I hope you don't lose your job over it."

"I'll second that," she said, her laugh was a violin glissando. "Way I look at it," she said, "if it serves the cause of justice, why not? If they are guilty of something they shouldn't get away with it—and if, as I suspect, they are not, where's the harm?"

"That's a nice way of looking at it," I said.

"Well, it just seems to me Harley Holiday gave you more of a thrashing than was necessary. Given he's not a rocket scientist and reacts perhaps on an animal level, he still over-did it."

"Think there could be another reason?" I asked.

"I think it warrants looking into."

"So—the secret file—think we could break in?"

"And make it look like an outside job?"

"Preferably."

"Not likely, finding the key is—well—the key," she said, giving me another glissando.

"Any ideas?"

She put her finger to the tip of her nose. "We could go in there late tonight—if you're up to it—and see what we can find."

"How late?"

"Lawyers work late—sometimes to midnight. I was thinking real late—one or two in the morning. But you should be resting and mending."

"I'll be okay—if I can stay awake that long."

"I have some ides," she said, with a twinkle in her melodious voice.

I liked the sound of that. "Did you find any more about Tushman's friend, Dick?"

"Not really. Mr. Tushman was on the phone with him today. Sounded like he was trying to reassure him of something—soothing—but that's all I got. He used to be called Richard when I started, then suddenly it was Dick. Not that that means anything. Dick and Mr. Tushman go way back, apparently. I heard a rumor Dick has AIDS."

"Have you seen Dick since they got back from California?"

"No. And I used to see him once a week or so. He'd come in for lunch with Mr. Tushman. They'd go out sometimes, but sometimes they just ate in his office—sent out for something.

He was looking pretty frail the last time I saw him, about two weeks, I guess."

"He wasn't at the reenactment," I said. "Morely Tushman seemed protective."

"He is that."

"How can we find out about him?"

"Hmmm. Might be tough."

"Nothing in the files?"

"I doubt it. We can certainly look."

"Tonight?"

"No time like the present," she said.

The telephone rang. I knew it had to be Bomber, and I didn't want to answer it. It was one of those decisions I had to make in a hurry. I didn't want Joan to hear me stutter, but I didn't want to miss a call from someone I had given my number to—someone who might prove helpful to the investigation. So I said, "Do you mind if I answer that?" and Joan hopped off my lap, and I bounded for the phone on the desk.

"Hello?" I said. When I heard the voice say "Tod?" uncertainly, I thought I must have gone white—probably the last person a man wants to communicate with while in the presence of the woman of his dreams is his mother.

"Oh, hi," I said, being careful not to let "Mom" slip out, with enough lack of enthusiasm to turn off the least sensitive soul.

"Is that you, Tod?" she asked. "You sound…different."

"Maybe the Chicago air."

"Must be," she said, "your father tells me you've been hurt. I just wanted to be sure you're all right."

"Oh, thanks, yes—I'm fine."

"Was it bad?"

"Wasn't good. I'm healing nicely."

"I tell him till I'm blue in the face—that kind of work is not suitable for a sensitive soul like you—you're an artist—

a musician. You don't want to be in any predicament that's liable to get you hurt—but I might as well be talking to the wall. You sure you're all right?"

"Sure," I said—how can you be sure of anything? I rationalized.

"Well, good," she said. "It's nice to talk to you."

"Me, too," I said, hoping the brevity of my contributions would send her the message I didn't really want to chat at that particular moment.

"I don't suppose you've had much opportunity to make the acquaintance of any nice young women there?" It was a question, though it sounded more like a statement of fact made in resignation of the larger, overriding hopelessness.

"Well…" I said dragging it out in a vain hope she would get the picture and hang up. It was not to be. "I wouldn't rule it out."

"Oh Tod!" she exclaimed in close to ecstasy. "That would be so wonderful!— Oh," she said, "oh, my goodness—you don't mean she, I mean, there is someone there with you now?"

"I wouldn't rule that out completely."

"Oh, well, dear me, I'll let you go then, if you promise to tell me all about her."

"Well," I said, but feeling in my bones a danger with her having this info—"perhaps I will—if you promise not to tell Bomber."

"Tell Bomber? But why not?"

"It could cause complications."

"Oh," she said, "oh, yes."

"Yes! Yes!"

"Well don't worry on that score. It will be our secret—and I'll do what I can to stall here."

When I hung up, I noticed Joan was studying my face, and I didn't think it was medical curiosity. She was asking who I had been talking to with only the glance, not the words. Now that Mom was no longer a presence, I decided to tell Joan.

"It was my mother."

"Oh," she said, "how nice."

"She was asking if I'd by any chance met any nice girls. Mom's old fashioned. Still calls you girls."

"That's fine with me. Nothing wrong with 'girls'."

To kill the time before our clandestine visit to Morely Tushman's office, we went to a fast food chain and killed some fast food—then went to her place to play more duets—Pablo de Sarasate's *Air Bohémien,* some Shostakovich preludes, Debussy's Sonata No. 3 in G minor. The time flew by, as I noticed it seemed to with Joan.

Before I knew it, it was midnight, and the appointed time to set out on our breaking and entering caper. It would be easier than most such operations because Joan had a key to the premises, but what she didn't have was a key to the private files of Morely Tushman.

EIGHTEEN

WITH ALL THE CHICAGO LAKE frontage, some fog was inevitable. The moon was in its Hey-Diddle-Diddle-the-Cat-and-the-Fiddle-the-Cow-Jumped-Over-the-Moon phase, but it showed through the soup only intermittently. Joan was driving her car so we could get in the parking garage and case out the cars to see if any partner or associate might be working late.

When she turned on the ignition the music poured out of her car radio.

"Isn't that Beethoven's Violin Concerto?" I asked.

"Um?" she said, as though distracted. "Yes—third movement."

"Really good playing," I said, listening to the perky melody from the solo violin.

"Think so?"

"Yes—don't *you?*"

She wrinkled her nose. "I don't know," she said, "I keep thinking I could do better."

"You?" I laughed. "Of course you could do better—if someone would give you the chance—full orchestra—the works." Then something nagged at my consciousness—something about her reacting—"Who's playing? Do you know?"

"Yes," she said, "I know—" then fell silent, humming along with the melody.

I ratcheted my eyes in the direction of the pretty driver of the car. She was smiling as though at a private joke.

"So who *is* it?" I said, realizing the answer as I said it.

"Me," she said. "It's a CD of me with the Cincinnati Orchestra. Like it?"

"I love it. I'm speechless," I said. "I'm just honored to be in the same car with you—let alone playing the piano for you."

"Not *for* me. We are playing together."

"Wow. How many concertos have you done?"

"Just that one. I'm going to trade on it for the rest of my life."

"I get it. You snare the boys into your car, and the CD goes on and they can never look at another girl."

"Oh, yeah," she said, "like the eligible men are just bursting Chicago at its seams. Men with musical sensibilities? Lot of them prefer their own kind—"

"Hmm, like Morely Tushman?"

"Exactly."

"Too bad," I said, but of course I was pleased.

When we reached the parking area, she said, "I don't know all the cars, but the partners have reserved spaces," she said. "Not that any of them besides Mr. Tushman knows my car."

There were no cars in their reserved spaces.

"Anybody walk to work? Take a taxi?"

"You never know," she said, "anything is possible, anytime." We parked a long way from the firm's spaces.

She'd brought her pocket pen-sized flashlight, and we had a discussion about turning on the lights in the office or not. If someone should come in and find us rifling the files and Tushman's office for his key to this private file with a flashlight, it might seem more suspicious than if we were just there to pick up something Joan forgot.

"Yeah," she said, "something that couldn't wait for a

couple hours for me to get when I returned to work in the morning." We got on the elevator. "As catburglars we leave something to be desired."

"You know what I think," I said, "I think you are risking too much. Why don't you show me the layout and let me take the risk? What could happen? A couple of weeks in jail and a little embarrassment. If they caught you there you'd lose your job—so why don't you stay at your desk as though you were a very conscientious secretary while I look for the key."

She brought her upper lip up to touch her nose. "It shouldn't take that long."

The office was dark—she decided not to turn on any lights, but used her pocket flashlight to guide us to Morely Tushman's office—she went right for his desk and opened the middle drawer.

"God bless Mr. Tushman," she said. "He's so trusting."

There were keys in the drawer, but none of them fit the private file, which was a neat wooden contraption on wheels behind the desk.

"Now what?" I asked.

She sighed, "Well, it was a fun trip. Next stop, Mr. Tushman's place—climb in the window, rummage around for keys—bring them back, try them, then return to Mr. Tushman's abode before he wakes."

"Yeah," I said, "great idea."

"In the alternative, why don't we look around here—we might get lucky."

"Sure," I said unenthusiastically, "but if we do find a key lying around here, what are the chances there's anything important in the files?"

"If there weren't, he'd have given me the key."

We looked everywhere in the closet, under the desk, under the file cabinet—nothing.

"Think," I said, "didn't you ever see him open the file—
or any surreptitious movement in the direction of a nice key
hiding place?"

She scrunched up her forehead in thought. She thought a
long time. Her eyes went to the uniform pictures on the wall.
She started with a daring motion to attack the pictures, not
unlike a bird of prey. On her third or fourth picture, she
grabbed it like all the others and lifted it away from the wall
without detaching it from its hook. "Voila!" she whispered her
exclamation, as she gingerly plucked a shiny brass key from
its routed-out pocket in the back of the frame. She held it up
in front of her winking eye, "Ta tah!"

She moved gazelle-like to the wood cabinet, inserted the
key in the lock and clicked it open. She shined her flashlight
on the contents and began rapidly pulling file folders out and
laying them on Morely Tushman's desk.

I stood beside her and took some of the envelopes and
opened them. The first one I came to was marked simply
"Madame".

Inside were handwritten scrawls on note pad sized paper—
along with some of the same on that ubiquitous yellow legal
paper. They seemed to me to be notes from telephone conversations.

<u>Furious!</u>
<u>Shabby treatment</u>
Hassle

"What did you find?" I asked.
"Lot of cryptic notes. Almost like code. You didn't expect
it to be that easy, did you?"
"It never is—"

In a huff
Out of Joint
He'll be sorry!!!
Terrible table
Underground memory short

Another note—

Otto: <u>She makes a Shakespearean tragedy out of
everything. Ah well, she won't live for ever.</u>

There were more notes, but they made no sense.

Joan went through the other folders. "Here's one on poor
Dick," she said—when we heard the door from the hall open,
followed by the sound of footsteps.

We froze—hastily put the files back, returned the key to
the picture frame. By unspoken agreement, we both went into
the closet just in time to hear the office door open, followed
by thrashing sounds. We both held our breaths—and I admit
I liked being so close to Joan—closeted with her, so to speak.

Was someone ransacking the place—someone trying to get
into Tushman's secret files? Someone with an approach not
as delicate as ours?

My heart was beating crazily; Joan's was too. The dark,
suffocating closet compressed us to a fortuitous immobility.
We were both afraid to make a sound. As our eyes adjusted
to the darkness, we looked into each others eyes where we
easily saw the mutual hope that no one opened the door.

On an irresistible impulse, while looking into her eyes, I
slid my arms around her and moved my lips to hers. It was a
quiet passion that held us together—silent, still, shutting out
the fear.

The noise seemed endless—people were talking as though

they had no fear. Then we heard the sound of a vacuum cleaner and we exhaled our terror in unison.

We waited for a few minutes after we saw the light under the door go out and heard the door shut in the outer office. We must have counted to sixty before I ventured to turn the door knob thoughtfully provided inside the closet.

Quickly I checked the outer office. It was dark, without a sign of a soul. I returned to Tushman's office, and Joan and I began reversing our hasty retreating process and went back to work on the files with the flashlight.

Joan withdrew another folder labeled:

~~Richard~~ Dick

Inside we found medical records that indicated he wasn't doing so well. AIDS, which if I counted correctly, didn't give him much time. I'd have to interview him—but how?

We looked like one armed paperhangers, got everything we thought pertinent, and Joan took the stack to the room down the hall that housed the copy machine. I stayed put, checking to see if we missed anything. When Joan returned with the copies, we replaced everything carefully and hastened down to Joan's car in the parking garage.

We didn't relax until we were out of sight of the John Hancock building. Then Joan said, "Not a bad night's work."

"You were fantastic," I said. "Sure you don't have experience in second story work?"

"I do now," she said, "I guess we should go to bed."

"Sounds good," I said.

"To *sleep*," she said.

"Are you tired?"

She wasn't.

NINETEEN

AS SOON AS WE got in Joan's apartment, I began to wonder what we might have missed.

"I don't know," she said. "Obviously we didn't get what he has in his mind but didn't write down—the stuff he doesn't want anyone to know."

"And how are we going to get it?"

She fluttered her eyelids, "Feminine wiles?" she asked. "I'm afraid Mr. Tushman is not susceptible."

"Do you ever just—you know—talk to him? Does he ever reveal anything?"

"No, to both questions. Morely Tushman is not the sort you just talk to, and he never reveals anything. He's the ideal lawyer-client privilege attorney."

"Good for his clients—not good for us."

She spread out the copies on her dining table. "So what do you make of this?"

"Well, it looks like Madame Claddington was not an easy client. Lot of complaining—I'm a little surprised that Otto Underwood is a client, though I don't see what the significance is."

"Apparently she complained about her table at one of his fundraisers."

"That would fit. She was kind of difficult. Out of joint—in a huff—okay, but what's this 'He'll be sorry'?"

She frowned, "Don't know."

"She was the one to be sorry—were she alive to be sorry.

But here—this one—what do you make of 'Underground memory short'? Do you have a subway here?"

"We have the El—for elevated—we don't go underground here. We think that's for moles."

"Yeah—moles—could that be it? Underground a code for moles—a mole being someone who infiltrated an organization?"

"Whose organization?" she asked, "His presidential campaign?"

"Maybe," I said, "maybe he infiltrated someone else's—a modern day Watergate."

"'Terrible table'—I guess that's simple—she didn't like her table at the fundraiser."

"Maybe. If that's what they were talking about. Of course it makes some sense, the Madame wouldn't like any table that wasn't with the guest of honor."

Joan had copied all the handwritten scrawls in Madame's folder, though the words were cryptic and some were illegible, and puzzle as we did, we couldn't make any sense of them.

"You know," she said, "London has an underground. You don't suppose that's a reference, do you?"

"I don't know. She's surely been to London."

"You know Dick is English—lived in London."

"No, I didn't—could there be a connection?"

"Poor Dick. It doesn't look like he is long for this world."

"Tushman take it hard?"

"Well, he never discusses his personal life with me, but I do see signs that it's wearing on him."

"They live together?"

"They didn't always, but my sense is when Dick started slipping, Mr. Tushman moved him into his place."

"That was nice."

"Yeah—there must be some risk, don't you think?"

"I guess—if there is, why is Tushman taking it?"

"Love?" she said.

"Love to," I said.

She laughed, "Darn it."

"We didn't find the Krondike agency in his private file."

"No. I'll look tomorrow, see what I can find in the 'public' file."

We both seemed to get drowsy at the same time and fell into a chaste bed. When I awoke in the morning, she was gone. A note invited me to help myself to the refrigerator and told me cheerily she was off to work—dutifully and conscientiously, because this was no time to make waves in the workplace.

Armed with Dick's address from the file in his lover-companion's office, I trundled out to the nicer edge of town, where I presented myself at the door of an impressive Tudor house while trying to look like a hospice volunteer.

The door was opened by one of those older, white haired women, a little plump, but her extra body fat keeping the wrinkles from her face—one of those happiness sowers who had devoted her life to the care of the infirm. A nurse who sowed cheer on infertile ground—it was a lovely calling. She brightened at seeing me, causing me to believe I was a bright spot in the middle of her shift.

"Hello," I smiled as disarmingly as it was possible for me to. "I'm Teddy Grimm from hospice. I've come to look in on Dick."

"Well, how nice," she said, expanding her arms in a gesture of goodwill and welcome. Oh, I thought, would that all my disguises were so easy. Then a frown come over her face that I thought spelled trouble.

"But you don't look grim," she said, with a patronizing sadness.

"Why thanks," I said, as though I had been genuinely complimented.

"Well, Dick will be glad to see a man," she said.

"Oh?"

"Yes, I don't think he likes women very much."

"Why not?"

"Oh, you know," she made a helpless, fluttering gesture with a hand. She lowered her voice, "I don't mind telling you homosexuality is not natural and Dick is paying the price. It's an affront to God."

"You're religious," I said, not as though I had discovered a cure for cancer, but as a flat, unarguable premise for more conversation. "Get 'em talking" was Bomber's motto. No telling what you'll learn.

"Oh, yes," she said beaming, "and very proud of it."

I nodded. I decided against reminding her that there was something in the Bible about not judging your fellows unless you wanted to be in the same pickle. But then looking at her, I decided there was not a lot of fodder for judgement. Unless you want to include homophobia.

"Have you discussed your opinion on the matter with Dick?"

"Oh, my, yes—have I!"

"How does he take it?"

"Well, I guess I'd have to say not well. Not well at all. He considers me a meddling busy body. I wasn't hired for my opinions, he says, and he'd thank me to keep them to myself."

"Oh, dear."

She nodded with purpose.

"I take it he's not doing too well, or they wouldn't have sent for me."

"Oh, no," she said nodding, then thinking better of it and shaking her head. "He's not—not well at all. You ask me, you came none too soon."

"Can I do anything for you—get you anything to make your job easier?"

"Oh, no, thank you. Mr. Tushman gives us everything he needs."

"He must be fond of Dick."

"Oh my," she said, "I'd say *so*."

"And Mr. Tushman is good with him—with Dick?"

"Very solicitous, yes. It's heartbreaking, really. Though I'm on duty only the hours Mr. Tushman is off at work, I do get to see some interaction, and he always seems so considerate—courtly even."

"May I see him?"

"Well," she said as though that were a novel idea, "he should be delighted."

"He doesn't get many visitors?"

"None. His whole world seems to be Mr. Tushman."

She led me up a dark wooden staircase—mahogany perhaps. The upper hallway was gloomy, and it had a lot of old furniture that might have come from Frankenstein's house.

At the door to the bedroom, with drapes drawn against the sunny morning, the nurse said "Dick—a Mr. Grimm to see you, he's from hospice."

From Dick's reaction as I invaded the sanctity of his sick room, I thought he might be already dead. He was as gray as a cadaver in the half light of the bedroom, where he occupied a double bed like a mummy whose shroud had just been removed. On closer look there appeared to be some breathing going on, but it didn't seem to be to any purpose.

"Doing all right?" I asked, wondering how a real hospice worker would handle it.

At length without otherwise stirring, he opened one eye and drew in a few minutes' ration of air.

"Hospice," he grumbled in a gravelly voice, "you came to the right place."

"Ah," I said, "Dick—do you want to be called Dick or Richard?"

A half smile pulled at half his mouth. "Ah, sometimes I have trouble remembering. Richard, Dick—I've been both. In a way, Dick is a scandalous name, what with all its connotations. Richard has more dignity, if you don't think of those Shakespeare Richards. So Dick it is—not because I don't need the dignity, not because I've anything in particular against Richard the second or third, but because at this juncture I'm trying to hold on to any shred of youth and vitality I may have once had. Dick is a man of fecundity—pizzazz, energy—*sexuality!*" he said as though he had been groping for the proper word and suddenly found it. "So I'm Dick again in a fleeting attempt to get hope to triumph over reality."

"How are you feeling?"

"Exhausted. I haven't talked so much in ages."

"Oh, sorry."

"No, that's quite all right. All I do is lie here anyway. I'd much rather drop over dancing or doing something, but I don't have the energy to get out of bed."

I think my face was suitably long when I said, "It must be rough."

"It's no fun, but you resign yourself. Like anything else in life—the inescapable reality sets in and you just go with it. Adapt or die my mother used to say, and I'm in no position to argue the point."

"What does the doctor say?"

"Not much. I won't let him hoodwink me. I have a month or so—maybe less. But, you know something?"

"What?"

"I'm up for it. There's life and there's being an invalid, and that's no life. All these people playing at keeping me alive—making me comfortable. Wonderful—comfortable is what you have when happiness is beyond question."

"Well, I've seen a lot of terminal patients," I lied, "but you have one of the best attitudes."

It worked. I could tell he was pleased. "No options," he said, modestly. "We're all given a shot at the big game of life. What we give and what we get don't often balance. All lives come to an end one way or another. My immune system gave out. Can't fight off the germs anymore. Some get cancer that eats away at their cells and flesh, or their hearts go south," he shrugged. "Different sauces on the same old dish."

"Do you have everything you want-books, magazines, tapes, CDs? I can get you some if you'd like."

"No, thanks," he said. "Morely takes good care of me."

"Morely?"

"Yes, Morely Tushman. He's a prominent lawyer in town—perhaps you know of him? He's very active with charity and the important people."

Did I notice a flicker of distaste in that description? "Afraid I don't," I said. "I try to keep a respectable distance between lawyers and me."

"Not a bad idea," he said with a smirk, "but I can't complain. Morely's been aces with me."

"How so?"

"Well, this is his house for starters. He took me in when I began to fall apart."

"When was that?"

"I noticed after we come back from our trip west."

"Oh, where did you go?"

"Long story," he said. "We went with one of Morely's clients. A crazy woman who wound up getting shot on the trip."

"Dead?"

"Yeah," he said, "dead."

"Where was this?"

"A place called Angelton, California."

"I've heard of it. Nice?"

"Oh yeah. She had a nice spread all right. She'd never been there—she kept it pristine—flowers daily—had a crew keeping it just so in case she pulled a surprise visit."

"So someone shot her?"

"Yeah—"

"Who?"

He didn't answer right away. Finally he licked his lips. "One of her staff, apparently. Little communist or something, resented her obscene wealth."

"It was obscene?"

"Not to me. You can't be too rich for my taste," he said. "Anyway, when I got back, I started going to pot."

"Smoke pot?"

"No—I mean the deterioration was noticeable. I was weakening already before we went, and I tried to beg off, but Morely wouldn't hear of it. Do me good, he said. Didn't."

"I'm sorry to hear that—but this murder intrigues me," I said. "Was she sleeping or what?"

"No. Watching fireworks. It was the Fourth of July."

"So you *saw* it happen?" I said, astonished at the thought.

"Yes…no. The others did. I was inside. Wasn't feeling well," he said, sighing, as though it reminded him of his depressing condition. "But things…" he said, then paused at the difficult memory, "are not…always what…they…" he trailed off. I thought I saw his lips form "seem," but I couldn't take it to the bank—or the courthouse.

"Thanks for coming," he coughed. "I'll have to ask you to leave now, I'm worn out."

"I'm sorry—I stayed too long."

A rueful smile covered his pale lips. "Nah," he said, "I'm going to have a long time to rest—an eternity, really."

On my way out, the happy nurse couldn't thank me enough for coming. "You'll come again, I hope," she said, "He so enjoyed having someone to talk to who didn't scold him for his unnatural acts."

"I don't know," I said, "I only go where they send me."

Back at the hotel, my phone rang. I hoped it was Joan. It was Bomber instead.

"Boy? Get back here on the double. All hell has broken loose—the commie could not be dissuaded from demanding a speedy trial and waiving all possibilities for delay. I told him your investigation was not complete. Cut no ice with the thick-headed pinko. I'm sorry I ever agreed to take his case…"

After all my years with Bomber—at home and in the office, I learned to read his thoughts by the terms he employed. The quaint military phrase "on the double" for hurrying was put into use by the master trial lawyer when he thought the going was going tough, tough, tough.

I tried to stall my return with the need to look into Zachary Roseleer.

"What in the Sam Hill is this?" he said. "Since when do you want to put off coming home?"

"Only when I'm n-not finished with my in-investigation."

"Zachary Roseleer works for Otto Underwood—that's the hope right?"

"Right."

"But Otto Underwood is a *Californian,* remember? His offices are *here.*"

There was no more stuttering, because there was no more arguing. Oh, I tried to think of a million ways to plead for time to go back to Dick, and Harley Holiday, and Netta, but Bomber would not hear of it. "Are you deaf, Boy? The case is starting Monday. Move it, boy—double time!"

TWENTY

"Tod," JOAN WHISPERED into the phone, "that creep Harley Holiday is following me around."

"Does he know you know?"

"Oh, he doesn't try to hide it."

"Then it's just to intimidate us."

"It's working," she said. "After I saw what he did to you…"

"I don't think he'll harm you—I'd let him know you recognize him—maybe smile and wave."

"I'll try—see you tonight," she said, and hung up.

I always experienced a desolation when Joan hung up the phone.

But two minutes later it was ringing again.

"Good news, kid," Bomber said on the phone. "Bonnie has fiddled with the internet and gotten a lead on Zachary Roseleer. She's a whiz with that thing," he said with a happy pride in his voice—as though one good turn could justify keeping that shapely airhead on the payroll.

"What did she f-find?" I asked.

His answer was not music to my ears—"I'll put her on. She'll tell you."

My first thought was I could put to rest any fantasy I might have about Joan Harding replacing Bonnie Doone as Bomber's secretary—and if I asked him to hire a secretary for me, he'd laugh me out of the office. Bonnie Doone came on the line. "Hiya, Sweet Meat," she said. "What's the scoop in Chicago, baby?"

Demeaning was Bonnie's middle name. If our sexes had been reversed, she'd have been on the carpet for sexual harassment. As it was, I, being of the so-called stronger sex, had to take anything with a smile she dished out.

I was gritting my teeth. "Zachary Roseleer," I said, "you have something?"

"Oh, do I ever," she said, with the subtlety of a kindergartner's crowing about getting to pass the cookies. She fell silent—I never liked her better than when she was silent, but I was eager to hear what she had on the long lost Zachary Roseleer. "So?" I asked. "Are you in the mood to share it with me?"

"Show and tell time, is it? Put up or shut up?"

"I couldn't have put it better myself."

"All right, Joy Boy, hang on to your hat—Zachary Roseleer is a sort of an underground political consultant to the stars. The guy who tells you what you don't want to hear about things you don't want anyone to know. Has two successful big ones to his credit, but he becomes so *persona non grata* for his dirty work that he changes his name every go around."

"Where does he hang out?"

"There's the rub, Sugar Bones. He doesn't. He flits from place to place putting out fires—when he isn't starting them."

"Any idea his connection to the Madame?"

"Oh, oh, whoa there—down, boy—that's your department. I don't want to rob you of your prerogatives—step on your toes. You'd be out of a job before you know it. Not that a third grader couldn't do your job better."

"Thanks a million, Miss America," I said. "I'm sure if Bomber is looking for third grade mentalities to help out, you'll be at the top of the list. Any indication this Zachary might be conversant with firearms?"

"Guns, you mean? What a swell way to put it. Go to the

head of the NRA! Guns don't kill people, Sweet Meat, *people* kill people."

"Yeah, and is this Zachary noted for that kind of work?"

"Gracious me, that's your job, as I said. Isn't this internet just the cat's pajamas?"

"Yeah," I grumbled, "it might be, if it gave us a lead on where to find him."

"Start with Otto Underwood, numbskull. Do I have to draw you a picture?"

There were a few more barbed unpleasantries before we hung up.

As the intrigue stepped up, so oddly did my spirits. I found myself hoping Zachary Roseleer would lead to some need for further investigation so I could prolong my time in Chicago.

Loose ends time. I called Netta to ask about the computer Harley Holiday had taken from the Madame. She said there was nothing on it. She herself was not up on computers and the Madame never touched it.

Joan and I decided on an all-night jamming session for my last night on earth, as I chose to characterize it. And I didn't mean I thought I was going to heaven.

Harley Holiday was stationed at her house when I arrived. Brazenly, I sauntered over to his car. "Hi, Harley," I said. "How's it going?"

"Fine," he said. Dare I speculate that he appeared a mite frightened? Certainly not from fear of physical harm, but the fear of the unknown, as though I might psyche him out.

"Just to let you know," I said, "I'm going to be here tonight. We won't be doing any investigating. Tomorrow morning, I fly back to California. You're welcome to come along if you think it would serve some purpose," I reached in my pocket for my ticket, causing him to jump as though I were going to pull a gun on him. When he saw the ticket, he seemed to relax.

"We told Morely Tushman I was leaving, I'm sorry he didn't tell you."

"Hey," he said, throwing up his hands, "I only work here, *capisce?* Do what I'm told."

Our final night of music, I'm embarrassed to say, got rather silly. We played the usual duets, violin sonatas and what have you, but it was increasingly apparent the music was turning morose. Tempos were dragging, brilliance of tone was ebbing and suddenly for no reason I segued into *Marcia Funebre* from Beethoven's Piano Sonata, Opus 26. Joan played irreverent riffs on the theme, moving from morose to inappropriate, jazzy figures.

Staying with Beethoven in what might have been depressed periods, we did the Funeral March from his 3rd symphony—the *Eroica.* Then for an encore Chopin's funeral march from his Sonata 35 #4 in B minor.

Being funeral-marched out, we fell into bed, where I must draw the veil of privacy.

The separation in the morning was not an easy one.

Joan made buttermilk pancakes with whipped egg whites that floated across my tongue. We sat at her tiny kitchenette table—space was at such a premium in big cities. We held hands across the table between the maple syrup and the orange juice.

"Tod—I don't want you to go."

"I don't want to either. But one positive effect it might have is you should get to keep your job with me out of everyone's hair."

"A lot of good I'll do you—they'll be watching my every move—probably bugging my phone."

"You've done your bit," I said, "Of course, I'll call you everyday—and if anything develops I won't be opposed to hearing what it is."

We embraced at the last minute and decided she should not

come out with me in case Harley Holiday was still hanging around.

She watched me from her doorway until I disappeared around the corner to the elevators.

When I reached the street, I was surprised to see Harley Holiday still on duty—didn't he ever sleep? I found my car and got in, started it, moved out into the traffic and checked the rearview mirror.

I had gotten onto the highway to the airport and had just gotten used to the idea of being followed—he just wanted to make sure I got on the plane, I thought—when I heard the roar of acceleration and saw him pulling up beside me. Traffic was heavy going toward the airport but Harley had enough maneuvering room to make this threatening gesture. I, however, did not have enough room to evade him. I slowed down. He slowed—I changed lanes, moving to the right, he changed with me. I was beginning to think he was up to his old intimidation when I casually glanced in his direction and found myself looking down a barrel of a pretty respectable pistol.

This is it, I thought. Just when I've found the love of my life. Typical! I quickly began driving erratically, so he couldn't get a clean shot. Not that a dirty shot would please me. I jammed my brakes, half hoping I would be rear-ended to attract attention. No such luck.

Harley Holiday slowed, I changed lanes, trying to get on his right side—make the shot more difficult. Cars were coming between us.

Suddenly he was on my left, the cars around us having dispersed—the gun raised, pointing at my head. I slowed and on an impulse blew my horn, attracting some coveted attention. Harley snapped his head, and for an instant I was afraid he was going to squeeze one off in anger. I kept lurching in the car and swiveling my body around to make a more difficult target than a sitting duck.

I was so terrified I couldn't take my hand off the car horn. It got me a lot of angry attention, but everyone was looking at me rather than at Harley Holiday. I frantically pointed at the gunman, but only the occasional driver looked his way. The gun fell to his lap. I hoped one of them would get on one of their ubiquitous cell phones and call the police. The horn blowing dispelled the immediate threat but not the long-term danger. I hung back and Harley stayed just enough ahead of me that I could make a sudden move for an exit and he was beyond it.

I got back on the highway at the next opportunity—checking for my adversary. I didn't see him. I was turning to get off at the airport exit when I thought I saw his car parked, waiting for me. I swerved back onto the highway and took the next exit. I drove up to the unloading area—propped open the trunk, got my suitcase and left the trunk lid up and ran into the car rental counter, told the young woman my story—"Sir, you can't do that," she said, "all cars must be returned—"

"Yes, yes," I said. "It's life or death. I had a man pointing a gun at your car and he's probably sitting at the car rental lot waiting for me right now—sorry—charge me extra—do what you want—" and I slapped a twenty dollar bill on the counter and ran to the check-in counter.

I looked at the clock and saw all those diversionary tactics had taken their toll and I was very short of time. I ran from the check-in counter, lugging my bag with me, and had the honor of being the last one on the plane before they shut the door.

I looked around the plane—no Harley that I could see, unless he had worked himself into the hold somewhere.

When I sat back in the last seat on the sold-out flight, I found myself between two individuals, a man and a woman, who might have benefited from some dietary restrictions. The space left for me after they staked out their territory would have been commodious for a strand of dry spaghetti, but not much more.

Needless to say, I didn't move too much for the duration of the flight. And the kicker was they were married!

I offered to change seats with one of them, but they both expressed happiness where they were, and proceeded to spend a large part of the flight talking over me as though I was—well—a strand of dry spaghetti.

It irked the daylights out of me until I heard one of them say, "You see OU's climbing up the polls?"

"Yeah—I think he's going to win."

"OU, kid!" said the other. It was difficult for me to tell who was talking, they were built so much alike and their bulk obliterated any distinguishing characteristics.

"Excuse me," I said, "are you talking about Otto Underwood, the presidential candidate?"

They looked at me as though I was a pancake short of a breakfast. "Oh you, kid?" one of them said. "Who else would we be talking about?"

"I'm sorry," I said, "I just never heard of him being called that."

"You do know the expression OU, kid?"

"I've heard it—something out of the twenties wasn't it? Like twenty-three skidoo?"

"Can't prove it by me. I wasn't around in the twenties, and from the looks of you, neither were you."

"Too true," I said. "Can you tell me anything about this OU, kid? I don't know much about him."

"Well, where you been, boy? You got your head in the sand or something?" His voice was loaded with aggression so I decided he was the male.

"I'm afraid I'm a babe in the woods about politics, but I'd like to learn."

"Well, son," (they made me feel right at home with this Boy

and Son stuff, like Bomber was talking to me), "Otto Underwood's just about the most wonderful candidate ever come
down the pike."

"How so?"

"Well, he's a moral man," the window seat said, "I mean
he says something, you kin take it to the bank."

"OU, kid!"

"What about foreign policy?"

"Butt out."

"Mind your own business," one of them said.

"How about if we are attacked—or our interests abroad
are?"

"Well, Otto Underwood is death on radicals, you better
believe it! An' with all these bombings—this is where the wars
of the future are going to be fought—one on one."

"United States against them," the other one chimed in.
Sounded simple. "Ain't another candidate anywhere's got
this tough stance on the radicals. Anybody knows it's gotten
out of hand. Otto Underwood's the one with the backbone to
put a stop to it."

Before we landed, I casually reopened the topic. "Oh, by
the way," I said, "the name Mrs. Anna Claddington mean
anything to either of you?"

They tried to think. It seemed a major undertaking. "Can't
say it does," they said in virtual unison.

TWENTY-ONE

BOMBER SENT BONNIE V. DOONE to meet me at Angelton Airport. A taxi would have been nicer, but all things considered, it was an astute move on Bomber's part. Bonnie V. Doone *can* drive a car. It's one of her more developed talents. It's always a miracle when gorgeousness can be useful.

"Yo, Sugar Lump," she said from the car at the curb where she was illegally parked, "hop in—Bomber's bursting to see you. All Hades is breaking loose."

I got in next to her, though my instincts were pulling me to the nether regions of the back seat.

Bonnie was built with a body Michelangelo would have chiseled had he cared for women. I couldn't help comparing Bonnie's structure with that of my new love Joan Harding. Bonnie dressed like she'd just stepped out of one of those girly magazines—with a kind of physical perfection that put off any serious contender. Joan was real—dressed practically and attractively without any obvious thought of being alluring.

That was alluring to me. When you've got it, you don't *have* to flaunt it.

Mercifully, the ride from the airport to our Victorian on Albert Avenue was not that long, and the airhead could fill the air with the wisdom of her tender years, which was just one cut below a high school linebacker.

When Bomber heard the front door he bellowed, "Get in here, Boy! On the double!"

Bonnie grinned like the cat that swallowed the whole birdcage, and threw off a snappy salute. I dropped my suitcase in place in Bonnie's outer office/reception area and straightened up to face the music.

Bomber started the moment he saw me step in his uncharacteristically open door, and (of course) closed it behind me. One of my responsibilities as underling to the great Bomber Hanson is to be a sounding board. Pianos have sounding boards, so do violins. It is what resonates so you hear the music. My function as a sounding board was more like a punching bag—to absorb blows. I know more than once I'd felt punch drunk after serving my time across the desk from Bomber Hanson, attorney-at-law. King of Torts.

"I've had the humiliation of my life," he shouted, as though he were pacing in front of a jury of deaf mutes. "Appearing in court and being forced to protest that my client's wishes are counter to his best interests. Judge McCoy rules as any sane judge would that I know what's best for my client, and the kid goes berserk and says he demands an appeal—not only is he ornery, he's stupid to boot. He wants the speedy trial the constitution promises him," he says. "Favorite reading matter in the slammer that constitution—which by the way would be bonfire kindling if he had his way government-wise. More of 'em read it that under*stood* it—*before* they got locked up, our jails might not be so overcrowded.

"Judge says 'Haste makes waste, sir.' Yes, swear to God he called the punk 'sir.' 'Sir, you have one of the most experienced attorneys in the country; it'll behoove you not to go against his judgment. These things take time for preparation—for *your* sake.'"

"'Then let me out of jail and take all the time you want,' the kid says."

"Judge McCoy fixes him with his most unhappy glare. 'Mr. Espinal, you don't talk to an officer of the court like that.'"

"'Nobody tells me how to talk. We're brothers—I recognize no authority.'"

"'You'd be in tough shape under communism then,' McCoy said, and I could have kissed him. He's a bleeding heart liberal. Deep down he goes for that share the wealth *schtick*—brothers under the skin—from each according to his ability, to each according to his need—the blueprint for our graduated income tax and welfare schemes. But, I got to hand it to old McCoy, he knows the difference between communism and compassion. The whole thing was unreal." Bomber was worked up, as though the indignity had just happened, when it had transpired three days before. Unreal—but a taste of what's in store for us.

"I'd be out of there in a second, if I were a quitter. I should probably be institutionalized for taking this case—and may well be if I keep it. Judge McCoy lectured the punk on courtroom etiquette, but it was clear—though the punk said he *un*derstood—that he lacked the good sense to go along with it."

It was kind of fun seeing Bomber so harried. It didn't happen often.

"So the upshot," he said, "is we're on. Speedy trial here we come. Confucius should have said, 'Speedy trial is sloppy trial,' but the kid is so bull-headed he equates innocence with acquittal. He's told me as much. So we are on a tremendous spot. It's hard to win these hopeless cases *with* sufficient preparation—impossible without. So here's the jury roll—" he said, handing me a couple of pages of typed script. "Get us some pinko commies, socialists, left wingers—freedom of speech nuts—even if you do, this loudmouth is so obnoxious he could terminally offend a jury made up of twelve clones of his mother.

"So," he said, sitting back as though exhausted by his tirade, "anything new?"

I shook my head. "Other than almost getting killed on my way t-to the airp-port, n-no."

"Who?" Bomber asked, startled at the news.

"Harley Holiday, the b-bodyguard who tackled our client on the Fourth of July."

"Tell you something?"

"You mean b-besides my unf-fitness f-for this line of w-work?"

He waved a hand of dismissal as though my thought were hardly worth consideration. "I speak of the guilt or innocence of my client."

"There's s-something they d-don't want us to know."

"I'll say!" he boomed. "Now all we have to do is find out what it is."

That exchange was Bomber in his essence: it was *his* client, but when it came to *my* work, it was *we*. Every once in a while he masters the obvious—all we have to do is find the real culprit.

"Any weak links in the eyewitness ranks?" he asked.

"The chauffeur is not willing to c-categorically say he saw Inocencio shoot her."

"Of course not. None of 'em saw him, they were looking at fireworks—lots of noise and commotion; distraction. So the question is, why are they all swearing to a lie?"

"Yeah."

"And how long before they get to the driver and he swears on a stack of Holy Bibles that he saw it too?" he asked. "So, Boy, you told me everything you have to report on Chicago?"

I must have turned every shade of red at that one. I opened my mouth to stammer but nothing came out, thank goodness, because I didn't know what to say. Had Mom talked to him about Joan after all? Then I had an inspiration, "I did g-get s-some inform-mation by quasilegal methods," I said.

He held up a hand, "Don't compromise me with methods.

You know my stringent requirement that all information be obtained in the strictest conformance with all applicable laws—that are known to you at the time." He dropped his voice: "Unless, of course, expediency in the service of an innocent client should dictate otherwise."

"Of course," I said with a smile. He had extricated me from my embarrassment. It was no good telling him about our enthralling duets. Understanding the aesthetic nature of the arts was not on his radar screen. I don't doubt he could have taught me a thing or two about prize fighting or skeet shooting, two things that had never caught my fancy.

He waved at the jury lists in my hand—his wordless dismissal.

Sixteen hour days were the rule for what was left of the week before the trial—five days and change. I turned over every public record on the list as well as tapping every relevant source I knew—including the ubiquitous Bonnie V. Doone and her wizardry with the internet. There sure is a lot of information about people on the internet, unfortunately a lot of it is about other people with the same name, and separating the wheat from the chaff is sometimes impossible.

Everyday I missed Joan Harding more. Memories kept breaking my concentration, and at times I feared my obsession would compromise the case. We managed to talk on the phone everyday—so long at a time I couldn't believe it when I looked at the clock afterwards. Perhaps the thing we talked about most was how to get her out to California to help on the case without costing her her job. We had not come up with a solution.

Here's what I found at the end of five days. I equated it with the Batan Death March to give Bomber a reference he could understand.

From what I could tell, there were a surprising number of liberals in town. But most of them in the jury pool were of the parlor variety—not card carriers, not many who would cheerfully march to a gas chamber singing the Russian National anthem.

The biggest surprise was to find Bill Michaels on the list. Michaels was a columnist for a local throw away who never saw a democrat he couldn't love nor a republican who had any redeeming social value. The chance of the district attorney ever allowing him on this jury was as they say, slim to none. But I fantasized how much fun it would be if Webster—our local defender of the citizenry—ran out of preemptory challenges and tried to argue with this judge to have Bill Michaels removed for cause. A real hoot, but not too bloody likely, as they say across the sea.

None of the judges were buddy-buddy with Bomber for obvious reasons—and in a criminal case the judge's sympathy was usually with the county because most of them had come up in the ranks from district attorney—McCoy had been a public defender. McCoy was a champion of the downtrodden—the huddled masses yearning to breathe freely. Of course, McCoy, like all the rest of the judges, did not suffer Bomber's courtroom antics gladly, and he had a temper that could be set off in a moment at any perceived hint of disrespect for the bench in general and for himself specifically.

For Bomber, I graded the prospective jurors from one to ten as the Americans for Democratic Action committee might, with ten being Joseph Stalin and watering down from there to Jesse Helms at one. Of course it wasn't scientific, but it was some indicator of a predisposed mindset for each—those I could determine.

I didn't find any ones or tens—but Bomber was not disposed to take anyone five or under if he could help it—and you couldn't always help it, depending on how the names came up—and I'd marked one person a nine (Bill Michaels, the columnist) the rest came out as follows:

8   14%
7   20%
6   21%
5   30%
4   11%
3   3%
2   2 persons
Unknown 15%

So, Bomber had the best odds perhaps ever from a pool of prospective jurors, with about fifty-five percent acceptable and probably eight percent or so of the unknowns, putting the acceptables at almost two-thirds. Of course, that was if he could keep Inocencio's mouth shut for the duration of the case.

We may have had less likeable clients, but I can't remember who they might have been.

TWENTY-TWO

PRESIDENT JUDGE KELLER graciously gave up his main court-room with the high ceilings and the generous seating to ac-commodate the anticipated crowds interested in Angelton's crime of the century (the third or fourth trial in the last fifteen years so designated). It was a space out of a King Arthur movie—the founding fathers of this coastal burg were into old. Everything was made brand-new to look old. Were they after class and respectability, or was it a fear of the untried and unknown that motivated them?

I was assigned to give Inocencio a final pretrial pep talk in the courthouse holding tank. Bomber and I both thought the task was not only thankless, but hopeless too.

Inocencio was sullen on the wooden bench in the tank. He left no doubt of his victim status. He was not wearing the jacket or tie Bomber had bought him, and I saw another hopeless cause in trying to get him to. I tried anyway. I sat on the bench next to him to assume a palsy stance. "Ready?" I asked neutrally.

"I want to get it over," he said.

"You *will* wear the jacket and tie, won't you?" I asked. "Ap-pearances are so important, and Bomber wants you to have every chance of winning this thing."

"He is not man enough to tell me this himself?"

"He's man enough, Inocencio—he's trying to win your case with insufficient time—thanks to you pushing for a speedy trial."

"You take my place in this hellhole? I wait. I don't kill nobody! I'm totally innocent."

"It may surprise you, but I believe you are innocent. So does Bomber. We also realize we could be wrong. But what matters is that all twelve of the jurors believe you are innocent. Of that, they have to be convinced. Doing it right takes time. Rushing it, like you've forced us to do, is not going to help you. Way I see it, you owe us one."

"What?"

"Keep quiet in court. If you hear something you don't like, don't blurt out your opinion. Tell Bomber or me at the first opportunity. We're going to give you a pad to write on if you have something you want brought to anyone's attention."

I looked in his eyes. He held them steady—no promises there.

"All right, I know what you're thinking, and I hate to tell you but you're wrong. All life is, perhaps unfortunately, salesmanship. And a large part of salesmanship is getting people to like you. Nobody likes a wise-mouth."

"I don't kill nobody!" he protested again.

"You know that verse—

Here lies the body of John Jay,
He died maintaining his right of way.
He was right, dead right as he sped along,
But he's just as dead as if he were wrong."

"Funny," Inocencio said.

"Not funny at all," I said. "I can easily see them leading you off to a life in jail—or worse—perhaps a lethal injection—with you singing out at the top of your lungs, 'BUT I'M INNOCENT.' The slammer is full of guys singing the same tune. Who knows, maybe you can get a chorus together to give one-song performances."

"You crazy!"

"Yeah? Well let me tell you what your problem is. You think you know everything, and you don't know a fraction."

"You do?"

"Heavens no, but I'm willing to face my limitations."

"What's that?"

"I know I'm no trial attorney. I wouldn't be any good standing up in court to plead your case. So I don't do that kind of work. But you know all about the law, the courts, the psychology of jurors. You could write a book. You remind me of the saying—'He is often wrong but never in doubt.' Well you can take my advice—Bomber's advice really—and sit in court with your mouth shut, as do ninety-nine percent of the accused, or you can make a jackass out of yourself as you did in the motion hearing with Bomber. In case you don't already know, Bomber's fuse is not generous. It doesn't take much to tip him—you do it, you'll be defending yourself."

"Way it looks, I could do better."

"Oh yeah, sure, wonderful," I said, exasperated. "See what I mean? For your sake I won't tell Bomber you said that, I'd recommend you didn't either."

He glowered. It came naturally.

I stood, clapped him on the shoulder like a good buddy. "Okay," I said, "we're ready to go. Jury selection is first. It can get tedious—same questions over and over. Bomber is a master at telling who's for us and who's against. Big part of the game, so remember—patience and forbearance. You give those prospective jurors every reason to love you—because some of them will *be* jurors. And—please," I said pointing to the jacket piled on a scarred table, "wear the jacket and tie."

"Why?"

"It's a psychological thing. You look so great no one could imagine you shot anyone."

"I didn't!"

"Yes, yes," I agreed, "Salesmanship!"

Ten minutes later the marshal brought Inocencio into the courtroom. He *was* wearing the jacket, and the tie was approximately under his collar and looked like a two year old had tied it. Bomber rolled his eyes when he saw him. I was pleasantly surprised—I thought I'd made important inroads. When Inocencio sat down, I leaned over him and whispered, "Thanks, let me straighten your tie."

He glowered, but he let me fuss with it, and I managed some improvement.

The jury panel was brought in—about fifty of them—then the judge. Some judges treat their job in relation to jurors as a popularity contest. McCoy was one of those. All smiles with the "Good morning, ladies and gentlemen," then sliding into the palaver about the goodness of jury service, the privilege to give something back to our wonderful society, blah, blah, blah. They never bought it. You could tell by their faces that some were resigned to it (those whose companies paid their salaries) and some in search of a loophole to weasel out of it (those who weren't being paid).

Judge McCoy asked if anyone had a hardship that would keep him from serving. Surprisingly, no one came forward, probably for two reasons: (1) Bomber put on such a good show his juries were in demand and (2) people liked to take part in celebrated cases, such as this; the newspapers were giving it constant ink, declaring it a case of economic disparity, of good vs. evil, of youth vs. age, man vs. woman—all of them presupposing our client was guilty.

There were the usual questions about anyone being related to or having personal knowledge of any of the principals, the accused, the attorneys—no one did.

Each attorney got to address the panel in an effort to weed out those who might be predisposed to favor the other side.

Bomber kept his remarks brief. He said this was a case that

would depend heavily on eyewitness testimony. Could these blessed jurors find it in their hearts and minds to realize that eyewitness accounts were notoriously inaccurate, and that too many people had gone to their deaths or languished in jail because of erroneous eyewitness identifications? Would they be able to remain objective in the face of multiple witnesses who claimed to have seen the defendant commit the crime if we in fact showed there was reasonable doubt they had seen anything at all?

Of course they all said yes—sure we're all fair and open-minded—but we made a note of those who hesitated and those who protested too much. But Bomber had planted the seed.

Bill Michaels, our rabid liberal columnist was called in the second batch of prospective jurors. Webster made quick work of him to Bomber's amusement but not surprise.

Bomber leaned over to me at the defendant table and whispered in that husky audible whisper of his, "Let's hope he goes back to his paper and writes something scathing about being unceremoniously dropped from this too-political trial for political reasons." (He did—in such a cutsey, self-agrandizing way it may have had the opposite effect.)

It took us two and one-half days to impanel a jury and two alternates. Politically, Bomber figured we did okay—seven to four for us and one unknown on the main panel. Though he didn't say so, I suspected Bomber was a little disappointed that the level of intelligence was a touch higher than he might have chosen. His appeal was going to be more emotional than intellectual. And, of course, the verdict had to be unanimous, meaning he had to get not only our seven, but also the enemy of five, to win.

In his opening statement to the jury, District Attorney Webster Grainger III took up the eyewitness theme, after reciting circumstances of the case which he called "facts," but Bomber would attempt to belittle as "facts as the D.A. sees them."

"It is fair to say, ladies and gentlemen of the jury," Web said, "I have never had a case with more eyewitnesses. It was a small gathering on the beach, in a controlled space. The attendees were positioned in such a manner—on which they all agree—in which the bullet could only have come from the defendant's gun. The case is virtually open and shut. But look for my opponent to raise peripheral and unrelated issues. He is a master at obfuscation. And the more hopeless his case, the more smoke and mirrors we can expect. We have five eyewitnesses to the crime. We had six, but Madame Claddington didn't live to identify her assassin. Now, my opponent will likely trot out all the so-called scientific studies that purport to show that, in some cases, eyewitness testimony can be less than perfect. We will not argue the studies. But there is a dramatic distinction you should look out for. And that is this: In those cases—Mr. Hanson will try to introduce over my certain objection—the person identified was a stranger to the eyewitnesses. In this case, everyone of them had met the defendant and had seen him standing where he was when he pulled the trigger—seen him there for perhaps ten minutes or so—he was not someone who ran to the scene, did his foul murder, then ran away. No, in this case the accused was tackled in the act by two brave men—at least one of which will be a witness here. He will tell you they saw the defendant throw the murder weapon in the ocean. Further, we will tie the defendant's position to the ballistics report, emphasizing he was the *only* one in position to commit this tragic, senseless, cowardly murder.

"Why did he do it? It was simply a class thing. Madame Claddington was rich—beyond comprehension perhaps. The defendant is a self-avowed communist. The victim got her wealth through robust capitalism, and that made him mad. Not much of a motive for murder you may think, but it was enough for him."

Bomber rose laconically to his feet. "Your Honor, I have been the soul of forbearance during the district attorney's opening remarks. I doubt there is a soul in this courtroom who knows better than the district attorney that opening statements are limited to a recitation of the facts of the case that he plans to prove. He seems to be making arguments more appropriate to the closing statement, and I am just wondering if that is because he fears that this proper order of things will not be to his advantage. Like maybe he thinks saving his argument for his closing will be too late."

"All right, Mr. Hanson," Judge McCoy said. "Enough. I'll sustain the objection I assume you are making. Just tell us what you intend to show, Mr. Grainger."

Web stood flat-footed with a wry expression on his face. "Indeed, Your Honor, and I shall prove my case through my witnesses. I will have no further remarks at this time."

"Hallelujah," Bomber said under his breath.

"Mr. Hanson?" Judge McCoy directed his attention at my father who isn't in heaven.

"Yes, Your Honor," Bomber said. "With the court's permission, I will save my remarks, if any, to the opening of the defense case."

You could tell Judge McCoy felt he had been flim-flammed, but he had nothing to say.

TWENTY-THREE

INOCENCIO HAD MADE IT THROUGH the jury selection without an outburst, but he sat there like a keg of dynamite waiting to explode. I patted him surreptitiously on the shoulder and said, "Good work," when I thought no one was looking. I don't think he was pleased.

After the lunch break, District Attorney Webster Grainger called Avery Knapp to the stand. He was a police detective sergeant who had taken less than scrupulous care of his body. He was cool, man, cool as he sauntered to the witness chair, taking time to turn and smile at Bomber en route.

Avery was a casual, laid-back witness who had been in this seat many times. He wasn't about to get his dander up about just another murder. Webster had him establish the murder scene—he was the officer called to investigate Madame Claddington's death. Webster used a blackboard to diagram the place where Avery Knapp found the body—with a line drawn showing the bullet's approximate trajectory.

"So, looking at the body from the house, with the ocean in the background, would it be fair to say the bullet entered Mrs. Claddington's head from her left?"

"It would be fair to say that," Avery said, with only the gentlest suggestion of sarcasm in his tone.

"And that the killer would therefore have been standing to her left?"

"Yes."

"You saw no evidence the body had been moved?"

"No."

Bomber didn't jump on the double negative. It suggested that he saw *some* evidence. Webster must have been asleep, because he didn't correct him.

When it came Bomber's turn to cross-examine the witness he rose from our table and said "Sergeant Knapp—"

"Yo, Bomber," the Sergeant said with a smile of familiarity—as though they were old fraternity brothers reunited.

"We know each other, do we not?"

"Well," he said startled that the question would have to be asked. "Sure…yes."

"Will you tell the jury the nature of our acquaintance?"

"You got me my divorce."

"Satisfied were you?"

"Ecstatic!"

Webster jumped up. "Your Honor, may I approach the bench?"

"You may," Judge McCoy said, then watched the three of us cozy up to his fortress.

"Your Honor," Web began when we all stood leaning in one fashion or another on the judge's bench, "I don't mean to be nit picky," (translation: I'm going to nit pick, but I want you to take it seriously) "but the relationship of the witness with Bomber is a bit off-putting. I expected at any moment the learned attorney would jump in the policeman's lap and kiss him—"

"On the cheek only," Bomber said, winking at McCoy.

"See what I mean?" Web yelped, *sotto voce*.

"Are you making a motion?" the judge asked.

"Yes," Web said, stiffening his back, "I move Bomber excuse himself from questioning this witness."

At first I thought it a laughable suggestion, then I got a sudden foreboding that stopped the blood in my veins.

"Oh, Webster," Bomber said, "do you want to make such an issue about this minor witness?"

"He's *not* minor," Web protested, as though Bomber had insulted him personally. "None of my witnesses are minor. They are all building blocks to mounting a strong case for the state—"

"You know," Bomber said evenly, "when you take off like that, I want to grab old glory and wave it right along with you. But, I am the attorney for the defendant; who do you want to cross-examine this vital witness, Betty Crocker?"

Judge McCoy smiled, then frowned. "Bomber, that's out of order."

"Well, Jesus Jenny," Bomber said, faking an anger of his own, "if the district attorney wants to make a mountain out of a molehill, shall we all run for bulldozers, or shall we tell him we have enough mountains already?"

"And I suppose," Web said, "if it were up to you we'd have a world of molehills—"

"Oh my—" Bomber said.

"Gentlemen," McCoy said, "settle down. Webster," he said, looking at the district attorney as though trying to reason, "are you sure your case will be compromised if Bomber asks the questions?"

"Yes!" Web was unflinching.

"Very well. Tell me, Bomber, what was the nature of your dealings with Sergeant Knapp—a divorce case? Anything else? I didn't know you did divorces."

"I don't," Bomber said. "He asked me, I tried to tout numerous others who specialized in domestic bitchery, including, if you can believe it, some *women*. He remained adamant—"

"So why did you do it?"

"Oh, I have a soft spot in my head for officers of the law.

It's a lousy job—enough stress to end any marriage. His wife hired a shyster who threatened to absolutely bury him. He was about to be taken to the cleaners by that shrew he must have been in love with at some point—and if she didn't clean him out, some lawyer would. Cops aren't rich, so I did it."

"He came out all right?" Judge McCoy asked, interested in spite of wanting not to be.

"Oh yeah—look at him, he's happy as a clam—"

"Paid you?"

"Yeah, sure—I got five-hundred bucks out of it."

"Five-hundred?" Web was astonished. "You did it in half an hour?"

"Ever heard of *pro bono?*"

"Hear of it? It's all I do!"

It was hyperbole of course, but I knew what he meant. The district attorney's salary for a year was ten to twenty percent of what Bomber could earn on one case.

Somewhere in all this digression and irrelevancy, I saw a light bulb go on in the judge's head. He was looking at me. I didn't like the look. "I suppose there's enough reason to have someone else ask the questions of this witness, though I could instruct the jury to disregard—"

"But we know the psychology," Web said.

"Yes, okay—let your associate ask the questions, Mr. Hanson."

I almost fainted dead away on the spot. My mouth dropped open so far I must have looked like the Grand Canyon at sunset. The best I could do was shake my head, for my vocal cords were out to lunch.

"Why not?" the judge asked, as though there could be no reason at all. "Would that be acceptable to the district attorney?"

"Perfectly," Web said. It didn't increase my estimation of him. He was fairly gloating at the prospect of me falling on my face. I saw myself drowning the courtroom in spittle as my terror turned torrential.

Bomber, bless him, caught on right away. "Tod has no courtroom experience," he began.

McCoy cut him off. "He's a licensed member of the bar in good standing. Am I correct about that?" he said, looking at me. I nodded. It was the best I could do.

The judge threw out his hands as though that was the end of it. "Surely *you* have no objections," McCoy said to Bomber.

"I don't, but I'm not the only consideration here."

"The district attorney already agreed," Judge McCoy said as though there couldn't be another consideration.

"If we could have a short recess to go over it," Bomber said, stalling.

"Okay—make it short. Just give him your questions—he can read them. Surely there isn't much to ask—the direct was straightforward."

"Yes, Your Honor." Bomber could be humble pie.

The judge declared a ten minute recess, and I was hoping for more like ten years. Before we left, Bomber (humbly) asked if there might be options.

"Get another lawyer in here? You can do it, but practically speaking—with the delay and the cost to you—I don't see it as feasible. Up to you."

As soon as we were alone in the conference room of the courtroom, I said "I'll p-p-pay f-for the l-l-lawyer-er."

"Now, Tod," he said in his best, albeit rusty, soothing manner, "you can do it. It's not all that different from conducting an orchestra, which if I'm not mistaken you did in school—before I knocked some sense in you and got you signed up for law school. It's a piece of cake, anyway. Just a few questions to create a doubt—*reasonable* doubt, you understand."

I understand he was mimicking the code of the criminal

courts—that was all the case we had at that juncture. Our goal was to create doubt—and you did it with every witness. I shook my head.

"Aw, Tod, here, I'm going to write the questions. What would you do if I tipped over cross-examining some miscreant? Surely you'd step into the breach like a good soldier."

"Surely n-n-n-not—this is n-n-not our ag-agree-ment."

"Emergency measure, my boy. A stupid ruling—not enough off center to get a mistrial from the appellate court perhaps, but a nuisance just the same—come on," he said, taking his yellow legal pad in hand and scribbling a few questions. "Gosh, any young associate should give his eyeteeth for an opportunity like this—" his tone was so reassuring, but it wasn't reassuring me.

"I'm n-not one of th-them—"

He looked up from the pad. "Help you if I stayed in here?"

I opened, then closed my mouth. I was always astonished when Bomber displayed some sensitivity toward me. Any flash of humanity, no matter how brief, buoyed my spirits. I felt myself weakening, and I didn't like it.

"So let me p-pay for another l-lawyer to d-do it?"

He looked up with a smile of astonishment. "You sell a symphony?" he asked, unabashedly belittling the salary he paid me. "Look," he said, when I didn't respond—how could I? "I don't know why I'm encouraging this, you're liable to take to it and be so good at it I'll be out of work."

"Not b-bloody likely," I groused.

He kept writing the questions on the yellow paper as though my participation were a *fait accompli*.

When he finished his list of questions, he looked up, pasted on a sickly smile and handed me the list. "I'll be out in the hall," he said.

TWENTY-FOUR

I MOVED INTO THE COURTROOM with legal pad in hand, but didn't realize I was moving. I set the pad on the defense table and glanced at Inocencio who was already seated, trying to hide my trepidation from him lest he lose his confidence. The glance was sufficient to tell me he knew the score, and if I'm not completely mistaken, he had a twinge of sympathy and encouragement, not to say fear, in his return glance.

I didn't trust myself to sit down—I thought I wouldn't be able to stand back up—so I laid the tablet on the table without looking at it. For some reason, I thought looking at Bomber's questions would be like looking at Bomber while I spoke, which would result in an exponential increase in precipitation.

Judge McCoy was a "remain seated" judge. A lot of those judges were in the guise of democracy in the courtroom—an idea that could be fatal with a defendant like Inocencio Espinal. I prefer the "Please rise," from the bailiff—a little respect can go a long way—but I guess I'm old fashioned. Today I would have welcomed it because I was already standing.

Judge McCoy looked at me curiously—then seemed to let his eyes wander looking for Bomber—a thin self-satisfied smile struck his lips for an instant that was like an eternity to me.

"All right," Judge McCoy said, a touch *too* self-satisfied for my taste, "are we ready to proceed, Mr. Hanson?"

I lifted my head far above my level of courage. "Yes, Your Honor."

Judge McCoy smiled the smile of contentment. "Proceed," he said, I thought rather grimly, but I wasn't that rational. "Introduce yourself to the jury."

I turned to face that stern collection of faces that seemed intent on devouring me with their looks. "Hello," I said lamely—what a great start. "I'm Tod Hanson. I'm the associate of Bomber Hanson—the legend of the courtroom—and, coincidentally, his son. So you can imagine I've lived my professional life in his shadow—and I like that just fine. I've never done this before—spoken in open court—and, you might have guessed, I'm terrified."

With that those stone faces turned to happy jello—big smiles all around—and suddenly I felt as though I belonged. I also felt Judge McCoy was indulging me more than was absolutely necessary—as was District Attorney Grainger. So, with this newly felt luxury, I turned to face the witness, without notes.

"Sergeant Knapp, were you at the scene when the shots were fired?"

"No, sir," he said. He called me "sir", and I suspected he was old enough to be my father. I turned to the blackboard with the diagram. "You testified from what you saw after the crime was committed that it looked like the bullet came from this direction, is that correct?"

"Yes, sir."

"How close can you pin the place the gun was fired—from what you observed?"

Sergeant Knapp shifted in his seat. "Well, that's difficult to say. It would depend on a lot of factors."

"What are they?"

"The exact position of the victim's head when the shot was

fired. It can only be speculated generally. She could have turned it any number of ways before she was hit."

"That would allow for a rather wide range in the position of the killer?"

"Yes, sir." It was obvious Sergeant Knapp was bending over backwards to help us.

I went to the board and took up a piece of chalk. Pointing to the line Webster had drawn to show the projected trajectory of the bullet, I said, "Now, Sergeant, let's assume the victim was found here." I marked the spot Webster had drawn with a larger X. "Is it true the closer the killer, the easier it is to mark his position?"

"Well, yes, sir." The sir came a beat later than it normally might have—as though had it been someone else questioning him he might have omitted it.

"And, consequently, the further away the harder to tell precisely?"

"That's correct, sir."

"So let me take the chalk to the approximate position the accused was standing—would it be fair to say he could have been—say ten feet on either side—from your observation at the scene?"

"I couldn't say. It could have been ten feet, fifteen feet— five—I don't know."

"And did you observe a bank or cliff? Let me rephrase that. What can you tell the jury about the topography at the crime scene?"

"The land behind the house—where the principals were congregated—is flat, for perhaps thirty to forty feet, then it drops down to the beach—oh, say four to seven feet at various places."

"Thank you, Sergeant. From your observation at the scene of the crime, would it be fair to say it is possible that the fatal shot could have come from below the bank?"

"It's possible."

"And that a person there could have been concealed due to the height of the bank?"

"Yes," Sergeant Knapp said, "that is possible."

"And, again, the further from the victim, the wider the range—so that he or she might have been anywhere—let's say for argument's sake—anywhere in this approximate range," and I drew generous markings for a good distance, "perhaps fifteen feet on either side of the trajectory line—oh, like so," I said casually. "Would you say in your long and varied experience as a police investigator that we are talking a possible ball park here?"

"Yes sir, I would," he said with such force of expression that I thought the jurors must be taking that as the true theory of crime. "Reasonable doubt is what we're about," Bomber had said. It was all we had.

"Oh, and, Sergeant—have you found the murder weapon?"

"No, sir."

"What steps were taken to find it?"

"We had the beach and ocean dredged in a radius based on how far a person could throw a weapon of the caliber that fired the bullet—then added fifty percent beyond that to be safe."

"And were you at the scene for the dredging?"

"Yes, sir."

"And no weapon was found?"

"No, sir." True, that question had been asked and answered and Web could have legitimately objected, but I think he was so stunned that I wasn't spitting all over the courtroom that he was tongue-tied. He was letting a number of things slide by he would have blasted Bomber for. Perhaps he had seen the overwhelming sympathy on the faces of the jurors as I had, and decided against rocking the boat with minor infractions.

"Now, Sergeant Knapp, you testified you found one bullet

lodged in the skull of the victim, Anna Poritzky Claddington, is that correct?"

"Yes, sir."

"Find any shell casings?"

"No, sir."

"Did you look?"

"Yes, sir."

"Was there any evidence of more than one shot being fired?"

"No, sir."

"In your expertise, sergeant, how much time would it take—approximately—to take a careful aim at the target and get off a clean shot, such as the one that killed Madame Claddington?"

"A crack shot could do it in a second or two."

"How about an inexperienced gunman?"

Sergeant Knapp smiled. "I don't think he could do it at all."

"Why not?"

"Oh, to get a shot like that with a pistol, considering the kick and all, takes a pretty steady hand—one with some experience with side arms."

"Do you have any knowledge that the defendant here had that kind of experience with guns?"

"No, sir, I do not."

"Did you investigate that area—the defendant's expertise with guns?"

"No, sir."

"Why not?"

"Again," he said, shifting in his seat. "Eyewitnesses. Besides which it's hard to trace a Mexican immigrant's past."

I nodded sympathetically. "Did you check the defendant for powder burns on his hands?"

Avery Knapp blushed. "No," he mumbled.

"Why not?"

He shrugged. "Thought it was a slamdunk—again, all those eyewitnesses said the defendant shot her." He shrugged again.

"Did you happen to *notice* any powder burns on his hands?"

"No, sir—"

I stood, swaying gently on my feet, just staring at the witness, nodding my head slowly—to which I finally added—when I was sure the judge would wait no longer, "No powder burns…" then I looked at the judge and said, "No further questions."

The courtroom was so silent I thought everyone had left—probably bored by my dull performance.

Then a voice from the back of the courtroom cut through the silence:

"Bravo!"

It was Bomber.

TWENTY-FIVE

AFTER THE DISTRICT ATTORNEY asked Sergeant Knapp a few questions on re-direct, none of which cut into our establishing of doubt, Judge McCoy asked us to come to the bench for an off-the-record conference. Bomber took the longest, having to come from his perch in the back of the courtroom.

"Young man," Judge McCoy said, "that was a fine cross-examination."

"Thank you," I said, bowing with suitable humility that was in no way faked.

"You can be understandably proud of him, Bomber," Judge McCoy said, "but you know better than to disrupt a courtroom with your sentimental outburst."

"Yes, Your Honor," Bomber said, "I…couldn't help myself…I meant to stay out in the hall, but I just couldn't. I just handed him the questions and I'd no idea he had time to memorize them—I thought he'd read them. But no, not my boy—what a presence!"

"I don't know what you're talking about, Bomber, the boy never looked at your questions."

Bomber's eyes popped, and he whipped his head to look at my face. His lips were holding a wondrous smile.

"Bravo," he said, very quietly, and we resumed our seats.

The jury sat in silence for our bench conference, but their attention was rapt. They couldn't hear most of what went on, but Bomber had a way of sending signals with his looks,

glances, and expressions so they usually got the gist of it—
except in cases where he didn't want them to.

Once again Bomber had Web to thank for overreacting.
Our ploy—though it almost killed me initially—won the
hearts of the jurors. You could tell they were pulling for me
all the way.

The rest of the session was devoted to the coroner who testified the victim died of a bullet wound to the brain—the
bullet entering here and lodging there—complete with a
diagram on the board that Web had thoughtfully furnished.

Bomber didn't ask the coroner any questions. We had no
argument with how she died, only with who killed her. After
he announced he had no questions for the coroner, he leaned
over and whispered to me, "Gotta let some more time pass
before I try to follow that tough act of yours."

The ballistics expert from the police department, Wystan
Van Vert, was next.

Since the gun had not been found, he could only testify that
he had examined the bullet that had been removed from her
brain.

"Can you speculate on the kind of gun it could be?" Web
asked.

"Oh, no," he said, fairly chortly. "There are hundreds of
guns that fire that kind of bullet."

"Did you try to match the bullet to any gun?"

"No, sir. No gun was found…to my knowledge."

"And if a gun is found, can you at that time match this
bullet to it?"

"If the gun fired this bullet, I can match it." The D.A.
nodded, apparently satisfied with that meager gruel. "Your
witness, Mr. Hanson," he said.

"Thank you," Bomber said, then paused as though considering his first question.

"No further questions," he said.

I looked over at the district attorney and found him looking perplexed. He looked at his watch, then at Judge McCoy. "Your Honor, may we approach the bench?"

"Yes."

We hiked up there where Web recited his tale of woe. "Your Honor, I scheduled my Chicago contingent next, but apparently I miscalculated the length of Bomber's cross-examinations. In my experience these were extremely short. Not that this isn't a blessing, you understand. Why weren't there *any* questions of the coroner *or* Van Wert?" He seemed truly confounded by it all, and he took the opportunity to blame Bomber for his loose scheduling. The judge frowned, but there wasn't much he could do as Web claimed he had no other witnesses who could be sandwiched in. So we all had to suffer with the rest of the day off.

Judge McCoy dismissed the jury and as they marched out Inocencio jumped up, "Where are they going, these Nazis?"

"Sit down, punk," Bomber said, with excessive force. "Those people are going to decide your fate—you don't call them names."

"Look, they march a goosed step like Nazis. The day is not done. Where is my speedy trial? Your Constitution it give me a speedy trial. If they go home these Nazis—I rot in jail."

The marshal moved behind Inocencio, to forestall any sudden move he might make against anyone in the court-room.

Judge McCoy was not a happy man as he glared down at our client. "Young man," he said sternly, "you will get every guarantee in the Constitution in my courtroom. But you have to earn them with your civil behavior. I will not tolerate these childish outbursts from you—I can easily have you bound and gagged if you persist—or I can put you in another room to watch on TV."

"My right is to face my accusers—I tell them anybody say I shot anybody is lying."

McCoy's lips were tightly set as he nodded a nod I could see concluding a death sentence: short, curt, and stern. "Mr. Hanson, take him into the conference room and talk sense to him. I'm serious—any more of his antics and out he goes. Be sure and fill him in on how the jury will react to any physical restraint he forces us to put on him."

"Yes, Your Honor," Bomber said, clearly not relishing the prospect.

"I'll send the marshal along," Judge McCoy said. "He can stay inside or outside the room, as you choose."

"Outside will be fine," Bomber said, as the marshal put handcuffs on Inocencio and led him to the conference room, off the courtroom.

Inside, with the door closed, Bomber said, "You really did it this time, kid. You alienated—made very mad—every person who could save you."

"*I* am mad."

"Well, how nice," Bomber said. "You think anybody cares? Your job is to make the judge and jury *love* you, instead you are going out of your way for the opposite. And we've just begun with fairly harmless witnesses."

"They no talking about me. They talk like I kill her. They no talking about me."

"That's why we are gathered here, bozo, to establish your innocence."

"I *am* innocent."

"That's good news, but it isn't enough. We have to convince those twelve people you so stupidly called Nazis. That will not endear you to any of them—that I can promise you."

Inocencio grunted, and I wondered if he got it at all.

"Tell me something, Señor," Bomber said, and I was heart-

ened by his newfound show of respect. Then, of course, he
quashed it, "How does a punk kid like you get attached to an
outdated idea like communism?"

"At school. I had teacher. He was talking. It made sense."

"Yeah, but why is it you people who don't like capitalism
always flock to the U.S.? Why aren't you in Cuba?"

"They are poor."

"Communists are poor. You want to be rich, you're barking
up the wrong tree."

"This is rich country. Not enough people have much
money. It should be divided more the same."

"How are you going to bring that about? Revolution?"

"I'm not afraid to die."

"That's very gratifying—in case we lose this case—"

"There will be a revolution," Inocencio said with a snarl.
"People they will all be the same with money."

"Communism is dead, kid, haven't you heard? It doesn't
work! Tod, get him a copy of *Animal Farm*—it's a cute story,
kid—the animals take over the barnyard. The pigs are in
charge-the pretense is they will all be equal, only the boss pigs
decided some are more equal than others. You got to have a
framework-human nature is what it is. Altruism is sparse—
it's dog-eat-dog. All the communist experiments failed, yet
our capitalist democracy is going strong. Brook farm,
harmony, the shakers, the drunkards—all caput. Maybe our
ties to our hunter/gatherer past are still too strong." He shook
his head—"No, I'm afraid communism is the refuge of those
who can't produce themselves.

"So where are you going to fit in the scheme, kid? You
going to be one of the pigs or one of the horses?"

"Huh?"

"You gonna be a horse that pulls the load for the pigs in
government? Or one of the pigs yourself?"

"I don't care. As long as all the people is the same."

"Impossible, kid," Bomber said. "You're out of touch with reality. Life is not like that. You have to decide—then you have to take your chances on a bureaucracy that makes your own Mexican government apparatus look like a dream. Takes three or four years for Mexicans to get a social security number in the U.S. now—how long if we were commies? Incentive—you need incentive. Being a good Joe for people you never met doesn't cut it."

"You only want cars and houses and rich clothes. Television in every room!"

"Some do, kid, that's true. But they have to produce something for society. That society wants to get what they want."

"Too much you care about things."

"Right now I care about getting you your freedom. You want that or not?"

"I want."

"Good, then try to cooperate. Do what I say. I've been down this road many more times than you have—so let me suggest you stop fighting me."

The kid got a good smoldering look on his face, but he held his tongue.

The meeting adjourned and after Inocencio was led away in his handcuffs, Bomber turned to me—"Think we made any inroads?"

I shook my head.

"Me neither."

I had visions of a long, luxurious telephone conversation with Joan Harding in Chicago, modestly mentioning in passing my pinch hitting for Bomber and his unorthodox expression of approval from the back of the courtroom.

Instead I was greeted back at the office by the inimitable Bonnie V. Doone, the bearer of glad tidings:

"Speak of the devil, Sugar Lump," she said. "I found

Zachary Roseleer. Says he won't do us much good, but he's happy to see you anytime—here's his number."

We also found Alden Wagner, Madame's erstwhile partner in the antique business without much trouble. He has a shop on Santa Monica Boulevard in Los Angeles. I called, and he said he too would be glad to see me. But his tone told me otherwise.

TWENTY-SIX

THIS WAS A TRIP I would have preferred not making. Driving to Los Angeles I never found much fun—but if you hit it wrong it was a voyage through hell—very slowly.

By the time I pulled up to the address I had written on a scrap of paper, I thanked Dante for preparing me for the trip with his *Divine Comedy*.

The highrise apartment buildings on Wilshire Boulevard in Westwood struck me as lumbering giants going nowhere, perhaps because they were already there.

I got the VIP treatment with a space in the subterranean garage for my heap. Zachary was on the fourteenth floor—not bad—and the elevator was one of those fast ones.

Zachary Roseleer opened the door in maroon silk pajamas, though it was after three in the afternoon. He was a pudgy guy with tossled chestnut hair, which indicated some allegiance to a bottle. "Handsome Tod," he said, "come on in." He opened the door wide and padded in bare feet across some plush white carpet.

I followed as I corrected him, "Hanson, Tod, really."

"Good, good," he said.

When I cleared the doorway I saw a blonde woman I was inclined to call a bimbo, were I not at risk of defaming that interest group. Zachary was an expert at interest groups. Perhaps she was here for him to study the thoughts and opinions, prejudices and desires of single blonde women who automatically subtracted ten years from their age.

Blondie was twirling her hair between her thumb and fore-finger. She was sitting on her crossed legs on the couch watching TV. She was wearing a shortie nightgown with a silky gold robe thrown around herself haphazardly as a towel thrown on a hotel bathroom floor. Was the message here "We are lovely people who don't have to fuss a lot about appear-ances," or "You are an intruder not worth dressing for?"

Zachary sat on the couch next to his girl, and her hand drifted to his thigh as though drawn by a magnet.

"Sit down," he said, when he looked up and saw the per-plexed look on my face. I sat in a chair (white leather—all of it) opposite. He didn't ask her to turn off the TV, and since I was positioned opposite the viewing audience, I couldn't see what my competition was, but it was robust. Probably one of those afternoon shows where some aggressive woman inter-viewed partners in incest, or something less wholesome.

"Now, what is it?" Zachary said, not angrily, but not with any warmth either. "Madame Claddington, is that it? Someone popped her, did they? Harmless old biddy," he said, "but annoying sometimes, I gather."

"You gather? Didn't you see her shortly before she died?"

"An errand of mercy," he said, waving a hand. "She got all lathered up about a seat at a fundraiser. Didn't like her table—too far from the star—so the star—Otto Underwood himself—dispatched me to soothe her feathers. I guess her donation was not as grand as she'd imagined. Was still thinking in nineteen-fifty dollars, or something."

"Were you able to appease her?"

"Oh, who knows? In this business you are constantly treading lightly among egos. She had a big one, but she wasn't the only one, by any means."

"How much did she give you?"

"A couple grand," he said. "But it was a thousand a ticket minimum—and people were buying tables of ten—they got to sit closer," he shrugged. "Isn't it crazy what's important to people?"

"Yeah. But I suppose you could make a case that politics is crazy."

"You could," he agreed.

I smiled at the blondie. "Hi," I said trying to gain her attention, perhaps shame Zachary into introducing her. She didn't tumble. He interrupted their public petting to give her a gentle poke. "Hey," he said, "this is Tod Hanson—Bomber's kid."

"Oh, hi," she said as though she had just met a table lamp, and then she was back to her incest warriors.

"What else do you know about Madame Claddington?"

"Oh, nothing really. Rich Chicago widow. Meat packing or something, wasn't it? Putting out fires is one of my subordinate specialties."

"What's the main one?"

"Focus groups—telling the candidate like it is, from my experience with voters."

"Will you come to Angelton to testify?"

"Oh, why would I do that?" he asked, alarmed. "What I told you is all I know—you'd find that useful?"

"You were probably the last outsider to see her alive."

"I don't know about that, but it was pretty mundane stuff."

"Why even bother with her? You seem to be a pretty big guy in the organization, why would *you* be dispatched to a lousy two thousand dollar donor?"

He shrugged. "Because Otto thought she was good for a lot more, I guess."

"Did you try to get it?"

"Subtly. That was to come later. This was a softening up visit. Soothe the ruffled feathers. Next time—with enough dough—a seat at the head table. Wish I could tell you something dramatic, but it was pretty mundane."

"Tell me what you said—what she said. It may trigger an idea."

"An idea that *I* killed her?"

"No, no—something relevant to others in the case."

"Well, Jesus, I don't know. I started with some small talk, flattering, how lovely she looked."

"How did Madame Claddington become interested in Otto Underwood?"

He shrugged, "I came in after the fact."

"Your conversation with her didn't reveal any background? Why she gave two thousand dollars? Why she wanted to be closer to his table?"

"No," he said, but he suddenly seemed to take an interest in the TV.

"Were they lovers?"

He shot a look at me and forced a laugh. "At their ages?"

"Before. Years ago, perhaps. I understand she was quite a looker."

"I don't know. I wasn't born yet."

"She knew him, didn't she?" I tried to squint as though to see through his soul. "Way back?"

He squirmed. He stopped pawing his companion. She was so intent on the tele-tabloids she didn't seem to notice. "He may have said something. I don't pay much attention to that stuff. It's not my line."

"And she? Didn't she mention it? Isn't that why she was out of joint? Thought this was to be a big reunion or something special, and she's put at a table where she can hardly see him?"

He glared at me in a way that told me I was getting a lot warmer.

"Well," I said, into his silence, "I suppose I should be asking the big man himself these questions."

"You should *not!*" he shot at me like I was a clay pigeon. Then he quieted when he saw his companion twitch at his eruption—twitch without taking her eyes from the screen. "That is why he has me—"

"I'm sure if you could satisfy us we could forego the pleasure of the candidate's company," I said, leaving a loophole large enough to sail a battleship through.

"Well," he said, unsure he was doing the right thing by his boss, "she did hint at something a while back."

"Romance?"

"What else?"

"How did she reconnect with him? Who made the move?"

"She did—when his candidacy started to take hold—like so many others, she was attracted by celebrity. You'd be surprised how they come out of the woodwork. And if he loses, they crawl right back."

"So Madame Claddington called him? Said, 'I want to give you some money—just give me a good seat?' Was she on some kind of mailing list?"

"Don't know the details."

"Will Underwood?"

"You know, I'd love to give you what you want, but if it is a confession of murder, you're at the wrong place. They locked up a little commie, didn't they? Makes sense to me. Especially with all those eyewitnesses."

"You weren't one of them, were you?"

"What? Me? No way. Look, she was a very minor annoyance in the scheme."

"Did you know Morely Tushman is Otto Underwood's lawyer?"

He blinked. "Is that significant?"

"Just asking."

"He has a lot of lawyers. All over the place. You run for president, you'll have a lot of lawyers too. I understand your father's a lawyer and you probably are too, so I'll put my lawyer jokes on hold, but I got a ton of 'em."

"I'll bet. What's your favorite?"

"Scientific experiments. They're using lawyers instead of rats. Why? Three reasons: one, there are more lawyers than rats; two, you can become attached to a rat; and three, there are certain things a rat just won't do."

I chuckled politely. I'd heard it. I decided to join the fun. "What do you have when you have a thousand lawyers buried to their necks in sand?"

"Not enough sand," he said, stepping on my punch line.

"You do know them all," I said.

"And then some."

"Morely Tushman a lawyer like that?"

"I don't know him."

"Well, it does seem like Mr. Underwood has most of these answers. How about setting up an appointment for me to see him?"

"Can't be done."

"Won't take long."

"Long? What's long when you're running for president? Ten seconds is long. He's hopping every minute. Hardly time for eating, sleeping and the bathroom." He shook his head. "It's a killer, I can tell you."

"And I suppose the last thing he needs is an association with a murder case?"

"Association? What do you mean? How is he associated?"

"When we subpoena him to testify. That's association."

"You wouldn't!"

"No? Are you giving us any choice?"

"It's harassment."

"Yes," I shook my head sadly. "So much of the legal systems is devoted to harassment. That's why there are so many lawyer jokes—it's an easy way to think you're getting even."

"Only you aren't. Never can."

"Often seems that way. So let me talk to Otto Underwood. He can probably clear the whole thing up in five minutes, and we'll see the folly of calling him."

I reached into my pocket and pulled out the subpoena for Zachary Roseleer. "Oh, and this is for you, just in case we'll need you."

"What? This piddly info I have warrants a schlep to where is it? Angelton? Give me a break."

I twitched my head once. "You get me to the man with the answers, we may tear it up."

He looked at it and frowned. "He's got serious stuff to do, man," Zachary Roseleer lamented.

"Murder is a serious charge," I said.

"I'll see what I can do."

I left the consultant and his consort fondling on the couch. They were, I decided, seriously well suited for each other.

Seriously.

It was a short drive to Alden Wagner's antique shop on Santa Monica, fashionably afield from the more fashionable Melrose.

Wagner's shop was a cluttered storefront with more depth than width. I don't know antiques from Mozart, so I couldn't asses the quality of his merchandise.

He gave me half a smile as I forked my hand over his glass counter and made the introduction.

He found a chair for me, and I sat at the open end of his counter. There were no customers in the shop.

The glass case was perhaps eight feet long and was full of smaller items like ink wells, cosmetic cases and assorted jewelry. On the bottom shelf was a silver mirror tilted just so, offering, I thought, an opportunity to look up women's dresses. Being the Sherlock Holmes that I am, this indicated

Alden Wagner's orientation was closer to Madame Claddington's than to Morely Tushman's.

"What was your last contact with Madame Claddington?"
I asked when we were settled in our chairs.

"She left a message on my machine. I hadn't heard from
her in simply ages."

Simply ages? Perhaps the mirror was just a mirror.

"What was the message?" I asked.

"Mysterious, as usual," he said. "She said she had info that
could change the course of history."

"Did you tell anyone—or save the message?"

He laughed. "What? Some nutso pronouncement from that
crazy old bat?"

"So that's a no?" I asked like a lawyer.

"That's a no."

"Why do you think she called you?"

"We used to gossip all the time. I was her buddy—till she
got tired of me. That's the way it was with the Madame. Life
with her was a roller coaster. You never knew what to expect."

"Did you call her back?"

He made a face. "I'm afraid I'd had it up to here with the
Madame. When we were working together, I had to kiss her
behind—'Madame this' and 'Madame that'—but, as they say
in the Bible, 'Now that I am a man I put away childish things.'
Talking to Madame Claddington just isn't my idea of a good
time."

"Any theories on her murder?"

"I don't do theories," he said.

Next stop, Otto Underwood.

TWENTY-SEVEN

I CALLED THE CAMPAIGN OFFICE of Otto Underwood. He wasn't in, they couldn't help me reach him, and he was too busy to see me anytime soon.

I flipped the yellow pages until I found the closest process server. I called—he was in; I drove over and gave him the subpoena for Otto Underwood. If he wouldn't speak to me, he could answer Bomber's questions in court. Of course he would resist, but as Bomber would tell him when he called, a contempt of court citation for ignoring a summons in a murder trial wouldn't play too well in the papers.

On the way to the freeway, I passed a phone booth at a gas station. I pulled up, got out and placed my call to Chicago. A friendly recording told me what time it was where I was calling. Eight-o-six p.m. Nice to know. Joan would be home I hoped, and able to speak freely.

She answered, cheerful as ever. "I hoped it was you."

I laughed, "As opposed to another solo offer with a symphony?"

"Those come in the daytime, silly," she said.

"Four to five times a day lately," I said. "If there were any justice in the world…"

"Speaking of justice, how's the Hanson quest for truth and justice going?"

"Swimmingly. Have they stopped following you, Joan?"

"Oh, yeah. They left with you. My father always warned me about hanging out with shady characters."

"Always pay attention to what your father says."

"Right on," she said. "I'm feeling helpless here—in more ways than one—what can I do?"

"Think you could find out anything about Dick and Morely Tushman?"

"Romantic stuff?"

"No—well, that could be a basis for something. But how did they meet? What was their attraction? What did they have in common? Friends? Or, maybe just a good background on Dick. His interests, connections, skills."

"Any idea how to go about it?"

"Phew!" I said. "There's the rub. I'd start asking around for people who know them—but you're hardly in a position to do that."

"Maybe I'll do the cat burglar trick again—tonight," she said. "I have a feeling we've only scratched the surface."

"Yeah, but would he keep incriminating stuff about his friend lying around?"

"We'll see. Maybe a lead of some sort. Well, I'll call if I find anything." We ended the call with some endearment. I always felt good after talking to her.

I got home in one piece before eleven—two a.m. in Chicago—and doodled on the piano forming ideas for my violin/piano duet, waiting for the phone to ring. It didn't. I conjectured the possibilities. Joan was snooping long through the night. She was home in bed, thinking it was too late to call me—or worst of all, she had been caught and was languishing in a cell at the police station. I realized that horror story was not likely, as the firm would eschew the notoriety connected with an arrest.

That didn't keep me from staying awake worrying about her. I finally fell asleep and awoke too late to catch her at home. Since the Chicago troops were scheduled to appear in Angelton at trial today, I thought I'd risk calling her.

I could tell by her voice when she answered at the office, she was not alone. I whispered, "How did it go?" and she answered, "Still working. I'll keep you posted," and we ended the brief call on that note.

The morning at the courthouse yielded a sighting of three witnesses from Chicago: Morely Tushman, Harley Holiday and Netta Forsley. Morely Tushman was the first at bat.

Before the district attorney questioned Tushman, Bomber asked Judge McCoy to instruct all Web's other witnesses to wait in the hall. Not that they weren't all well coached in what Web was going to ask them, it was his own cross-examination that Bomber hoped to keep from them.

Sartorially, Tushman was, as usual, impeccably turned out: A navy pinstripe suit, doubtlessly pressed after he arrived in Angelton, custom made French-cuff silk shirt with his initials on both cuffs. From time to time, Morely Tushman would tug at his sleeves to make sure the position of cuffs to jacket sleeves were just so. His tie was maroon with a paisley pattern so no one would accuse him of pandering to modern fads.

By contrast, Bomber looked almost like a soldier in the army of the homeless that so enjoyed the courthouse lawn—as well as the library, inside and out. Well, that's an exaggeration, not many of them wore suits. Bomber seemed to care about as much for clothes as they did, and if it weren't for Mom's stern intervention, he'd go out of the house wearing two different shoes, a mismatched pair of pants and jacket, and a clashing shirt and tie. Mom's goal was to neutralize his impossible color sense, something like disarming land mines. When she succeeded, she struck a blow for peace and domestic tranquility, and when she failed it was a natural disaster.

Web's early questions to Morely Tushman were softball, self-serving sallies into never-never land. What a fine man he was to come here from Chicago in the cause of truth and justice. "I try to do my bit," Morely Tushman said, with a modest tilt of his head.

Rather than make a boorish but obvious objection, Bomber rolled his eyes at the judge—who didn't seem to like the attempt at one-sided intimacy.

"Mr. Hanson, are you logging an objection or just rolling your eyes?"

Bomber stood as though every muscle in his body had gone to sleep and was resisting awakening. "Your Honor, I don't wish to disrupt these orderly proceedings with a barrage of objections, no matter how legitimate they most certainly would be. But I can't for the life of me believe that the district attorney doesn't understand or acknowledge the basic rules of evidence or that he would engage in chicanery in an effort to subvert the honest workings of this honorable court to the indubitable end that justice is ill-served in his misguided posturing for a conviction, regardless of the guilt or innocence of his victim—uh, the defendant."

"Your Honor," Web complained, "he's making a speech."

"Yes," Judge McCoy said. "Do you wish to object or not?"

Bomber waved a magnanimous hand. "Oh, let him tell us how wonderful they both are. I'm sure the jury will continue to be endlessly fascinated."

"Mr. Hanson!" the judge snapped. "That's *enough!*"

Bomber bowed humbly. "I stand corrected," he said. I glanced at Morely Tushman who had not before seen one of Bomber's stellar humble-pie charades. Attorney Tushman seemed to be quite astonished.

Web resumed his questions, and, miraculously got down to business. Tushman told of the trip—of Madame's last minute decision to go to the house she had never seen—two thousand miles from her Chicago home—and how she wanted to bring her faithful staff along for a treat.

"How nice," Bomber whispered to me, in that patented

whisper that carried nicely to the jury box. Judge McCoy frowned at Bomber, Web made a sour face.

Next, Web put up the diagram of the Fourth of July backyard scene and Morely Tushman established who was seated or standing by leaving his witness box and putting the initials of Morely's beloved staff on the location of their particular X. Then Web asked him to draw an X in a circle to show where the villain was standing. Of course he said the defendant, but villain was implied in his tone.

When Morely Tushman finished his illustrated lecture, Bomber scrawled with dramatic flourishes of arm and wrist on his legal pad.

"Where's Dick?"

I responded with a smile—stutter free. Then Tushman went through his litany of the murder scene which seemed to us to have been so carefully scripted, rehearsed and espoused as to become a mantra. He heard the shot, saw his Madame slumped over.

"I looked over at the defendant and saw a gun in his hand. I yelled something—'Get that man'—or whatever—I was very emotional, that's all I remember."

"Then what happened?"

"They jumped him—Harley Holiday and Madame's chauffeur—just as the defendant threw his gun in the ocean."

"That's a lie!" Inocencio shouted out at the witness—and the judge gave him a stern admonishment and instructed Bomber to control his witness. Bomber whispered to Inocencio, "Look, kid, that wins you no points here. Cool it—let me handle him."

The kid's body was heaving. I'm pretty sure Bomber's heart was not in the reprimand, for decorum or no, I thought Inocencio's denial was quite heartfelt and effective. Then I noticed Bomber was surreptitiously patting Inocencio's thigh under the table.

Web decided on a little overkill. "Your Honor, I am sad to say I suspect defendant's counsel of aiding, abetting, encouraging and rewarding, if not outright coaching that kind of behavior, and I suggest a citation for contempt of court served on both attorney and client would not be out of line."

Now it was Judge McCoy's turn to glare at Web. No judge of my acquaintance liked to be told how to run his courtroom. Web did not press.

Bomber couldn't resist getting into the act—"Web, you should have your hands full running the district attorney's office, why don't you let Judge McCoy run his court?"

"All right, both of you," the judge said, "Ask your questions, Mr. Prosecutor."

There were more questions about how the trajectory of the bullet was consistent with Inocencio's position. Web had Tushman place the two staff members in the kitchen, then pointing to the diagram on the easel, asked, "So if the mortal bullet came from the direction of the circled X—the defendant Inocencio's position—in your opinion, would it have been possible for the shot to have been fired from the house?"

"It would not."

"Thank you, Mr. Tushman. No further questions."

"Mr. Hanson?" Judge McCoy said when Bomber just sat staring at the witness—an introductory, intimidating stare— "Are you ready?"

I could feel the vibes of Bomber champing at the bit, so I knew he was casting himself in a courtroom drama.

"Oh, *yes,* Your Honor," he said with a broad smile—"with great pleasure," and he rose from our table and moved toward the witness.

Looking at Morely Tushman watching Bomber approaching I had to say the intimidation had succeeded.

TWENTY-EIGHT

SOMETIMES ATTORNEYS who should make the best witnesses, make the worst. Is it overconfidence or the old saw about the prophet being without honor in his own country—or no man is a hero to his valet? Whatever it is, I suppose it is just another product of the genetic jumble. I expect Bomber on the stand would make a super witness, though that thesis is still untested.

"Good day, Attorney Tushman," Bomber said, smiling his put-'em-at-ease smile.

"Good day," he riposted from the witness chair, the smile somewhat more grim.

"You stated, I believe, you were an attorney licensed to practice before the Illinois Bar."

"That is correct."

"And as such, you have a healthy respect for the perjury laws?"

"Objection," Web said.

"Yes, you can rephrase that, Counselor."

"I'll let it pass," Bomber said. He'd made his point without requiring an answer. The answer was obvious anyway. Of course he *would* say he had a healthy respect for the perjury laws. Web, as was sometimes the case, made a technical point but lost the battle, emphasizing a point that should have been passed over.

"Would you mind listing again the people who traveled

from Chicago to California with Madame Anna Claddington?"

"Harley Holiday, her bodyguard, Netta Forsley, Madame's secretary, Peter Williams, Madame's chauffeur and myself."

"That's all?"

"All her employees."

"Yes, just so. But were there others, not in Madame's employment who came also?"

"Yes."

"Who were they?"

"Only Dick Funkhauser."

"And what was his relationship to the Madame?"

Here Morely Tushman slid into waxing poetic flights in an effort to stem the tide of inevitable reality. "Madame was a woman with a rare generous spirit. Dick had a terminal disease and had never been to the West coast, so Madame, bless her loveable heart, invited him along."

"How did Madame Claddington know Dick?"

"Through me," he said, and I think I saw a tear in the corner of his right eye.

"He worked for your firm?"

"No…he was a…friend."

"How did you meet him?"

"Objection."

"Sustained."

"All right—may we assume that the relationship was with you and not with the victim of this murder?"

"Yes."

"Had she ever met this Dick?"

"I don't believe so."

"And where was Dick standing on this diagram of the murder scene?"

"He wasn't there."

"Where was he?"

"Inside the house."

"Why was that?"

"He was too sick to be outside. Madame and I were afraid he'd chill and catch pneumonia."

"What *was* his illness?"

There was a dramatic pause—you could tell Morley Tushman didn't want to answer but knew he had to. His tongue moistened his lips before he spoke. "AIDS," he said.

Bomber stared at the witness curiously before moving on. "So by my count, the total number in the party accompanying Madame to California was five, not counting the Madame herself. Is that correct?"

"Correct."

"And how many of those five came to Angelton to testify this time?"

"Three."

"Including you?"

"Yes."

"Which two didn't come?"

"Peter, the Chauffeur and…Dick."

"Who decided who would and would not testify?" Bomber asked.

"The district attorney spoke to me about it. We agreed on the three of us."

"Was Madame's chauffeur one of the eyewitnesses called?"

"No."

"Why not?"

"Well, he could have come, of course. Economy was a consideration, I suppose. He, along with Harley Holiday, wrestled…the defendant to the ground. It was decided—in view of Mr. Funkhauser's condition—to save him the rigors of the trip."

"The same trip he made a few months ago?"

"Yes."

"It wouldn't be because Mr. Williams, Madame's chauffeur, didn't share your view of the events?"

"Objection! Calls for a conclusion, no foundation, and absolutely irrelevant."

"Sustained."

"So we are not to be blessed with the views of the chauffeur?"

"Objection!"

"Yes, Mr. Hanson, you know better. You also know you are free to call the man as a witness yourself."

"I just might do that," Bomber said. "And this—" Bomber made his face frown as though he were searching for the name, "—Dick—yes, Dick. As far as you know, he will not be on hand to give his views—?"

Judge McCoy cut Bomber off. "Same goes for him—you may call him."

"I'd like to explain," Morley Tushman spoke to the judge, who shrugged.

"All right," he said.

"Dick is too sick to make the trip. He doesn't have long left I'm afraid—" This recitation was taking a toll on attorney Tushman. "And he saw nothing. He was in the house, under blankets—warding off a chill."

"In July?"

"Nights can be cold in California, I'm told," Morley Tushman said ruefully.

"Did you wear a sweater?"

"No—"

"And you were outside?"

"Yes—but I wasn't sick."

"So Dick was on this Fourth of July trip for what reason?"

"Objection—asked and answered."

"Sustained."

"Well, you said Madame felt sorry for him—but did the trip do anything for him? It sounds like it made him worse."

"Objection."

"I mean, if he couldn't even go outside to see the fireworks?"

"Mr. Hanson!" Judge McCoy was angry. "There's an objection before this court and I'm going to sustain it. At any rate, you don't talk over objections, you wait until I rule."

"I stand corrected," Bomber said with his humble duck of his head. "Now Attorney Tushman, can you give me the background of the initial invitation to Dick to come on the Fourth of July trip?"

Morely Tushman looked blankly.

"Did Madame one day say out of the blue 'Let's take Dick to California'?" Bomber was trying to help him along.

"Not in those words."

"In what words, then?"

"We were talking about the trip. She asked how Dick was. I said not too good. She said, 'Let's take him to California.'"

"Were you and Dick lovers?"

Shock and consternation took over Attorney Tushman. "What?" he asked in astonishment, giving Bomber another opportunity to drive the nail home.

"Did you ever have a sexual relationship with Dick—"

"I *beg* your pardon."

"You don't understand the question? You want me to repeat it?"

"Objection, Your Honor." Web got up with laconic movements showing he wasn't worried about the question being answered, just about keeping things correct. "Perhaps we should approach the bar?" Another aw shucks toss off. As though he were trying to be Bomber without the steam.

Web was especially quiet at the judge's bench. He obviously didn't want any of it to leak to the jury—so I knew we could count on Bomber to whisper just louder than was necessary, so the judge would admonish him to "Keep your voice down," to which Bomber would reply "Sorry," lower his voice for a while, then seemingly inadvertently punch up a key word or two.

"Your Honor," Web said, "the witness's sexuality is so totally irrelevant to this case. We are all aware of desperate defending attorneys trying to smear everyone—the victim *and* the witnesses—in a desperate attempt to obfuscate the true, and in this case simple, facts of the case. Now Bomber is obviously attempting to tar this respected Chicago attorney with the feathers of homosexuality."

"Oh Web!" Bomber said, "What a neat metaphor—light as a feather—get it?"

The judge's glare showed Bomber what he thought of that comment. "I'm inclined to agree with the district attorney, unless, of course, you can connect this to something important."

"I don't understand what all this squeamishness is about. In this modern and enlightened age when we have gay pride day and gay parades—I mean where has Web been? You know damn well if some *hetero*sexual relationship had some bearing on a trial, it would be admitted. Now, I'm aware Attorney Tushman might desire to downplay, or even override, his—how do we put it so delicately now—sexual *orientation*. But we have a young man here whose life and liberty are at stake, and what are a couple of queers next to that?"

I winced. My breath stuck in my throat. Even though this audience was small, Bomber still managed to offend all of it. Of course, if I had to guess, I'd put my money on both Judge McCoy and Web as being more homophobic than Bomber, who really didn't care about race, color, creed, national origin, marital status or sexual orientation. But Bomber knew how sensitive everyone had become, and he loved to be outrageous. One of his favorite bumper stickers (not that he would have one on his Bentley) was *Nuke the gay whales for Jesus*.

Much to Web's chagrin, Judge McCoy ruled Bomber could ask the lover question.

"The question was," Bomber began when we were back at our tables at the feet of the judge—"were you and Dick lovers?"

There was a long pause in the witness box—Bomber didn't press and even looked away, giving him time to work up to the agony of an answer. Bomber was standing far from Morely Tushman, so the jury would have no interference with a full view of the witness.

Finally we heard a sigh of resignation. "I never thought representing the Madame would do this to me. Some time ago, Dick and I…were…intimate."

"Thank you, Attorney Tushman. Did you ever do any shooting with Dick?"

"What?" Tushman was shocked.

"Skeet shooting—going to a firing range? Either of you ever handle pistols?"

"I didn't. Surely you don't suspect…" he let it trail off to nothing.

Bomber picked it up. "Suspect what?"

"Nothing."

"Objection."

"All right. I'll sustain it. It's time for a new direction."

"Or *some* direction," Web said.

"Attorney Tushman, are you familiar with Otto Underwood?"

"Yes. I suppose everyone is these days."

"Thanks for your editorial. I'm speaking of a more, shall we say, intimate familiarity."

"If you are asking the same question, the answer is no."

"Let me rephrase—was Otto Underwood a client of yours?"

"I did some legal work for him."

"Would you be able to tell us about the nature of that work?"

"I'd say my work with any clients would fall under the lawyer-client privilege protection."

"Do you know Zachary Roseleer?"

Tushman frowned. "I don't believe so."

"He works for Otto Underwood—in his campaign."

"I don't know him."

"He may have used other names. Zachary Roseleer is it currently. He does advising on issues, puts out fires. Paid a visit to Madame Claddington before she died."

"I wasn't there."

"I didn't suggest you were. I'm just asking if you knew him."

"No."

"Now, let me change that to did you know *of* him? Did Madame Claddington mention him to you?"

"Not that I recall."

Ah, there it was—the all-purpose denial of the undeniable. Not that I recall—not that I can remember. It didn't help with the jury perhaps, but it helped our morale and our hope that there might have been some incriminating connection there.

Bomber turned to stage whisper to me, "I've gotten about all the honey I can from this lemon—we're beating a dead horse." He looked up and in full voice said, "No more questions."

On my nightly call to Chicago, Joan surprised me. I had

considered her search for info on Dick a longshot indeed, but
she teased me with information. "I have this gay friend—he's
going to do the bars—the gay bars, you know, and see if he
can learn anything. He says it won't be easy and not to get
our hopes up, but he'll give it a try."

TWENTY-NINE

NEXT DAY I SAW INOCENCIO reading *Animal Farm* before the jury came in. Bonnie Doone had gotten him a paperback copy.

"How's the book?" I asked.

"I don't like it," he said, in what I thought was a transparent attempt to keep his prejudice pure.

Netta Forsley and Harley Holiday didn't add much to the fund of knowledge. Both spouted the party line—one-hundred percent sure Inocencio Espinal threw a gun in the ocean. Bomber could have destroyed Netta with a couple of questions, but chose to let her pass. He was sometimes sensitive to overkill in the eyes of the jurors, and mercifully this was one of those times.

He saved the gunfire for Harley Holiday, a more worthy adversary.

"Mr. Holiday, are you acquainted with my son and associate Tod Hanson—seated here at the defendant's table?"

"Yes, sir."

"Can you explain how you know him?"

"He broke into my house—I caught him and decked him."

"Very nice, Mr. Holiday. Can you tell the jury how he broke into your house?"

"How?"

"Yes. Did he kick in the door—break a window—come down the chimney?"

That got a laugh from the audience, an indulgent smile from the judge and a frown from the district attorney.

"No—I guess the door was open."

"On purpose? As sort of a trap?"

"Objection. Argumentative."

"You may rephrase, Counselor."

"Were you deliberately leaving the door open and not answering knocks so you could deck intruders, as you so quaintly put it?"

"No."

"Just so happened?"

"Yes."

"You stated you were a security man and worked for the Krondike agency, and that was how you were hired as a security or bodyguard for the deceased, Madame Cladding-ton."

"Yeah."

"Did she tell you why she hired you?"

"Her chauffeur was getting as old as she was, and she wanted protection."

"Protection from what? Did she say?"

"We never talked about that," he said. "Mr. Tushman hired me. He told me she wanted a bodyguard. I should watch out for her safety."

"Well, what kind of safety? Were you to prevent her from falling in her kitchen? Tumbling down the stairs? Did you sweep the place for banana peels?"

He didn't like to have his line of work demeaned like that. "That's ridiculous," he said. "I went with her when she went out—like the secret service goes with the president."

"And why do they do that?"

"To prevent harm from coming to him."

"Someone shooting him?"

"Yeah, or trying to rough him up."

"So, you were hired to prevent her from being shot?"

"Any kind of physical harm."

"So, she must have thought someone was going to shoot her?"

"Objection! Speculative. No foundation. He doesn't know what was in her mind."

"But he just said he was hired to protect her from being shot. Apparently it didn't work, because she was shot in his presence. I'm simply trying to establish that."

"But he already testified she told him nothing."

"All right. I'll rephrase. Did *anyone* tell you Madame Claddington was afraid of being shot?"

"No."

"No? Afraid of being harmed?"

"No."

"She was looking for a *companion?*" Bomber asked with a hiked eyebrow.

"Objection!"

"Sustained."

"When did you meet the defendant, Inocencio Espinal, for the first time?"

"On the Fourth of July."

"At the fireworks party?"

"Yes."

"To your knowledge, had Madame Claddington met Inocencio before the Fourth of July?"

"I don't know."

"Were you there when they were introduced?"

"Yes."

"Did it seem to you it was a first meeting?"

He shrugged. "I guess."

"So, apparently, you weren't hired to keep the defendant from shooting her?"

"Objection."

"Sustained."

Bomber made his point. He didn't need to fight the ruling.

"What was it motivated you to jump on the defendant during the Fourth of July fireworks?"

"I heard a gunshot—looked over in the direction of the sound—someone yelled—'Get him!'—and I ran over with the chauffeur and we tackled him." He pointed at the defendant.

"Did you find a gun?"

"No. He threw it in the ocean before we got to him."

"You saw him do that?"

"Yeah."

"Did anyone—to your knowledge—go to the ocean to look for the gun?"

"I didn't."

"Why not?"

He shrugged. "Didn't think of it."

"Describe it please—the gun."

"Well," he shrugged again, "it was just a…a handgun."

"Yes. A thirty-eight? A colt automatic?"

"I don't know the brand. It happened so fast."

"And it was dark, was it?"

"Yeah."

"So it could have been a toy?"

He frowned. "She wasn't killed by no toy."

"Quite so, but I didn't ask you that. I asked if because of the darkness and the confusion what you saw the defendant throw could have been a toy pistol—or even a pretzel—or perhaps—" he paused to sharpen the jury's attention "—nothing?"

"Nah, it was a gun."

"Did you hear a splash?"

He seemed surprised by the question. "Not that I remember."

"So, maybe this thing that you say the defendant threw might not have made it as far as the water—and yet no one looked for it? Is that correct?"

"Well, there was the noise of the fireworks."

"Were you watching the fireworks?"

"Yes."

"So you didn't see the actual shooting?"

"No."

"All right, Mr. Holiday, did you see District Attorney Tushman's friend, Dick Funkhauser, at the Fourth of July party in question—where Madame Claddington was murdered?"

A nice connection, I thought. Bomber was full of mind games. Some found a home in the jury box.

Harley said Dick was on the living room couch covered with a blanket. Though it was July, he seemed cold. Harley couldn't remember if Dick had blankets before or after July fourth. He couldn't remember the layout of the living room or how many doors went outside from it. He said he never worked protecting presidential candidate Otto Underwood, and didn't know if his agency had.

"Now, in the last month, were you assigned to watch my associate at the defendant's table, Tod Hanson?"

"Yes, I was."

"Can you tell us the nature of that assignment?"

"Mr. Tushman said your son was harassing a sick man, and he wanted to see that it didn't continue."

"Who was the sick man?"

"Dick Funkhauser."

"And how was Tod supposed to be harassing him?"

"That I don't know. I was just supposed to see that he didn't go near him again."

"So you were stationed outside Dick's house, were you?"

"No."

"No? How did you manage to protect him then?"

"I watched your son."

"Followed him?"

"Yeah."

"And did you report all his movements to someone?"

"To Morely Tushman."

"To your knowledge, after that time, did Tod Hanson attempt to see Dick?"

"No."

"Now, Mr. Holiday, you stayed with Tod all the way to the airport?"

He nodded.

"Answer audibly please. The reporter—"

"Yes."

"And did you pull a gun on him on the highway between Chicago and the O'Hare airport?"

"No."

"No?"

"No. I don't do guns."

"Do you have a gun?"

"Well, yes."

"Did you have one with you on your ride to the airport?"

"I carry a weapon at all times. I have a license for it."

"Good for you."

"Your Honor!" Web bleated.

"Bomber!"

"I stand corrected. Was the gun you claim to have seen thrown toward the ocean similar to the one you carry?"

"I couldn't tell."

"No more questions."

"Redirect Mr. Grainger?"

"Thank you, Your Honor. Mr. Holiday, thank you for

coming all the way from Chicago to help us get justice in Angelton, California. I know it has been hard and I appreciate it."

"Call out the violins," Bomber stage whispered—several jurors smiled in our direction.

Web proceeded to try and establish Dick Funkhauser really was sick, which Bomber did not make easy for him—insisting through objections that the witness was not a medical doctor.

When he finished, Web asked to approach the bench. When we got there he asked the judge if three witnesses from Chicago could be excused to return home. Bomber said he might need them if the case continued to develop as he expected. Web protested it was unreasonable to keep them—an inconvenience.

"Inconvenience?" Bomber blustered. "My client, now *there's* inconvenience. What is a couple more nights in a plush hotel at the expense of the county next to the inconvenience my client is suffering?"

"Very well," Judge McCoy said, "by tomorrow morning give me a brief on what you plan to accomplish by recalling these witnesses."

"Well I can tell you right now. I plan to call the chauffeur, who mysteriously was overlooked by the prosecutor. I would expect the prosecutor himself might want an opportunity to rebut the chauffeur with his own witnesses, the ones he selected to call."

"Your Honor, this is a simple eyewitness case. Three witnesses, upstanding citizens all, saw the defendant shoot Madame Claddington then throw a gun in the ocean. What would satisfy Bomber? One more eyewitness—an old man with fading eyesight—too frail to easily travel? No. I say Bomber would not be satisfied with one hundred eyewitnesses."

"You're on the money, Web. Eyewitness testimony is notoriously unreliable. I merely suspect the chauffeur is not as dead certain your version of things is how it all came down—as they say in the street."

"All right, Bomber," the judge said, "put it all in your brief. I'll think about it. In the meantime, you may contact this witness and produce him if you like."

"Thanks, Your Honor."

Judge McCoy adjourned for the day and Bomber gave me marching orders. "Get the chauffeur out here as soon as possible, and check out that the distance to the ocean at the tide prevailing on the night of July fourth, twenty-eight hundred hours." He liked to tell time in military terms. "Time the route from the living room couch to the spot where Dick could have shot Anna Claddington—and back. My guess, it's less than a minute each way." Then he added as though it were an insignificant request, "Oh, and do the brief."

I reached Peter Williams by phone. He was jolly and cordial, but didn't want to make the trip. He said his health was okay, but he wasn't crazy about flying—but finally—without threatening subpoenas, he said, "If you think it will help justice, why, I guess I'm in no position to turn my back on that."

With that good news—Bonnie Doone got him a ticket for the next day. I told her to make it first class.

"Bomber will scream bloody murder," she said.

"Let him," I said, realizing she would probably ignore my request.

Then I set off for the murder scene.

THIRTY

My CALL TO JOAN that night was pleasant but not productive. Her friend the cellist was making the gay bar scene, but not having much luck garnering gossip on Dick and Morely Tushman. He was still trying, and both hoped he would get a break someday.

I told her about our day in court, and she was skeptical that Harley Holiday was so naïve about Otto Underwood. "This isn't that big a town, and the Krondike agency is as inbred as Pitcairn Island."

"I read that book too. Fascinating," I said.

"Well, I'm going to do some checking on Harley Holiday and Otto Underwood. Sounds like Harley is going out of his way to be devious."

District Attorney Grainger's first witness the next morning was Lupé Fernandez—Inocencio's boss. He was nervous and brought an air of the hang-dog to the stand.

Eleven years he had served the Madame, he said, without ever having seen her. He took his orders from Morely Tushman, "That lawyer," was the way he put it. Nine months before the Fourth of July did he meet and hire Inocencio Espinal, the defendant. "He replaced his cousin."

Lupé had little to contribute to the district attorney's cause. He was in the house when the murder transpired and he didn't see it happen. He admitted he didn't like Inocencio very much. He did intimate a vague conversation where Inocencio said he'd like to see the Madame dead. Inocencio blew up, the Judge reprimanded him.

Carlos Vargas came to the stand dressed in his casual finest. He looked more frightened than Lupé had.

On the stand he passed himself off as a friend and confidant of Inocencio Espinal. Web forestalled his expected questions from Bomber.

"Did you dislike the defendant?"

"Nah. I mean, it wasn't like Lupé or anything. I mean, Inocencio could drive you loco, but I kind of liked him."

"Can you explain why—or what you liked about him?"

"I don't know—he said a lot of crazy stuff, but some if it made sense."

"Explain what you mean, please. What crazy stuff?"

"Oh, about money and how not many had so much and there should be some way to spread it around more."

"Did he ever mention Madame Claddington in this regard?"

"Yeah. He said she was what he talked about. She had all this money to throw away and all these people didn't have enough food."

"Did he have any ideas how to get the rich to give money to the poor?"

"He said Castro had the right idea. You take it at gunpoint if they don't give it."

"Did the defendant ever suggest harming Mrs. Claddington?"

The muchacho fidgeted in his seat, stole a futile glance at the defendant and said, "The day we met her, before the fireworks, he said we like animals in the zoo. Across the street is a zoo. He said Señora Claddington was the zoo boss and she throws us her garbage to eat and someone should shoot her."

"What did you say?"

He tossed his head. "I laugh. I said 'You gonna do it?'"

"What did he answer?"

"He said, 'Maybe. Be a better world—if her kind was out of it.'"

I glanced at Inocencio who was visibly straining to stay in control—his neck muscles tightened to ropes.

"Did you see him with a gun?" Web asked the witness.

"Not in his hand."

"You mean you saw a gun on his person but not in his hand?"

"Well…I saw a big mountain in his pants," he said, gesturing with his hands and swallowing a smile.

Bomber groaned, one woman on the jury lifted her hand to cover her mouth.

"Where were you during the fireworks?"

"In the kitchen with Lupé."

"Did you see anything unusual that night?"

"Unusual? Yeah. I saw Inocencio shoot the Madame."

There was a murmur in the courtroom. Inocencio leaned toward the witness and had his mouth open when Bomber's arm shot out to restrain him.

"I looked out the window, and I saw Inocencio's arm come up and it was like he shot her."

"With a handgun?"

"Objection—he's leading the witness," Bomber said, "and now that he's got the question out the witness knows what answer he wants."

"Sustained."

"Okay," Web said, "Did you see what he shot her with?"

"A handgun."

"I rest my case," Bomber said.

"All right," the judge said, not without sympathy, "the jury will remember the district attorney suggested the answer, the question was objected to and sustained, then when an acceptable question was asked the defendant answered as it had been asked in the first place. You may keep that in mind during your deliberations. You may proceed, Mr. Grainger."

"Thank you, Your Honor," Web said as though he had just been done a favor. "All right, Carlos, did you see him—the defendant shoot Mrs. Claddington?"

"Yeah, I guess I did."

"Thank you."

When it was his turn, Bomber came out of the gate at a full trot.

"Let's be clear on this shooting business—you saw Inocencio's arm come up and he made a gesture like he was shooting, is that it in a nutshell?"

"Well—I thought I saw a gun."

"You were standing where for this?"

"I was in the kitchen."

"Where in the kitchen?"

"At the window."

"Why were you at the window? I thought you were helping Lupé."

"I wanted to see the fireworks."

"But you looked at Inocencio instead?"

"Yeah—I guess at that moment."

"Did you have any discussion with the district attorney about your testimony here today?"

He looked uneasy. It was a question every attorney prepared his witness for, yet they were all pretty uncomfortable with it.

"Yeah, he just told me to tell the truth," he said, as though he had opened a bottle of faux truth serum.

"Ah, very noble indeed. Did he tell you anything else?"

"Nah."

"No? Where did this discussion take place?"

"In his office."

"So you went to his office?"

"Yes."

"Get there on your own?"

"Yeah."

"How long did it take you to get there?"

"I don't know—fifteen minutes—maybe."

"Did you wait at all before you saw the district attorney?"

"Yeah."

"How long?"

"I don't know—half hour maybe—I was early," he added, as though to shield the district attorney from culpability.

"All right, so you've got say forty-five minutes to an hour invested so far—fair enough?"

"I guess so—"

"And another fifteen or so to get back to work?"

"Something like that."

"And when you are finally ushered into his office he says something like, 'Hi Carlos, how's it going? Just tell the truth—goodbye'?"

There were a few titters of merriment, the witness blushed and hung his head, but gave no audible answer.

It wasn't difficult for Bomber to outclass an unschooled immigrant, but unless it served his purposes, he didn't hold back. "So you probably discussed some other things, didn't you?"

"I guess."

"What were they?"

"I don't remember exactly."

"No? May I refresh your memory? Specifically, you discussed what you saw, didn't you?"

"I guess."

"Remember? Think—"

"Yeah—okay—I guess I told him what I saw."

"Which was?"

He shrugged. "Like I told you—Inocencio says he want to shoot her—and maybe he would."

"Maybe?"

"Yes."

"Did the district attorney suggest any of your answers?"

"Oh, no," he said, without adding "perish the thought," but it was implied.

Bomber and I looked at the jury at the same time. They were catching on.

"Now, Mr. Vargas, I believe you said Inocencio had—how did you characterize it—? 'a big mountain in his pants.'"

"Yeah."

"Did you work that phraseology out with the district attorney?"

"The what?"

"Phraseology. I'm sorry—those words—how you said them. Did you discuss them with the district attorney?"

"I don't remember."

"You may have thought of that yourself?"

"Yeah."

"The big mountain in his pants?"

"Yeah," he snickered.

"Is that how you explained it to the police?"

"Huh?"

"When you called them to report Inocencio's death threat?"

Web rose as a phoenix from the ashes—it was impressive—I could just see his trim body and million dollar custom tailored suit clear the dust. "I object, Your Honor, on the grounds that the question is without foundation."

Sometimes Web seemed overly fond of his image—like now. Bomber looked over at the district attorney as though he were having trouble fathoming what he was talking about.

"Well," Bomber said in amazement, "you mean you didn't lay that foundation? I could have sworn you did—one of your star witnesses hears a death threat—sees a big mountain in a man's pants. It is a given he drops everything and races to the phone to call the police. You mean he didn't?"

"Your Honor," Web was angry now, sputtering through his flushed lips, "I object—he's speechifying again, and his ridicule is highly inflammatory and prejudicial to the jury."

"You're being redundant again—and again," Bomber said.

"All right gentleman, simmer down. I'll sustain the objection on the technicality."

"*Did* you call the police?" Bomber asked, a great deal more astonished than he had a right to be.

"Nah," Carlos said shifting in his chair. The chair seemed to be growing more uncomfortable by the minute.

"But…but, why not?" Bomber was putting on his faux preposterous dumbfounded act. For this was a question that cropped up so often in criminal trials it sank to the level of a cliché: witnesses—often cellmates in jail—are forever saying someone threatened to kill someone else and the opposing attorney asks them why they didn't call the police—which they never do—implying that they certainly didn't take the threat seriously. To see Bomber railing against this witness, you'd think he'd never come across the ploy before. But the kid had a good answer.

"The cops wouldn't do nothing."

"You don't know that—the woman might be alive today if you had done your civic duty."

"Objection! Will you please tell Bomber to stop lecturing my witness."

"I shouldn't have to tell him," said Judge McCoy angrily, "and I'm not going to tell him again. The next time I'm going to cite him for contempt."

"I stand corrected."

Bomber had come out all right, in spite of the contempt of

court threat. Judges threatened that a great deal more often than they utilized it. Bomber didn't bother with a follow up—the kid apparently knew his business on the cops. Death threats rarely put a glimmer in the eyes of the police. The cliché answer is, "Come back when you have a body, then we'll look into it."

"So, you did take the threat seriously, did you?"

"Well," he squirmed, "yeah, I did."

"But not so seriously you thought of involving the police. Did you ask the defendant *not* to shoot anybody?"

"No."

"Why not?"

"Well—I didn't think that would do no good."

"Okay—so you went blithely into the kitchen, correct?"

"What does it mean, blithely?"

"Blithely—you went without a care in the world—to the kitchen, leaving a killer on the lawn in shooting distance of the woman you thought was his target."

"Objection—to his characterization of his retreat to his work station. Bomber is trying to put words in the witness's mouth, and I object to it."

"Okay, strike it." Bomber said, "You went to the kitchen, correct?"

"Yeah."

"And you left Inocencio on the lawn outside—where, if he had a mind to, he could shoot Madame Claddington?"

"Yeah."

"And as far as you were concerned that was exactly what he was going to do?"

"Yeah."

"So I'm wondering—don't you think that makes you an accomplice in the crime?"

"Objection!"

Judge McCoy appeared to be thinking it over.

"Oh," he said finally, "I guess it is stretching the rules a bit, but he may answer if he has an opinion."

The witness glared, "I don't have no opinion," he said.

"Oh, by the way, Mr. Vargas, did any of this come up in your discussions with the district attorney before the trial?"

"I don't remember."

"All right," Bomber said, turning back to the witness, "why were you in the kitchen during the fireworks?"

Web shook his head at the formation of the questions, started to rise to object, then changed his mind—he'd been doing quite a lot of objecting lately, and all this objection would result in was Bomber rephrasing the question. That would also serve to make the jury think he was afraid of the answer.

"I was helping Lupé get the food ready," Carlos answered after he was sure (and sorry to see) his side was not going to object.

"What exactly did you do?"

"Help him."

"Yes, you said. Did you cut carrots, peel onions, fry potatoes—what did you do?"

"Yeah, stuff like that."

The witness proved difficult to shake, though Bomber kept at him relentlessly—perhaps too relentless for the jury's liking. It was one of those times the King of Torts went over the line. The kid was not that believable, but it could easily be put down to Bomber's rattling him.

The defense didn't so much rest as run out of steam. It was not our finest moment.

Web tried to clear up some things—like how he never suggested how the lad answered any questions and how no favors were asked for or offered for his testimony.

Bomber tried again, but couldn't shake the kid, and I'm afraid, on balance, he did us some damage. It might have been a long shot that he was standing at that window watching Inocencio at that moment, but it wasn't impossible.

And with Web's best witness, he rested his case.

Bomber made the usual motion to quash the case because the prosecution had failed to develop a *prima facie* case, and it was, as usual, denied.

Inocencio looked at us with a look that reflected my thoughts. It would be nice, that look said, to have a miracle.

THIRTY-ONE

"So what happens now?" Inocencio asked Bomber when Judge McCoy declared a recess. We were in a conference room off the courtroom.

"Excellent question, me boy," Bomber said, not exuding as much confidence as I had seen in the past. "It is our turn to put on a case. I have just asked the judge to throw out the D.A.'s case because it wasn't strong enough to convict—he said it *was* strong enough for the jury to consider. Ordinarily, a defendant has *some* facts going for him—maybe an alibi— maybe a reasonable doubt case of mistaken identity. Or we find that someone else did it."

"I didn't!" he exclaimed.

"So you say," Bomber muttered, "I only wish there were some evidence to back it up. You know any reason why this last guy would want to frame you?"

"Two of them they don't like my politics. Carlos lied when he said he likes me."

"Little hard to get that into evidence," Bomber said.

"Is that lawyer," Inocencio said, "that Tush is trying to frame me up. Why he do that?"

"You tell me," Bomber said.

Inocencio shook his head. "I never know him. Why me?"

"Perhaps because you're an easy target, kid. Way you mouth off all the time. He got an unexpected bonus with your outbursts. What makes you such a hothead? You come here at no small expense and effort on your part—probably in the trunk of a car—then all you do is complain about our system. Exactly what's your beef?"

"Look at you people. Look at that Tush lawyer. His fancy clothes. You people and your spensive cars and big houses. *Things!* Things are *nothing*—the soul is everything. *Everything!*"

"Think Joe Stalin had much of a soul?" Bomber asked.

Inocencio ignored him. "Look into your soul when you drive your fancy car. When you go to your big house that would hold five poor families. Where are your feelings for your brothers?"

"Ah, am I my brother's keeper?"

"Criminals! You steal from the poor. All of the creatures of the earth deserve their share, not just selfish rich peoples! Your leaders they talk of poor people…to help…but they don't know what poor is—starving for food, nothing to do…no hope."

"Yeah," Bomber said, "you need robust capitalism to give them something to do—food *and* hope. But it's always good to hear the world view from Havana—this about the only pocket of communism left in this world. They changed the name of Siagon to Ho Chi Minh city to honor their communist liberator, then promptly went bustling, hustling capitalist. Russia is a hotbed of capitalism—twenty percent of the wealth of China is derived from Hong Kong—which is less than a half a percent of the land. Before long you may be the last communist standing. The talk of the soul is most edifying," (I know Bomber used big words that Inocencio didn't understand purposely) "but it doesn't put bread on the table. Face it, Castro's about the last hold out for your cause, so how are you going to bring about this world revolution?"

"I tell when I testify," Inocencio said.

Bomber stared blankly at him, "You're not going to testify."

"I…what?"

Bomber shook his head, "Too risky."

"I tell the truth," Inocencio said, as though Bomber had not only not laid down the law on the subject, but didn't exist.

"Believe me, boy, that is not in the cards. You have an abrasive, cocky way about you— It will only make the jurors mad." He shook his head once, again. "Life is salesmanship, boy—if a defendant testifies in his own behalf, he's got to have some sales ability. You don't have it. Believe me, it is in your best interest that you keep your mouth shut."

"And I could fry for it?"

Bomber nodded—"Deep fry," he said. With that Bomber walked out, and I explained Bomber's position in gentler terms.

"Hey, it's my life. I must have this right to tell the truth."

"You do, indeed," I said. "But it isn't that simple. If you cross your lawyer, he might back out of the case—or worse, finish it without putting his heart into it. I can tell you this about my father, he has given this his all. *He* believes you, he is just doubtful you can convince others—all *twelve* in this case. If *one* and only one thinks you are guilty, the judge declares a hung jury, and the case would most likely be retried—and I'm afraid without Bomber…"

"What? He's my lawyer."

"Yes—for the first round. If he fails to get you an acquittal he will be devastated, but he isn't likely to do it a second time."

"I'm going to tell judge I want to testify."

I nodded. "You can do that."

"What will judge do— If I say *I* want and Bomber *doesn't* want?"

"The judge will let you testify. He'll give you a lecture first about taking your lawyer's advice—that's why you have one—Bomber's one of the best—blah, blah, but if you insist, he will recognize it as your right."

"Okay—it's done then."

"Only Bomber will leave the case."

"Then you can."

"Me? Oh my—oh, no," I said. "I'm only an investigator—not a trial lawyer."

"You did good with that cop witness."

"Thank you."

"Bomber said." Inocencio added to cap his argument.

"But that was a one-shot fluke. No, I don't know all the rules and procedures—I'm not a persuasive person-my jury speech would be dull—and besides, the big reason I won't do it is I work for Bomber. He pays my salary. He says no—it's no. And finally, I have to tell you—I agree with him in this instance. You testifying will not help your case."

"So I should get rid of Bomber now?"

I thought a moment about this poor guy and where he came from and how his nature and ideas were formed. I couldn't feel superior—I'd had so many more advantages. And the funny thing was, I also believed him, though I had no idea how he could be innocent.

"Okay," I said, "here's what I suggest. You wait and see what kind of defense Bomber manages to put on. If you think after that that you *have* to say your piece, tell the judge then—maybe by then, Bomber will be okay with it. Just don't throw it all over until you have to."

Peter Williams, Madame's Chauffeur, was perfect on the stand. Bomber led him through his years with Madame. "I worked for her going on thirty-five years, and I loved her." Tears formed in his eyes.

"Was there any sexual intimacy?"

"Oh, no," he said as though he were startled, though I'm pretty sure Bomber prepared him for the question. "I had such respect for her. She was a lady."

"Did she treat you well?"

"Aces," he said, "yes sir, she treated me aces."

Bomber worked his way from esteem for Peter's employer to the night of the murder. Peter on the stand exuded goodness. He was just so happy and flattered to be included, he said.

"Did you hear from the district attorney?"

"Yes, I did."

"What was the nature of the contact?"

"He called me, introduced himself, and asked me what happened that night."

"And you told him to the best of your recollection?"

"Yes, sir."

"And did he ask you to be a witness for prosecution?"

"No, sir."

"No?" Bomber raised his eyebrows.

"No, sir."

"So if I told you the D.A. said he didn't call you as a witness because you were in ill health and couldn't travel what would you say?"

"Objection! Assumes facts not in evidence."

"Well, he's putting it in evidence," Judge McCoy said, and we were happily surprised at that. All I can figure is Judge McCoy was taken by the black chauffeur. Or he wanted a more even trial.

Peter laughed. "I'm here, ain't I?" he said. "Course, I don't run up and down five flights of steps like I used to, but I can still walk—"

Signs of amusement traveled over the jury faces.

"So, if Mr. Grainger had asked you to be a witness, you would have?"

"Certainly," he said, "want to do my civic duty."

"Well then, let's see if we can find out why Mr. Grainger *didn't* want you as a witness."

"Objection."

"Sustained. I don't like that at all, Mr. Hanson. You're pushing your luck here."

"I stand corrected," he said, followed by the ubiquitous ducking of the head to represent his eternal humility, but anyone who knew Bomber knew that was an oxymoron.

Bomber estimated where everyone was standing and asked, "Did you hear a shot?"

"No, sir—there was so much noise from the fireworks—"

"Did you see the defendant with a gun in his hand?"

"I didn't notice no gun."

"Did you see him throw anything in the ocean?"

"Can't say that I did."

"Now you and Harley Holiday, I believe, tackled Inocencio, the defendant, is that correct?"

"Yes, sir, that is what happened."

"How did you happen to do that?"

"He say 'come on get him—he shot Madame'—an' I turn and look an' Mr. Holiday is headed for the boy—and that boy, he looks dumbfounded, and we nail him."

"Did he move his arm in any way?"

"Sure did."

"How did he move his arm?"

"He was trying to defend himself. He throw it out like this," he demonstrated, "to put it between him and his attackers."

"Was he running away?"

"No."

"So to recap, Mr. Williams, from what you saw and heard personally that night, could you give testimony that would put this young man away for life?"

"Objection."

"Sustained."

"Did you see or hear anything that would indicate to you that this man murdered your employer?"

"No, sir, I didn't."

"When was the first you knew anything unusual had happened?"

"When someone shouted, 'He killed her,' and Mr. Holiday said, 'Let's get him.'"

"Did you meet the defendant before the fireworks?"

"Yes, sir."

"Notice anything unusual about him?"

Peter thought a moment, then broke into a broad grin. "Well, he wasn't black."

It got a nice laugh.

"Notice him carrying a gun?"

"No, sir."

"Notice any bulge…" Bomber paused for effect, "on his clothing, anywhere that could have been a gun?"

"No, sir, I did not."

"Thank you, sir, you have been a most forthright and honest witness. We appreciate your coming from Chicago to aid the cause of truth and justice—Mr. Grainger may have a few questions for you."

"Oh, Your Honor, please ask the jury to disregard Bomber's grandstand congratulations of his witness—as though he were the only witness to sacrifice and speak the truth."

"That's for the jury to decide," Bomber said, and sat down.

Judge McCoy said, "Your witness, Mr. Grainger."

THIRTY-TWO

THE DISTRICT ATTORNEY didn't do didley with his posturing and ridicule of Peter Williams—Madame's chauffeur.

It was the opening of our case on a hopeful note.

When Peter Williams left the stand, Web rose to tell the judge he had received a petition to excuse one of Bomber's witnesses, and Attorney Trevor Grimley from Los Angeles was in court hoping to be heard.

The jury was excused and Mr. Grimley came forward. He looked like the eastern prep school he attended in common with two presidents. His pleading was neither surprising nor original—Otto Underwood was a man busily trying to be president of the U.S., and this trial was so removed from anything he knew anything about, it would be sheer folly to deflect his daily assured path to the White House with this nonsense. Trevor Grimley was too suave to call it nonsense in front of the judge, but the implication was clear. Otto Underwood could simply not chance an unwarranted kink in his reputation by being dragged into association with a murder case he wasn't even remotely connected to.

Judge McCoy sympathized, but decided with a man's life at stake he would be making a mistake to not avail him of any avenue open to his defense.

One must never underestimate the appeal of power to a judge. The ability to make a presidential candidate dance went a long way toward compensating for the relatively poor salary.

Otto Underwood was scheduled to take the witness stand two days hence.

In the meantime, Bomber called an expert in eyewitness testimony who spoke convincingly about the errors—egregious errors—humans make in identifying their fellow humans. Bomber worked in how gestures can be misunderstood—for instance, a normal protective reaction of putting an arm up to protect oneself could be misconstrued as a gesture more or less consistent with throwing a gun away, and when that action fits the fact pattern, people tend to assume the truth of something not necessarily true.

Web, of course, did a nice job of minimizing most of this testimony. It was hard to say who, if anyone, benefited from the eyewitness argument.

Zachary Roseleer was next. He wasn't making any effort to hide his disdain for the proceedings. He was a man accustomed to working behind the scenes where the perpetual smirk on his face could not be seen by the general public.

Zachary gave his background before he went to work for Otto Underwood—other political candidates from all parties, based partially on focus groups of people who tell their concerns.

"So you tell the candidate what the people are thinking?"

"Exactly."

"And do you give your opinion—advice on what positions he should take?"

"I'm hired for my expertise," Zachary said, with a strange defensiveness.

"How would you characterize what you do?"

"I advise positions to take that will meet with public approval."

"And the candidates take your advice?"

A wry smile tweaked Zachary's lips. "If they want to win."

"Is Otto Underwood a candidate who wants to win—as you characterize it?"

"Objection."

"Sustained."

"They all want to win," Zachary said gratuitously.

"In your opinion," Bomber asked carefully, "would you rate Otto Underwood's will to win—based on your discussions with him—as high, medium or low?"

"High," he said, "very high—Otto Underwood is what I call a highly motivated candidate."

"On a scale of ten—"

"Ten!"

Then Bomber led Zachary through his reluctant visit to Madame Claddington. It was beneath him, you could tell from his expression. He claimed to have no knowledge of any special relationship between Otto Underwood and Anna Claddington.

"Wouldn't it be unusual, all things considered, if Otto Underwood and Madame Poritzky Claddington didn't have some deeper relationship—sending a man of your stature in his organization out to placate a two thousand dollar donor?"

"Objection."

"He may give his opinion."

"I really don't know."

"Well, had it happened to you before—that you were asked to placate any donor?"

"No."

"Has it happened since?"

"No."

"Now, Mr. Roseleer—think—Otto Underwood told you what his prior relationship to Madame Claddington was, didn't he?"

"Objection—asked and answered."

"Just want him to be sure."

"He didn't tell me anything."

"All right, Mr. Roseleer, let me ask you—if in your capacity as a campaign advisor to a presidential candidate— any presidential candidate—certain facts about his past were to come to light—how would you suggest to handle it?"

"Depends on what the facts are. If they *are* facts, how they can be proven?"

"Let's say in a case where a candidate has violent activity in his past. But only one person who knows about it is making noises about exposing him."

"Well, I certainly wouldn't recommend he have her killed."

Bomber paused to nod excessively, hoping, I suppose, Zachary Roseleer didn't have the good sense to retract or clarify his words. "Once again, I have to thank a witness for volunteering information I hadn't asked for. I did not suggest that this person was a *woman,* yet you saw fit to identify her as '*she.*' Were you referring to Madame Claddington, the victim in this case, by the way?"

"I was speaking generically," he said—then added, lamely I thought, "we always say 'he' when referring to an unknown, I thought I'd offer equal time to the women."

"Very nice," Bomber said, and quickly moved on before he could be censured for another gratuitous comment. "Then you suggested you didn't, or wouldn't, recommend Mr. Underwood—or a hypothetical candidate—have her killed. Were you by any chance referring to the *denouemont* of this case?"

"No."

"Then how was it you said 'I certainly wouldn't suggest he have her killed'? Isn't that what happened to *her* in this case? To Madame Claddington? Wasn't she killed?"

"Objection—compound question."

"Yes, well I can ask them one at a time if he can't remember them."

"Sustained," the judge said.

Bomber asked them one at a time—reaping the additional benefit of repetition and emphasis.

"Well," Zachary concluded—perhaps he was thinking of the facts in this case in his allusion. "But I can assure you, those thoughts, ideas, whatever you want to call them, never entered my conversations with Otto Underwood."

"With anyone else?"

"Anyone else?" Zachary seemed stunned at first—"I didn't talk to anyone else about Madame Claddington," he said.

"So in this case, just suppose Candidate Underwood had a past as Meteorite radical—and he was a member of the underground devoted to bombing buildings and utilities and what not, would you for example, counsel him to take a strong anti-radical stance in his campaign?"

"Well, that's a possibility—if he *was* actually anti-radical now, I wouldn't recommend he fake anything."

"So after you visited Madame Claddington roughly two weeks before she was murdered, and she told you she knew about Otto Underwood's murderous past and was about to expose it—what did you recommend?"

"Objection! Inflammatory, without foundation. Highly pre-judicial—"

"Sustained."

"No more questions." Bomber was forming a pattern. End his examinations with unsupported innuendo and an emotional, almost frightened, objection from the district attorney. It played so well for the jury, and the judge could tell them to disregard the question (as he did) until he was blue in the face, but the lasting impression was made.

The district attorney didn't bother to cross-examine Zachary Roseleer.

Instead, he asked to approach the bench, looking very pleased with himself.

"All right," the judge said. "We'll excuse the jury for the day. Thank you, ladies and gentlemen, I'll see you at nine Monday morning. Have a nice weekend."

Bomber groaned softly to himself, as he usually did at those harmless niceties you hear in everyday conversation. If it didn't serve some larger, specific purpose, Bomber was against it.

"Your Honor," Web said, "I'm pleased to report we have found the murder weapon. Ballistic tests have been made and the striations made on bullets fired from this gun match the bullet that killed Mrs. Claddington." Web wasn't going to call her Madame *ad naseum.* "I was hoping this would negate the necessity for Morely Tushman to return to testify on Monday."

"Not so fast," Bomber said. "We should throw in the case because you found a gun? *Where* did you find it? Who found it? When was it found? When did you get it?"

"I'm not on the stand," Web smarted, "and if I were, I'd object to the compound question. I suppose you'll be able to ask the witnesses those questions on Monday—or whenever Judge McCoy desires to hear the testimony."

"We're in the defendant's case," Judge McCoy said. "We'll have to defer to Bomber on this. Do you want to interrupt your case to hear this prosecution testimony?"

"No," Bomber said resoundingly, thinking any interruption would probably jar the jury and make more of the evidence than it perhaps deserved. It was clear the implication Web wanted to make was that finding a gun was tantamount to finding the murder weapon that the defendant had in his possession and fired at the time of the murder. That remained to be seen. I only wish I'd felt more optimistic.

The audience began leaving when the jury did, and there were only a few stragglers left in the old courtroom when we returned to Inocencio Espinal, our client at the defendant table. Bomber gave him the fish eye.

With a genuine whisper—the non-carrying variety—he said, "They found your gun."

Inocencio snapped his head as though awakened from an ugly nightmare. "What gun?" he said instantly, "I don't have no gun—never!"

Bomber studied his face, then patted him reassuringly on the shoulder. "Good work," he said.

"Hey!" Inocencio was angry. "You testing me? Trying a trick?"

"Maybe a small test," Bomber admitted. "You passed it."

"I want to tell truth on the stand," he said, angry at Bomber's little test.

Bomber shook his head. "No need, my boy," he said.

"But if it's a gun, everybody will think it's mine."

"Yes, they will," Bomber agreed. "That's good thinking, Boy."

"So, I must tell them the gun is not my gun."

"Not necessary," Bomber said. "I'm sure the good offices of the county have already been utilized to tie the weapon to you. Unless Web is trying one of his old surprises and you aren't telling me the truth, they have nothing—no evidence the gun is yours. The other possibility is they have solid evidence, you're lying, and testifying would do you no good at all. Either way, you on the stand is a no-winner."

"I want to talk to the jury," Inocencio insisted, still angry.

"Yes, well, if you are itching for another enemy, we can send for the judge on a Friday afternoon as he's leaving the courthouse for his weekend. At any rate, you need some time to consider your—shall we call it a nonnegotiable—demand? Because you'll be finishing the trial without your attorney."

"I can't take it no more—all lies!"

"Well, get used to it. It's all part of the game. You get on the stand under oath and Web will make a turkey enchilada of you—tie you in knots, get you to contradict yourself so you'll *look* guilty to the jury, even if you're not."

Inocencio opened his mouth to protest, but Bomber held up one hand to silence him and with the other signaled the marshal to come get the prisoner. "We'll talk about it Monday. I can't stop you from bugging the judge. *He* won't be happy about it. It really is up to you. Your decision should rest on one simple question: Do you want to win or lose?"

I'm not sure that was a concept Inocencio was digesting as he was led off to jail for the weekend.

After Inocencio was gone, we packed up and left the courthouse. When we were outside, I asked Bomber, "Were you serious?"

"Serious?" he said. "You ever know me to be *un*serious?"

"You'd quit the c-case?"

"Ah, that," he said with a sigh. "I do seriously believe if the kid takes the stand he will cook his own goose. The only question is, do I want to preside over his conviction? As my intellectual processes are presently constituted, I don't. So it comes down to would I rather be branded a loser or a quitter? What would you choose?" he asked.

"Loser," I said. "G-Go down fighting."

"Hmm," he said.

When we got back to the office, Bomber returned a call from his Korea buddy, Abner McNaughton. From all the information he could garner, Morely Tushman's law firm was in robust financial shape, and any mob connections they had were peripheral—no more than any other large law firm in Chicago.

Another hopeful theory bit the dust.

THIRTY-THREE

ON MY CALL TO JOAN HARDING that night, I heard from her mouth music as sweet as any that came out of her violin.

"Guess what, Tod? I've been rummaging around since my boss is out there on the coast, and I think I found something interesting."

"Oh?"

"A photograph of Otto Underwood—it looks like at some campaign rally—I can't tell where—maybe around Chicago. The reason I say Chicago is because guess who is in the picture?"

"Tushman?"

"Harley Holiday," she said. "That didn't strike me as so wonderful at first—Otto Underwood is in the background looking like he's giving a speech—Harley Holiday is in front, below the dais, and it looks like he's talking to someone, and I had suspicions—so I found a picture of Zachary Roseleer in the *Tribune* archives and matched it up and Bingo!"

"It's him?" I couldn't believe it.

"Sure looked like it to me."

"Can you overnight copies to us?"

"It's already done," she said.

What a gem she was. But I was again seized by pangs: "But…ah…your job?" I said. "When Morely Tushman sees the picture is there going to be any doubt in his mind where it came from?"

"Anonymous? Can you say it was sent anonymously?

Because it was, in a way. I'm the donor, and I wish to remain anonymous."

"Oh—okay."

"The photographer could have read about the case—the involvement of Otto Underwood is all over the news."

"You know who the photographer was?"

"No. It's not marked."

The next morning the press was out in force to greet Otto Underwood, candidate for president of the United States. TV cameras and earnest young women with microphones were made up and dressed to the nines. The stalwart men and women of the media tried their best to put the most sinister spin on Otto Underwood's appearance in court, asking him how he thought it would affect his candidacy. He smiled genially and said, "Hey—I'm not on trial, I'm merely a witness."

"Aren't you angry to have to interrupt your campaign to come here?"

"Not at all—I'm always campaigning. I'm campaigning right now. This is such a beautiful town, it's a pleasure to come back and see my many friends and supporters in Angelton. I've often said 'After Angelton, Heaven will be an anti-climax'—That is if I get to heaven—"

"Think you will?"

"If I don't have to sell my soul to the devil to win this nomination."

"It's been said winning your party's nomination this year is tantamount to winning the election. What do you think?"

Another broad smile. "In my experience, nothing is tantamount to anything. We take it one step at a time."

"What do you think Bomber wants with you here?"

"I have no idea."

"Speculation has it Bomber wants you for a boost to his

hopeless case—adding a touch of drama to a sinking ship. Care to comment on that?"

"Oh, my, no. I have more respect for the law than that. I'm sure he does too."

"He's defending a communist. You're on record as being tough on communists."

"Tough, but fair," he grinned. "I am second to none in my feelings for my country, and I have not stood idly by amid threats from abroad or within. I do not fear the communists—what's left of them—but I will not allow myself to get complacent either."

Otto Underwood knew how to play the press. He was a distinguished looking gent, and I studied his gestures and body language and decided he would not be an easy nut to crack. Those nuts that cracked easily did not last this long on the campaign trail—for what were the gallant men and women of the media if not nutcrackers?

Bomber, who usually didn't miss an opportunity to schmooze and spin with the press, took the side door into the courthouse—perhaps on the theory that given enough rope, Otto Underwood would hang himself.

I went in the main door. No one gave me a second look.

Otto Underwood on the stand looked presidential—regal, imperial. He was a presence—tall, fit, with silver, balding hair. I thought he had to fight not to appear looking down his nose at you. He seemed relaxed and refreshed, ready to cope with anything, and if he garnered a few votes in the process, so be it.

Even with the preliminary expository questions, it was apparent that Bomber was lulling Otto Underwood into a false sense of security—letting him blow his horn to his heart's content.

First Bomber went through the hostile witness routine. It

was simply a mind game and on Otto Underwood's behalf, Web objected.

"Do you feel hostile to the defendant?" the judge asked Underwood.

He smiled broadly—"I'm not hostile to anyone," he said.

Judge McCoy said, "Why don't the attorneys come to sidebar?" We marched up.

"Will declaring him hostile serve your cause, Bomber?"

"I think so," he said. "My client is a professed communist, and Mr. Underwood has made a name for himself as a violent anticommunist."

"Oh, Bomber," the judge said, "you aren't going to try to make this a political trial, are you?"

"You know," Bomber said, "if it were in my client's interest to try and make it a three-ring circus the Ringling Brothers better look to their laurels."

"Not in *my* courtroom," Judge McCoy said.

"Of course, Your Honor," Bomber said with his bogus bow.

"Before we go off half-cocked, why don't you ask the witness some questions—if I feel any hostility, I'll grant your request."

We resumed our stations. Bomber stayed on his feet.

"Now, Mr. Underwood, you don't want to be here do you?"

"That's not true."

"Well, you sent an attorney to quash your subpoena, didn't you?"

"Yes. May I explain?"

"Please do."

"I was annoyed at first, but I soon realized I had no right to be. I am running for the highest office in the land, and I don't want to shirk my civic duty. Even though I know nothing that could be helpful," he added as a parting dig.

"Nothing? May I determine that?"

"Certainly," Otto Underwood nodded so curtly it bordered on hostility.

"Do you know Harley Holiday?"

"I don't believe I do."

Bomber had him stand from his front row perch. "Do you recognize this man?"

Underwood frowned. "I don't believe I do."

"Never seen him before?"

More frowning. The wheels were churning. "Please understand I see thousands of faces a day sometimes, so I don't want to categorically deny anything. But I'm not acquainted with the gentleman. I'm sure of that."

"Could he have been a security guard at one of your campaign functions?"

"Possible, I suppose," he said. "I don't handle that myself."

"Who does?"

"Different people—"

"In Chicago?"

"I really couldn't say."

"Could it be Morely Tushman?"

"No."

Bomber plowed on. "Could Morely Tushman have gotten Harley Holiday as a guard without you knowing it?"

"I usually meet the guards—so we both know who we are dealing with. I suppose I have met hundreds of guards in my campaign, so I might have forgotten one or two."

"So Morely Tushman might have had something to do with security guards for your campaign in Chicago?"

"It's possible. I really don't know."

I had to give that to Otto Underwood—he wasn't stupid. I saw Bomber look down at the pictures of Otto Underwood with Harley Holiday in the front. It did not show any connection between the two men and Bomber decided not to use it.

"Mr. Underwood, where were you on July fourth of last year? At night?"

"I think, if memory serves me, I was at a picnic at the Elks Lodge in Long Beach, California."

"How long had you known Madame Claddington when she died?"

"Objection. Assumes facts not in evidence."

"I beg to differ," Bomber said. "Zachary Roseleer stated it."

"Hearsay."

"Oh, let him answer," the judge said.

"I'll ask—did you know Madame Claddington?"

"I did."

"Thank you. How long?"

"Well, I never knew her well, and I hadn't seen her for years. Lot of people come out of the woodwork when you run for president."

"And that's what she did?" Bomber asked. "Came out of the woodwork—like a termite?"

"I'm sorry, I didn't mean it that way. You just have an opportunity to renew a lot of acquaintances."

"Tell us when and where you met Madame Anna Claddington, please."

"I'm afraid the circumstances are hazy. I was probably in my twenties, so forty or so years ago. Was it at a party—some kind of gathering?"

"Someone introduced you?"

"I don't remember. She could have introduced herself."

"Or *you*—could you have?"

"Possible," he conceded.

"Remember what you talked about?"

"Lord no—all those years," he shook his head.

"Did you date her?"

The question elicited the first twitch in Underwood's

demeanor. "No—I saw her a few times, but I wouldn't call it dating."

"What would you call it?"

"Just that—seeing her."

"In social situations?"

"Well, when you characterize it that way, it sounds like wealth and power and high society. It wasn't anything like that. We just got together—a bunch of us kids."

"What did you talk about?"

"I don't know—what do kids talk about? Sports? Girls, boys, relationships, cars. Nothing unusual—"

"Politics?"

"Or memorable," Underwood continued, putting off Bomber's question.

"Politics?" he asked again. "Did you talk politics?"

"We may have. I don't remember specifically."

"If you did talk politics, what were your opinions—and hers, if she expressed any to you?"

"Oh I don't remember any specifics. I was more liberal in those days—as the young are wont to be. As we experience more of life, we see those things don't work and we search for things that will."

"Did Madame Claddington agree with you in those days?"

"Pretty much, as I remember it," he said. "As I say, it's all hazy."

"Did you keep up your friendship with Madame Claddington over the years?"

"No, we drifted apart. Then one day she up and married."

"When did you reconnect with the deceased? Madame Claddington?"

"Just this year. When I announced my candidacy she called to ask what she could do."

"What did you tell her?"

"Give money," he said, laughing.

"And how did she respond?"

"She laughed and said 'What, after forty years all I'm good for is a handout?' Well, we both laughed and had a good time." He shook his head once, pursed his lips, and made a pronouncement: "She was one grand lady, that one."

"I'm pleased to hear that. Did she give you money?"

"I believe she did. Two thousand for the tickets, wasn't it?"

"I'm asking you. If she gave that for a ticket, did she give you anything else?"

"Not that I'm aware of."

"Are you made aware of all the large donors to your campaign?"

"Supposed to be."

"But you don't know if you are?"

"Well, I do have a certain amount of trust, but with so much going on, you have to expect some things slip between the cracks."

"But you remember Madame Claddington's two thousand dollar contribution?"

"How could I forget it? Yes, I remember."

"How did it come about?"

"We sent a mailing for a Chicago fundraiser. A testimonial dinner that politicians like myself have found so useful. She responded."

"Did she attend?"

"Yes."

"Did you talk to her that night?"

"I did."

"About what?"

"She complained about her seat. She was too far away for an old friend. I told her I didn't do the seating, and it was done pretty much mechanically by putting those who gave the most in close proximity and working down as the contributions wore down."

"How close did two thousand get her?"

"Not close, I'm afraid."

"How close?"

"Oh, six or eight tables away, I'd guess."

"Did your explanation assuage her?"

"I'm afraid not."

"What did you do?"

"I sent Zachary Roseleer to see her—apologize—see if we could placate her."

"Did Mr. Roseleer report any success from the venture?"

"Alas, no. He said she was implacable."

"And two weeks later she was dead?"

Underwood said nothing.

"Is that correct?"

"Apparently."

"Now, your first meeting with Madame Claddington occurred in the sixties, is that correct?"

"I believe so. It's been a long time."

"If I were to characterize the political climate of the sixties, I would say it was somewhat rebellious for young people? Sit-ins in college administration buildings, civil disobedience. Lot of young people disenchanted with the establishment, would that be a fair characterization of what you witnessed?"

"As long as you are not trying to tar me with any sympathy with those rascals."

"Why, Senator, what a shocking thought," Bomber said this on the line between sincerity and sarcasm, putting the district attorney on the spot. If he objected to the implication of the tone, he would make it seem more important then it surely was, and Bomber would express great surprise that anyone could put such an interpretation on it. Bomber got away with a lot that way.

"But indulge my naïvete if you will. You said you were a liberal and those were liberal times?"

"I was not a lawless rabble rouser, just don't confuse me with that."

"I'm not trying to *confuse* you, I'm simply trying to understand where you fit in those times."

Wearily Web stood, buttoned his jacket, and said, "Your Honor, I am a patient man. Lord knows I've let Bomber explore grossly irrelevant areas. But we will sit here until eternity if I don't attempt to restore *some* relevance to the proceedings."

"You in a hurry to hang my client?" Bomber snapped.

"Please, enough, Bomber," the judge retorted. "Are you leading to something other than the witness's political beliefs forty years ago?"

"Am I leading to something? I hope to tell you I am. I am, for starters, leading up to getting my client off this trumped-up charge."

"Bang!" The gavel shook the large courtroom. "That is an inappropriate remark, Mr. Hanson—you know it is—highly inflammatory—strictly your opinion. The jury is to decide the charges. No, you know better and I know better and I will have no more of it. The remark will be stricken from the record and you will apologize to the court—the district attorney and the jury."

Bomber bowed elaborately to each and said, quite gratuitously, I thought, "I stand corrected."

"And do you apologize?" the judge insisted.

"I apologize," Bomber said. I thought the whole scene accrued to Bomber's benefit: the judge's overkill—God knows he'd been provoked enough—and deliberate humiliation of Bomber in front of the whole room. But Bomber had a way of turning those slights to his advantage as the wounded party.

"All right," Judge McCoy said, "I'm inclined to give you

leeway to defend your client, but my patience is not infinite—
so let's get to a connection here pretty quick."

"Yes, Your Honor. Now, Senator Underwood, are you familiar with underground organizations in the sixties? Groups
like the Meteorites?"

He frowned. "I may have heard of them—I certainly wasn't
a member, if that's what you mean."

"I'm relieved to hear that, Senator—I didn't ask if you
were, but you just saved me a question. To your knowledge,
what were the goals and methods of those groups?"

"Weren't they the ones who went around blowing up buildings and things—like terrorists?"

"Is that a question to me, or your answer?"

"Yes, I'm not sure I'm giving you what you want."

"I only want the truth, Senator. That's all—it's that simple."

"Well, the truth is, I'm not that well versed in those extrem-
ist movements."

"You never associated with any of them?"

"Certainly not!"

"And by the same token, Madame Claddington would have
had no knowledge of your association with the underground?"

"Not if her knowledge was correct."

"Did she say anything to you about the underground?"

"Not that I remember."

"Can't say an unequivocal 'no'?"

"No! Yes, I can say no."

"She's dead—we can't ask her, can we?"

"Objection."

"Sustained."

"Do you believe the underground in the sixties were
radicals?"

"From what I know about it, yes. Believe me, I am tough
on radicals—no one tougher."

"So, I suppose you understand the mentality of radicals."

"Yes, I do."

"Can you explain that mentality to the jury?"

"Individuals or powerless groups of individuals seek power and attention to their cause. Bombings, assassinations, and mayhem…bring them recognition they wouldn't otherwise get."

"Are you aware of the political philosophy of the defendant in this case?"

"He's a communist, isn't he?"

"He professes to be. Do you have any more questions for me, before I resume my own?"

"Objection."

"Sustained."

"How do you stand on communists?"

"I'm tough on any outfit that wants to bring down our government."

"And you include the remaining communists in that view?"

"I do."

"Do you know my client?"

"I do not."

"Do you wish to judge him without knowing him?"

"Objection."

"Sustained."

"You don't like communists very much, do you, Senator?"

"I don't like communism—it is a godless philosophy counter to everything this great country of ours stands for."

Bomber bobbed his head up and down. "You don't like communists then—do you?"

"No, I don't."

"Want my client to be convicted?"

"If he's guilty. Certainly!"

"Is that an opinion you held forty years ago?"

"What? Forty years ago? I was young—perhaps more naïve than I would have liked. But I was always a patriotic citizen, always unalterably opposed to anyone who had designs on overthrowing the greatest government in the history of mankind!" You could see Senator Underwood waving the American flag while fireworks filled the air. He was *that* convincing.

"Even when you were a radical member of the underground plotting to blow up buildings yourself?"

"Objection!"

"Sustained—strike the statement from the record."

"No further questions," Bomber said.

THIRTY-FOUR

DISTRICT ATTORNEY Webster A. Grainger III asked Otto Underwood, "Did you kill Anna Claddington?" "No." "Were you on the premises of the murder scene July fourth?" "No." "Did you arrange to have her killed?" "Of course not!"

When we got back to the office, there was a message for me to call Joan Harding in Chicago. I retired to my closet office to do so.

The great lift in her voice when she said, "Oh, hi!" told me she had good news. "You know the guy who was doing the gay bars for me?"

"Yeah."

"I think he hit on something. A guy who knew Dick Funk-hauser said he was a world class shot—some kinds of medals when he was at La Salle."

That was news—a touch of reasonable doubt, but not admissible in court since it was hearsay. And had we a prime source—Web would scream it was irrelevant and it would be a toss-up whether we'd get it admitted or not.

I explained our position and asked if there was any chance we could trace it back to Dick practicing at a shooting gallery or some direct, admissible testimony. She said she would try.

I took the news to Bomber, who seemed pleased just at the portent. Then he waved a hand at the chair opposite him. "Sit down, my boy," he said, in an expansive good humor.

"I'm bound to say that Chicago operative of yours has done us yeomen's service. How can we ever thank him?"

I must have blushed. Bomber paid it no mind. "I thought you must have paid him, but I don't see a sou on the expense account. Now we're going to have to ask him—" he paused as though an alien thought had just crept into his mind "—or I suppose it could be a she—to come to Angelton to testify."

My heart jumped and sank at the same time. It jumped at the thought of seeing Joan again, and sank at the thought of her losing her job identifying the photocopy of her boss's notes.

Bomber looked at me. "Be difficult, would it?" he asked gently.

I nodded.

"You understand why, don't you?"

I nodded.

"It's not a frivolous request. We need foundation to make the evidence admissible. Where did it come from? Morely Tushman's note about the underground will only help us if we get it admitted."

"C-c-could do that," I said.

"You?"

"I was with h-h-her when s-she, w-we, found it."

"You *were?*" He sat back thoughtfully. "I may have under-estimated you, me boy," he said.

Naturally my mind was racing. If I took the stand and Bomber asked me questions, I'd be spitting all over the court-room. Bomber knew what I was thinking, but kept quiet about it, as he always did about my stuttering in his presence.

"May I know who *she* is?"

"Morely T-T-Tushman's secretary."

His eyes lifted like a drawbridge. "Oh," he said like a sinking ship. "Probably lose her job?"

"Probably."

"Hmm," he ruminated. "The kid isn't worth that," he said.

He paused again. "She's the anonymous source of the picture, I suppose."

I nodded.

"We can't establish that with you, can we?"

I shook my head. "Why do you w-want the picture?"

"To impeach Zachary Roseleer. And Harley Holiday. I'd say we were getting really close to reasonable doubt. If he didn't do it, someone had to—who would it have been?"

I didn't have to say anything. I knew what he was thinking.

"Then there is the little matter of the notes of Morley Tushman where the word 'underground' appears. You saw what I tried to do with that. I can't wait to get Morley Tushman back in the saddle to ask him what it meant. Of course, I don't expect him to break down slobbering like they do on TV—any more than that presidential candidate did. They'll lie all day long in court—perjury is so hard to prove, so burdensome to try. Web doesn't have the stomach for it, that's for sure. We can create doubt, me boy, but we have to have the tools. I think we have them—it's only a question of utilizing them."

He paused to raise a thoughtful finger to his lips.

"How tough would it be for her to bring us the original?"

"She'd have to steal it. Could wind up in j-j-jail—after c-certainly l-losing her job."

"No theft—a matter of borrowing evidence for a court proceeding. No designs on keeping it. What do we have to do to get her out here?"

There was the real question—on the floor at last. I was on the spot. If I was too eager, I could kiss goodbye any thought of Joan coming to Angelton short of a miracle. I took a deep breath and finally got out the answer. "A job."

"A job?" he said, astonished. Then he thought a moment. "Well, I guess if she's going to lose hers that makes sense. Don't know anyone offhand who needs a good legal secretary—especially one who just lost her job from turning on her boss, but let me think about it. Oh, I see," he said, looking at me. "You're thinking we could use another hand about the shop. Well, you know my penchant for staying small—this would be counter to that and against my judgement. I don't suppose a large witness fee would move her?"

"I d-doubt it." I was toughing it out with Mr. Tough. Joan would probably come and testify for nothing, but I didn't see any percentage in telling Bomber that.

"Hmm," he said. "Well, I'll be thinking of a solution. On one condition."

"What's that?"

"You don't breathe a word of this to your mother—not until it's settled. If there is any skirt within a mile of you with a smile on her face, that woman goes bananas. It's positively unhealthy."

The next morning in court, Judge McCoy refused to accept the photograph into evidence because, he said, there was no foundation, "Where did it come from?" he asked. "At least we can expect an answer to that, can't we?" We were at the sidebar. Bomber was saying, "Let the jury know it came to us anonymously—they can reject it if they want. Let the district attorney put on experts to say if it's a composite or not."

"I should go to the trouble?" Web said.

"Winning is trouble sometimes," Bomber said, "I got news for you. You also have a rich uncle picking up your costs. We aren't so fortunate."

I attribute it to Bomber's uncanny knack of timing that he didn't show his hand on Morley Tushman's notes at that moment. He could tell Web was itching to say something, so he paused long enough for the district attorney to say—

"Your Honor—I have a request to make in Mr. Tushman's behalf. His friend and long time companion, Dick Funk-hauser, died last night, and he would respectfully ask to be released from his obligations here so that he might make funeral arrangements and settle his affairs."

Judge McCoy waved a deferential hand at Bomber. "What do you say?"

Bomber frowned. "I'm very much afraid I need him."

"For what?" Web demanded, "You can't just keep these out-of-state people sitting around. Can we have an offer of proof, Your Honor?"

"Well I'm not inclined to inhibit any defense that can be reasonably justified. Are you telling me this is something that can be reasonably connected to something relevant?"

"Yes, Your Honor. It goes to reasonable doubt."

"There he goes again," Web said, slapping his forehead. "It's a fishing expedition, Your Honor. That's all it is."

"Look," Bomber said, "before you get carried away, I am willing to be as accommodating as possible. He wants to go to a funeral, fine—it could also be arranged for this weekend. The only thing is, I have a document I want to question him about, and to get the proper foundation will probably take some time—bring a witness from a Chicago."

"Chicago!" Web whelped. "The murder occurred here."

"Your grasp of the real issues astonishes me, Web," Bomber said to Judge McCoy's frowning forehead.

"Thanks, Bomber," Web said.

"Your Honor, I'm willing to leave it up to the district attorney. I will question Attorney Tushman now about the document that seems to be in his handwriting. Of course, if he denies it, I'll have to call some handwriting experts."

"Is the document original?" Web asked.

"It's a photocopy."

"Oh, I'd object to that."

Bomber threw out his hands in the "What can you do?" gesture. "I'll be glad to produce the original if I can, but it may take more time—certainly necessitating Attorney Tushman's coming back from Chicago."

"Your Honor—may I consult Mr. Tushman before we decide?"

"Certainly. We'll recess until tomorrow morning."

We went back to our tables. Bomber whispered, "Can we get the original?"

"I'll try—" I paused—not only for effect but to gather my thoughts—and courage. "L-lose her j-job-no qu-question."

"We'll deal with it…if she produces," he said. But he didn't say how.

As soon as I got back to the office, I called Joan. She was gratifyingly amenable. Joan was alone in her office.

"In the cause of truth and justice and all that," she said, "I must do my civic duty, despite all advice to the contrary here."

"From whom?"

"My father for one. My mother too. They say I'm crazy to throw over a good job like this. Say not only will I lose the job, but I'll be black-balled all over town. All the more reason to spread my wings and fly west, young woman," she said paraphrasing Horace Greely. "They don't know how much I've missed you," she said, warming me from head to toe.

"You're too good to be true."

"Bosh—I didn't tell you the clincher."

"What's that?"

"The LA Philharmonic is having auditions for fiddlers."

"Fantastic!" I said. "If there is any justice in the world, you'll get it."

"And your innocent client will go free—"

The conversation veered to the personal. She asked how my violin/piano piece was coming.

"Lento," I said. "Too many distractions."

"Maybe you need a muse."

"Ah…"

"Oh, by the way, watch your fax machine."

"What for?"

"I contacted La Salle for Dick Funkhouser's shooting records, and they're being faxed to you." She paused. "Now the only decision I have to make is how to sing my swan song—and when. Do I sneak off into the night and leave Mr. Tushman a sweet letter ignoring my theft, or do I face the music and mention it in the letter? Or do I really stand tall and confront him when he comes back—tell all and wait to be led off in handcuffs? The more I hear myself say that, the less appeal it has. You think I'll go to jail?"

"Maybe you shouldn't *do* it?" It was one of those half statements, half questions that I didn't want her to accept.

"Shouldn't do it," she said with a mirthless chuckle, "I've already *done* it."

"But, you haven't risked everything on testifying. You could just put the notes back, and I'll tell Bomber you couldn't risk your future with a possible theft charge. I mean would the LA Phil hire you if you were Heifitz and had a felony on your record?"

"I'm afraid to find out."

I went to tell Bomber the news in his office.

"Yeah," he said. "I take it this—these 'notes' were not lying on her desk."

"No."

"She had to go seek them out—maybe even purloin a key, as Web would have it?"

"Yes."

"Hmm. Could make a case, I suppose, that she simply didn't want to bother her boss in California—in the time of his bereavement."

Bomber's strategy was to keep the pictures for Joan to identify. He decided against calling Harley Holiday again. His denials were on record, he would only weasel out of them. If he wanted to somehow set the record straight, Web could call him as a rebuttal witness. It would appear more dubious that way.

Before I left for the day, I heard the humming of the fax machine. It was the astonishing shooting records of Dick Funkhauser from La Salle.

It was a little after five when I got home that night to the cozy hovel over the garage at the ocean. I couldn't help comparing my decor to Joan's Chicago apartment; and, except for the ocean proximity, it didn't fare too well. I did fantasize about her living with me here, I just didn't know if it would ever come to pass.

I couldn't have been in the room five minutes when the phone rang. It was a breathless Joan. "Free at last," she said, "thank God almighty I'm free at last."

"Reverend King?" I asked.

"I just got home," she chuckled. "Mr. Tushman came right to the office from the airport—which was okay, because I decided I had to face him and tell him I was off to new and exciting ventures. I could tell by the tightness of his jaw he had his suspicions, but didn't quite know how to reprimand me without seeming to admit some kind of guilt—and I don't know if he *is* guilty of anything besides being a lawyer. What is the real story? Do you know?"

"I don't. I don't think Bomber does either. He's trying to build this scenario where Dick Funkhauser rises from the couch, goes out and shoots her, then returns while Harley Holiday, who is in on it and Peter Williams who isn't, tackle our innocent client."

"Why?"

"Because she threatened to blow the whistle on Otto Underwood and cost him the presidency."

"You buy it?"

"Reasonable doubt," I explained. "But it looks like the

media has picked up on it-a little slower than we might hope—
if there's anything there, I expect they'll find it."

"Why would Madame Claddington blow the whistle—
even if he was radical in his past?"

"Why would she do it? Vanity—all is vanity, isn't it?"

"Oh, I don't know that I'd want to be that pessimistic."

"The theory is she died for her sins. The big one was vanity.
She was insulted at the table they gave her for Underwood's
Chicago rally. Then Underwood sent an underling to assuage
her anger—which I'm told could be world class—instead of
going himself—further wounding her already weakened
vanity."

"Think she probably threatened—possibly half in jest—to
tell all about his past?" Joan asked.

"I think so. I can just see the pow-wow in the politico's
camp: 'But she was probably just kidding.' 'Can we take the
chance?' 'But murder is so much worse. Especially if she was
kidding.' 'Face it, she's had a rich full life—what's left for
her? She always did like the limelight. This would be her
fifteen minutes of fame.'"

"I don't want to believe it," Joan said.

"Let's hope the jury does," I said. "Are you packed?"

"Just about. Can you pick me up or should I get a taxi?"

"Are you kidding?" I asked. "I'd come for you if all I had
was a bicycle—and when you see my car you may wish I had
a bicycle."

She laughed, and her laugh gave me the wings of a sparrow.

"Are you ready to testify?"

"I can't claim I'm looking forward to it."

"And hear your ex-boss testify?"

"That might even be harder for me. I'm the one put him in
that spot."

"I have a feeling he can handle it."

"How?"

"Lie."

"In court! A lawyer?"

I laughed. "It wouldn't be unprecedented. For verily it is said, what is a lie if you're wrapped up in murder?"

"Do you think he is?"

"Ask me after we hear him testify," I said. "Oh—I almost forgot—we got the stuff from LaSalle—you know, Dick Funkhauser's marksmanship records."

"Good shot, was he?" she asked.

"The best. I never saw so many perfect scores. Can you imagine a guy hitting a bull's eye the size of a dime from one hundred feet time and again? I couldn't hit a barn door," I said.

She gave me her flight information.

I worked on my violin/piano duet far into the night. For some reason I wasn't sleepy.

THIRTY-FIVE

WHAT A WEEKEND! If only I weren't so shy and reticent about personal matters, I could tell some tales.

Monday was a banner day in court. There was so much electric tension in the air, you'd think everyone knew what was afoot.

The district attorney made the usual fuss about not having notice Joan Harding was going to appear.

We were at the judge's sidebar. Bomber was saying, "Hey! You wanted foundation for the stuff, we're giving you foundation. What would you have done had I been able to tell you this woman was flying out here from Chicago before I knew it myself? She arrived Saturday. This is the first time I felt optimistic enough to say anything. But hey, I'm willing to consider stipulations or a recess until you can pull yourself together."

It was vintage Bomber, and Web's tail sank between his legs as he allowed he could cope with the hardship.

"The defendant calls Joan Harding to the stand," Bomber said, so triumphantly I pictured him tooting a horn in *Aida*.

She was so beautiful, moving with such grace as she did to the stand. I'm sure my love and admiration were telegraphed to the jury. I couldn't help it. If any of the jurors missed it, Bomber did not. He leaned over me and whispered, "Want to ask the questions yourself?"

I shook my head in terror. That would be the *worst*, I thought.

Joan sat on the chair in the witness box, folded her hands in her lap, and smiled at me. Lord, such an exciting woman.

I had introduced Joan to Bomber before court, and he outlined his questions to her. I hadn't wanted to make an opera out of it, even though Mom was bugging me to bring her to dinner.

"For heaven's sakes," Bomber'd said, "let her get settled first. Testifying in court is no easy chore, especially when it cost you your job." That last bit may have been exaggerated, but it was only a matter of semantics.

Bomber asked the opening questions like an old friend—not much different from his handling of any friendly witness. I so hoped he could minimize my involvement, but there really was no way to tell the story without it. Web would pounce on it, so Bomber had to usurp Web's prerogative, and usurp it he did.

"Miss Harding, can you tell the jury how you came to be involved in this case?"

She nodded as demure as a maiden in church. "I met your son and he swept me off my feet." She looked at me and smiled. I smiled back, and stole what I hoped was a surreptitious glance at the jury. All eyes were on me. I remember thinking how corny it must have sounded—but as Bomber often (too often for my taste) said, "If corn will move a jury, plant me a couple of acres."

"Goodness gracious," Bomber said in mock surprise. "Whatever did you see in Tod?"

She smiled that irresistible smile again. "Well," she said, as though anyone would know, "he's so kind and thoughtful, considerate and compassionate—and we have music in common. He's a fantastic composer—we played duets." Bomber was beaming. Web was itching to object, but he knew better, and I was just blushing again. Bomber leaned over to whisper to me after Joan's answer, "Let's see Web do something with that."

Bomber knew displays of secrecy always piqued the jury's curiosity. "Speculation," Bomber said, "always added to reasonable doubt."

From there it was a piece of cake getting Joan over the nitty gritty of the theft of her boss's notes and laying the foundation for Morely Tushman's notes and the picture of Otto Underwood, Harley Holiday and Zachary Roseleer. Bomber also had her establish the trail that led to the obtaining of Dick Funkhauser's marksmanship records from La Salle University. And with soap opera aspects out in the open, I had a feeling the jury would have forgiven her if she had confessed to an ax murder in the cause.

When it was his turn, Web began by trying to be careful not to be too heavy handed in disparagement of what the jury had surely come to think of as true love.

"Miss Harding, how did you like your boss?"

"Objection," Bomber said easily. "She has already testified she has resigned her position."

"Oh, yes, she did quit, didn't she?"

"If you want to put it in those crude terms," Bomber said, "and before you ask, she has already testified she liked her boss and her job, and she was enlisted in the cause of truth and justice by an act of conscience. Asked and answered!"

"Uh!" Web yelled, really angry—and who can blame him? Bomber was testifying and out of order. Of course the trick with those kind of shenanigans was to steer clear of alienating the jury. It was a risk, and I was always amazed at how often Bomber survived it.

"All right, Miss Harding," Web said, "you sold out your boss, didn't you?"

"Objection."

"Sustained."

"Miss Harding, you claimed to have had affection for your boss, correct?"

"Oh, yes."

"Was there sexual intimacy?"

Bomber smiled and let it go.

"Oh, no," she said. "Mr. Tushman wasn't oriented that way."

"Uh, I move that be stricken from the record. It is nonresponsive. I didn't ask about his 'orientation.'"

Judge McCoy stared at the district attorney for a moment. "Well," he said, "you may not have asked it, but you asked *for* it. I'll let it stand."

"But, Your Honor, her response demeans a member of the bar in good standing."

"Then don't ask questions that have little if any direct bearing on the case."

Web opened his mouth to respond, then closed it again. Whenever he tried to be as provocative as Bomber, he got into trouble.

"All right, Miss Harding, did you think your act of cooperating with defending counsel in this case, was not an act of disloyalty to your boss, Attorney Tushman?"

"No, I didn't think it was disloyalty," she said.

"No? You went into his private files without his permission and produced documents you thought damaging to the state's case."

"But Mr. Tushman wasn't the defendant. I didn't think he had any personal stake in the matter."

"Why get involved in the first place?"

"An excellent question, Mr. Grainger. These days people seem to avoid involvement don't they?"

"I ask the questions," he snapped.

"Oh, sorry. But for me your question is not a simple one. It's a philosophical thing. See, I met this young man, and I'll admit, I was smitten—still am," she said, smiling in my direction. "He told me the effort he was making to get answers to his questions in Chicago, and the great difficulty he had getting cooperation. Then I met him for lunch, and he had been beaten to a bloody pulp. I knew I had to do something for him, so I offered to help," she shrugged her pretty shoulders. "A woman's instinct, I guess."

"But didn't you have qualms about ethics? Turning on your boss?"

"I don't think I *turned* on him, as you suggest. I had no inkling then, nor do I now, that he was guilty of anything. We were merely looking for hints that might help solve the mystery."

"Why didn't you just ask him?"

"You have to know Mr. Tushman. He's a very proper man. He would think of his clients first."

"Exactly!" Web said. "Wasn't attorney-client privilege involved? Didn't you break that trust?"

"Well, I'm not an attorney. Mr. Tushman would naturally feel that way, but I wouldn't. I'm sure he wouldn't want an innocent man convicted, and his attorney-client privilege restrictions could keep him from letting the truth out."

"You sound like a noble woman," Web said sarcastically.

"Why, thank you," she said with a smile that flummoxed him. "But, I don't see it as noble. It's just a small gesture to save an innocent."

Web bobbed his head in derision, "Sort of like the milk of human kindness?" he asked, mocking her.

"Exactly!" she said and beamed. Web was no match for Joan, and though he continued to try to paint her as an ungrateful shrew, she continued to parry his thrusts and turn them to her advantage. She was a *star!* Of course, I might be prejudiced.

When the district attorney gave up, Bomber rose for redirect questioning, but instead made a little heart-wrenching speech.

"Thank you for submitting to this ordeal, Miss Harding. I know how difficult it is to do the right thing, to make the sacrifices you've made to come here from Chicago—leave your job, which was no longer tenable, in the cause of justice—"

"Your Honor," Web snapped. "I move that be stricken from the record. Save it for his closing argument."

"Yes," Judge McCoy said. "Do you have any further questions, Bomber?"

"No further questions," he said.

Both Joan and Bomber were beaming. So was I.

Now it was Morely Tushman's turn. He was immaculately turned out as usual, but in more somber tones, befitting, I suppose, his bereavement over the loss of his long-term friend, Dick Funkhauser.

He sat in the witness chair, adjusted his shirt sleeves and cuff links and went through the preliminaries with a reminder from the judge he was still under oath. Perhaps it was his dark suit, but his pallor seemed more ashen than usual.

Bomber moved closer to the witness. It was as though he wanted to get as close as possible to Morely Tushman to contrast their respective sartorial splendors: Tushman out of *GQ* magazine, Bomber the street person.

"Attorney Tushman, did you trust your secretary?"

"Yes, I did. That's why—"

Bomber held up his hand. "You gave your answer. It was a simple yes or no answer. Thank you. Before July four, let's say, had she given you any reason to mistrust her in any way?"

"No."

"Did she in fact have access to your papers—legal documents, letters—notes? You weren't hiding anything from her, were you?"

"No," Tushman frowned, darkly suspicious about the direction of the questioning.

"Now, what was this secret cache of papers you held in a special safe?"

"Confidential things—lawyer-client privilege things."

"Let me be clear. All your documents that were privileged you held in this safe?"

"No."

"How did you decide which?"

"I suppose if I thought they were more sensitive than the regular communication of the office, I put them in the safe."

"Extra protection from prying eyes?"

"You could say that."

"Attorney Tushman, what does the word 'underground' mean to you?"

"Below ground."

"Does it call to mind any other definitions?"

"Not offhand."

"Think, please."

"Well, I guess the London subway is called the Underground."

"Good. Others?"

"Others?"

"Other definitions of the word 'underground.'" Bomber was in his bullying mode. I hoped the jury didn't find it insensitive in light of Morely's bereavement.

"I suppose it could be used for a secret."

"Can you give us an example?"

"There was the underground railroad," he said, as though he'd had an epiphany. "That was kind of a secret railroad—it wasn't a railroad really—just a way of getting slaves north."

Bomber smiled indulgently. "Anything else?"

"Nothing comes to mind."

"Take yourself back to the sixties. Does the underground mean anything to you in that period?"

Tushman pinched his eyes. "You know, I think there was something, but I'm not recalling it."

"The Meteorites in the same period—mean anything?"

"No-o-o," he drew it out as though he were really trying.

"If I told you the underground was a loose collection of anarchists, who made bombs to blow up buildings—and some of them blew themselves up—would that jog your memory?"

"It does sound familiar—the Meteorites were one of the groups, were they?"

"Attorney Tushman, I ask the questions here. It's the way we practice law in California."

I noticed a couple jurors shifting uncomfortably in their seats. It was such a gamble, Bomber's take-no-prisoners schtick. All he could really hope for was a major blunder from a witness, but that was an especially long shot with a man of Tushman's experience.

Bomber showed Morely Tushman the original document he'd had admitted to evidence—the one Joan and I filched from Tushman's secret stash where he quoted Madame linking Otto Underwood to the underground.

"Attorney Tushman, I show you a piece of paper with some handwriting on it. Can you identify it?"

Tushman took the paper and examined it carefully—then turned it over to make sure there weren't any surprises on the other side.

"It looks like a note I made on a telephone conversation with Madame Claddington."

"It's your writing?"

"Yes, it appears to be."

"Do you remember the circumstances? What was the conversation that led you to make that note?"

"I don't really remember. I often made notes—sometimes they were little more than doodles—a release for tension, an antidote to boredom."

"You quote Madame Claddington as referring to Otto Underwood's underground past. Can you explain it?"

"No—I suppose she meant it in the secret sense."

"What was the secret?"

"I don't know. She was alluding to something. She often did that—spoke in riddles. I don't know if it was intentional, or just her age."

"Is there anything else of significance on this page?"

Tushman looked again. "I can't see anything."

"Then will you tell the jury, Attorney Tushman, why you kept this note with your most secret papers?"

"No, I can't—perhaps it was a mistake."

"A *mistake!?*"

"Yes. It happens—got stuck to another paper perhaps."

"Oh really? Any idea what might have been on those it might have stuck to?"

"None whatever."

"Do you have any knowledge that Otto Underwood was a member of the underground in the sixties? Remember, you're under oath."

Tushman shot back, his face flushed with anger. "You don't have to lecture *me* about oaths—I am a practicing attorney."

"So tell me the truth so you can keep it that way."

"Objection! I move that be stricken from the record."

"Yes," Judge McCoy said, "strike it."

"Now, Attorney Tushman, I know you went to Chicago for the weekend—and I don't mean to be cavalier about your trip—but would you please tell the jury why you had to go back so suddenly?"

Tushman's eyes began to tear up. I could see Web making a move to object, but then deciding not to interrupt the poignancy of the moment. "I buried my…friend, Dick Funkhauser."

"Was he your lifelong companion?"

"Going on twenty years."

"We established before you were lovers—did we not?"

"Your Honor," Web said without standing, "I must object again to the relevance of this questioning—and it's been asked and answered."

"Sustained."

"I'm sorry," Bomber said with a stab at contrition, "perhaps we can explain it to the jury some other way—he was dependent on your hospitality for most of those years?"

"Yes."

"These last few years—after he was identified with AIDS—were especially difficult, weren't they?"

A sniffle. Then a nod. Then a more difficult, "Yes."

"Would it be fair to say Dick Funkhauser was grateful to you?"

"I suppose."

"In your debt?"

"I never considered it a debt."

"Did he?"

"Objection."

"Sustained."

"Did you have any conversations with him in which he expressed sentiments of that nature?"

"Objection—vague."

"Okay," Bomber said. "Did Dick Funkhauser ever tell you he was grateful for all you had done for him?"

"Yes, he did. He was an appreciative person."

"Thank you. But, am I right in stating he was not in your financial position?"

"That's right," he said, pained at the recollections.

"So if he wanted to reciprocate all the favors you'd done for him, it wouldn't be financial."

"Correct."

"Did you know your good friend Dick Funkhauser was an expert marksman in his college days at La Salle?"

"I didn't know him then."

"Did you find out later?"

He didn't answer right away—finally he shook his head. "I didn't know about that."

"His La Salle record?"

"Yes."

"But you knew he was a crack shot who could hit a bulls-eye the size of a dime from one hundred feet?"

"I don't think so."

"Look, Attorney Tushman, don't get cute—yes or no? Did you know Dick Funkhauser was a crack shot?"

"I may have known—he might have told me sometime ago that he was a shooter. I couldn't swear to it."

"Did you secure the murder weapon for Mr. Funkhauser?"

"Objection."

"Overruled."

"No, I did not."

"Where did he get it—do you know?"

"Objection."

"Sustained."

"Now you were also close to Otto Underwood, weren't you?"

Morely Tushman was shocked. "Not in the same way."

"No, I didn't mean that. In what way were you close to Otto Underwood?"

"Professionally."

"He was a client?"

"Yes."

"You were his only lawyer?"

"Oh, no. He had many."

"Why did he need so many, do you think?"

"I couldn't say. But he was running for president in fifty states and legal issues come up."

"As far as you know, were you his only Illinois attorney?"

"Yes."

"Did you pass on the comment made by Madame Claddington—about Otto Underwood not having a good memory of his underground years?"

"Objection! This is a mischaracterization of the note and the testimony."

"Oh, all right," Bomber said, giving the impression he thought the district attorney was being nit-picky. "Let me read you the note to refresh your memory—'Furious!, Shabby treatment, Hassle, In a huff, Out of Joint, He'll be sorry!!!, UNDERGROUND MEMORY SHORT, She makes A Shakespearean tragedy out of everything. Ah well, she won't live for ever.' Did you pass that on to Otto Underwood? The note you had put in your special, private safe?"

"I'm afraid my conversations with Otto Underwood fall under the attorney-client privilege."

"Madame Anna Claddington was your client, was she not?"

"Yes."

"And she's dead. Death ends the privileged conversations."

"But Otto Underwood is still alive."

"Isn't it a conflict of interest and against the cannon of bar association ethics to represent parties on opposing sides of an issue?"

"Yes, but Otto Underwood and Madame Claddington were not opposing litigants."

"Their goals were different, were they not?"

He frowned. "Not that I'm aware of."

"He wanted to be president, and she had information that could have stopped him."

"I don't know what you're talking about."

"I'm talking about the fact that Candidate Underwood was a member of the radical underground."

"Strike that from the record!" the district attorney yelled. "That is out of order and without foundation."

"It will be stricken," Judge McCoy said. "And Mr. Hanson, please do better."

"I stand corrected."

Bomber's theory of another gunman was an attractive one, but it was proving difficult to establish through witnesses. I feared it was eluding the jury.

THIRTY-SIX

JOAN AND I WERE HAVING the time of our lives. It was conducive to everything salubrious except sleep—and I had some difficulty keeping my eyes open in court.

When it was finally old Web's turn to cross-examine Morely Tushman he opened up with both barrels:

"Morely Tushman, are you as outraged as I am by your trusted secretary stabbing you in the back?"

"Objection," Bomber cut in, "he's testifying—asking questions with the answer already built in."

"As if you never did that," Web said, pointing a so-there finger at Bomber.

"Counsel to the sidebar!"

When we assembled loosely Judge McCoy let loose on us. "Gentlemen, you're better lawyers than you are showing me. Asking leading questions—suggesting the answer in the question, then asking it the right way which you knew all along with the answer already planted in the witness's mind. I won't have it. If you want to try the case in my courtroom you're going to have to act like grownups or I'll cite the lot of you for contempt!"

There was the contempt threat again—wielded like a powerless parent over a habitually errant child.

Back in position, the prosecutor regrouped. "Mr. Tushman, how did you feel when you found out your trusted secretary had secretly gone through your private papers?"

"Objection."

"I'll let him answer," Judge McCoy said.

"I didn't feel good, I'll tell you. I felt betrayed."

"Poor man!" Bomber whispered to me, jarring me awake. We were apparently at the end of Tushman's testimony. Joan was in the audience for the rest of the trial, and I'll never know how she kept *her* eyes open. Mom was dying to meet her, and we promised as soon as the trial was over.

The question Web asked Morely Tushman that made me shudder was, did Tushman consider having Joan indicted for theft? Tushman said he was considering it. Though Bomber had promised to defend her gratis, I was still skittish about it. Joan was left with the feeling the proposition was being offered as a bribe to the jurors. The prosecution had finally caught on to the charm Joan and I had with the jurors, so they devised this threat of prosecution to Joan. The idea being, I suppose, if Inocencio was convicted the documents would have had no import, hence no need to prosecute the perpetrator. If Inocencio was found innocent, they could blame it on the documents and would be angry enough to seek retribution in the form of indicting Joan for stealing the very document that made acquittal possible. The more real threat I didn't want to face—that Web would file a complaint against me with the bar association and try to get them to take my license. For the moment I was maintaining my position of denial. He couldn't…

I was awake for the next blow up.

After Morely Tushman was excused, Bomber said, "The defense rests."

"No!" Inocencio shouted, jumping up from the defense table. "I want to talk."

Judge McCoy banged his gavel. "I warned you about your outbursts, young man. If you want to testify, tell your lawyer, don't shout in court."

"He says no. But it is my right."

"Sidebar, Gentlemen!" Judge McCoy said.

After we assembled, Judge McCoy leaned over to Bomber, "Why don't you let him testify? This has run its course—get it over with."

"Two reasons," Bomber said. "One, it will blow the case. The kid has no sense of human relations. He will lose every single juror, and two—he testifies, I resign."

"Bomber."

"I'm working for nothing as it is. I don't try cases with clients who tell me how to try them."

"Aren't you being a little thin-skinned?" the Judge asked.

"My duty is to do my best for my client. I give it my all. My experience tells me this defendant on the stand would be a disaster—definitely counter to his best interests. I would not be performing my job if I allowed it."

"But," Judge McCoy said, not without sympathy—even with a touch of apology in his voice, "I *have* to allow it."

"I would object and note an exception for the record."

"Bomber," Judge McCoy implored, "you know darn well if I refuse to let him testify in his own defense, I'd be reversed in five minutes in appellate court. My hands are tied. I suggest we take a recess and ask him what he wants to say. He might surprise you—it could even work to your advantage."

A glance at the district attorney told me he found that a shocking thought.

We took Inocencio to the conference room.

"All right, kid," Bomber began, "you got your wish. You can testify. What do you want to say?"

"I did not kill her."

"That's all?"

"Yeah—you want to ask another thing, ask what you want."

"I don't want to ask anything. But you can bet the district attorney will ask you questions till the cows come home.

He'll try to confuse you—rattle you—make you look like a fool to the jury—catch you in inconsistencies and then call you a liar whose word can't be trusted. It's a no-winner. I think we've established reasonable doubt, but not so strongly you couldn't blow it by taking the stand."

"I don't tell truth they think I am hide something, they think I am the killer."

Bomber stopped to stare at his client. He'd just put his finger on the downside. He couldn't be as stupid as Bomber had thought. I could tell Bomber was having an unwelcome epiphany. "That's true," he said, with a deliberation that surprised both Inocencio and me. "I am however willing to take that chance in the face of the ugly alternative—the district attorney demolishing you in the witness chair, rendering you a puddle of melted butter in preparation for spending the rest of your life in jail. You consider that, you still want to do it?"

"Yeah, I do. I am not guilty. I am not afraid."

Bomber nodded, as though the boy were talking gibberish. He knew he couldn't stop him from testifying, he could only hope to minimize the destruction.

"Okay kid," Bomber said at last, "it's your funeral. So tell me how you'd answer these questions," and Bomber asked him the hard ones. I thought the kid did pretty well with the friendly forces, I could tell Bomber did too. Then he gave him some advice for coping with the enemy. That was going to be tougher.

Inocencio seemed confident when he took the stand and took the oath he didn't believe in. I hoped the jury didn't think he was too cocky.

After the preliminaries, Bomber asked him directly, "Did you kill Madame Anna Claddington?"

"No!"

It was a convincing "No" all right. Then Bomber asked him, "Inocencio, it was your idea to testify, was it not?"

"Yes."

"And I advised against it, didn't I?"

"Yes, you did."

"Will you tell the jury what I told you my reasons were for opposing your testifying?"

"You said I was a rough young man. I might say everything okay and still make somebody angry in the jury. You said the jury don't always decide on the facts…how they like the person it makes a big difference, and people might not like me. They could not like my politics."

"Anything else?"

"Oh yeah, you say you think I am okay with your questions—we are on the same side, but the district attorney would turn what I say, to catch me changing my answers and try to make it seem like I don't tell truth so the jury could think I'm a liar."

"And what did you say to those objections?"

"I say that's loco. I didn't kill nobody. Nobody knows that like me. I could go to jail for all my life. It is bad and wrong if I don't tell everybody I didn't kill nobody. It would be like if I did tell them I won't be in jail."

I wondered if Bomber would catch the double negative: "I didn't kill nobody," which of course, literally means I *did* kill somebody.

"So let's be clear again. Have you ever in your life killed anybody?"

"No!"

"Did you ever own or even possess a gun?"

"No!"

"One final question, Inocencio—are you afraid of the district attorney?"

"No! I ain't afraid of nobody. You tell truth, you don't be afraid."

"Your witness," Bomber said, grinning at Web.

Web stood, a wan smile on his face, as if to say, "Not afraid of me, eh? We'll see about that."

"Inocencio, do you trust your attorney?"

Inocencio was surprised at the question—apparently Bomber had not anticipated it.

"Yeah, sure," he said with an unconvincing shrug.

"Trust him to give you good advice?"

"I guess."

"So did you disagree with any of those reasons he gave you for not testifying?"

"No. I agree with them all."

"So why are you testifying?"

Bomber was about to object, but thought the kid could handle it—again. "Just like I told Mr. Bomber. I sit here and listen to people lie about me, and I can't take it no more. They don't like my politics—so okay—I don't like theirs either. All I know for sure is I don't kill nobody. I want people to be equal, I don't want to kill them."

"Are you familiar with a man named Joseph Stalin?"

"Yes."

"And Vladimir Lenin?"

"Sí."

"Communists, were they?"

"Yes."

"As you are also a communist?"

"Yes," Inocencio said, with his head high.

"Heroes of yours?"

"I don't have no heroes."

"Were you aware of the millions of people *they* had killed?"

"There were wars…"

"Their own people."

Bomber said from his seat, "You know this is a very nice history lesson, but unless Stalin or Lenin killed Madame Anna Claddington, it doesn't seem too relevant here."

"Are you objecting?" Judge McCoy asked.

"I am."

"I'll overrule it."

"All right, Inocencio," Web said, "those communists were responsible for the deaths of millions of their own people, so how can you say you are a communist, as though that would make it impossible for you to kill one person?"

"Stalin said, when one person dies it is tragedy. Millions die is a statistic. If Stalin kills millions, okay. *I* didn't kill nobody."

"So you say," Web said skeptically, "but realistically, didn't you find Madame Claddington a frivolous, useless member of society who represented capitalism at its worst? I mean, wasn't she a woman of obscene wealth whose money could have fed a hundred families or more?"

Bomber shook his head. "Compound—objection."

"Sustained."

"Alright, one at a time then. You pick which you want to answer first."

"Look," Inocencio said, starting to get angry. I crossed my fingers he wouldn't blow, "It would be a waste to kill her. She was so old she was dying. There is this saying, 'Never murder nobody who's committing suicide.'" (Warm smiles all around for that one. Not Web, of course.) The district attorney was maintaining a dead-serious demeanor, but Inocencio was still hot under the collar. "Now the husband, he was the capitalist pig who kills pigs to get rich giving fat to poor people— bacon, sausage, ham—killing her wouldn't do nothing for communism, and I didn't do it."

"Lot of people say you did kill her."

"Lot of people are wrong."

"Do you think they are framing you?"

"I object," Bomber said, raising a hand from his seat. "The defendant is not a mind reader."

"Yeah," he said anyway. "They are framing me."

"Are you familiar with the word paranoia?"

"No, I…"

"Imagining people are out to get you," Web explained.

"You think I'm paranoia get yourself in my place. I'm in a trial for a murder I didn't do…"

"Your Honor, *please* tell the witness to limit his responses to answers to my questions."

Judge McCoy dutifully did so.

Web got meaner. It was as though he were trying to try cases like Bomber did—but it was not Web's nature to be mean and aggressive and it came across as a terrible pose. But the meaner he got the tougher Inocencio was. He didn't rattle him—the district attorney caught him in only minor and meaningless inconsistencies which Inocencio was able to logically explain. All in all, the kid was a triumph, and when Web finally threw in the sponge, Bomber in a most uncharacteristic gesture actually stood to greet his penniless client as he returned to his seat at the defendant table—in full view of all he patted the obstreperous lad on the shoulder and whispered—the kind everyone could hear—"Good work."

"The defense," Bomber said with visible relief, "rests."

THIRTY-SEVEN

WEBSTER A. GRAINGER III, our august district attorney, or someone in his office—no doubt with Web's blessing—leaked to the newspapers the surprise finding of the murder weapon. Naturally the article was written as though this cooked the goose of our client—and ran along with a picture of Inocencio that made him look his demonic best.

Bomber came to court the next morning, armed with a copy of the paper. Before the jury came in, he asked Judge McCoy if he could speak to this outrage—this haphazard and blatant disregard for the cannon of ethics. This cheap shot to influence jurors. "If I'd known the district attorney was going to pull a trick like this, I'd have asked for a sequestered jury. And there isn't a scintilla of proof, it's all innuendo—pure and simple. It's a travesty on our justice system, a disgrace to anyone touched by the law—anyone hoping for a shred of fairness. On behalf of my client I ask that this outrage be exposed in the strongest terms from the bench—God knows verdicts have risen or fallen on much less than this."

Judge McCoy smiled indulgently. "Who are you turning on the charm for, Bomber? The jury is not in the courtroom—or didn't you notice?"

"Sorry, Your Honor, I just get carried away when I see flagrant abuses of the system—of trust itself. I'm doing my best for my beleaguered client and at the eleventh hour we're hit between the eyes with this too-calculated surprise. I'm bound to tell you, I think they had the gun all along—but try as they might they couldn't tie it to the defendant, so they opted for this last minute, baseless smear, in hopes the emotion would carry the day."

"I resent the implication," Web said in a huff.

"Resent away—you can't undo this damage."

"What do you want to do, counsel?" Judge McCoy asked, which I thought was a tacit acknowledgment of Bomber's tirade.

"I want the record set straight," Bomber said. "I want the district attorney to apologize to the court and jury for this skunk trick and I respectfully petition this court to tell the jury—now and in his charge to the jury—that this sensational bit of hokum is bogus. That there is not the slightest evidence that this gun was ever *touched* by the defendant, that inferences to the contrary are heavy handed, duplicitous and without the slightest foundation."

"Webster?"

"As usual Bomber is getting carried away with the sound of his own voice. We found the gun at the last minute. Would he have us suppress the evidence? I frankly don't think there is anything to apologize for. The fact that we have not been able to get convincing proof that it belonged to the defendant is self-evident and I'm sure Bomber will highlight that in the cross-examination as well as his, closing argument. Anything else is melodrama."

"All right," the judge said.

"And, Your Honor," Bomber said, "in the matter of the evidence itself, I move it be quashed for want of connection to the defendant at the bar of *justice*. It is inflammatory, highly prejudicial and without any foundation whatsoever."

Judge McCoy was on the spot. I think Bomber had a good argument, but a murder case without the weapon is a hard sell. They found a weapon—when and how remained to be seen. He decided to let the gun come in, but would instruct the jury in his charge of the absence of any connection, if that proved to be the case.

The witness was one of those kids who makes even me feel old. It was obvious Web had cleaned him up as best he could, but I half expected the kid to answer his occupation was surfer.

"I'm just kind of hanging out at the moment," he said instead.

"Have you held any jobs?" the district attorney asked.

"Oh yeah. I washed some dishes at the Café La Mer, I did some security guard work, a little bartending at private parties. Nothing too steady."

"Very good."

If we thought that was Web's idea of very good I'd have to acknowledge some slippage in my esteem for him, which in any case was not over the top, but somewhat higher than Bomber's.

The question revealed the kid—whose name was rather incidentally Eric Johnson—had not found the gun himself, but had been mysteriously handed it by a drifter at the beach. (I notice Web didn't ask Eric if he would characterize himself as a drifter.) The guy said he'd found it on the beach behind the house where the murder happened and thought nothing of it until the case hit the papers. Apparently, he was sleeping on a pile of the papers when he turned over and read the article. Now the drifter felt he would be suspect himself, and he wanted to be free of the gun and let them do with it what they wanted. He wanted out. So Eric took it off his hands, thought of trying to sell it or hock it, but then got the idea *he* could be a suspect, so he just decided to turn it into the cops and tell the truth.

Web let the narrative run and decide to let it stand on its own.

"Your witness," he said to Bomber.

Bomber could have made corned beef hash of the kid, but instead tried to make a few points through the dubious circumstances.

"Mr. Johnson," he said glowering over the lad who was already showing alarming signs of discomfort, "when exactly did you come into possession of this gun?"

"I don't know exactly—a couple of weeks ago."

"Could it have been six weeks?"

"Six? Gees, I don't know. Time flies for me sometimes."

"So if I said six, you couldn't argue?"

He shrugged. "Guess not."

"Eight?"

"Oh—I don't think it could have been that long."

"But you aren't sure?"

"As I said…"

"Time flies," Bomber finished his sentence.

"Your Honor," Web interrupted.

"Yes, Mr. Hanson, let Mr. Johnson answer his own questions."

"Very good," Bomber said. "So you held on to this gun for six or eight weeks?"

"No, I didn't say that. That's just when I got it."

"How long *did* you hold on to it before you took it to the cops?"

"Couple days."

"Couple days?" Bomber was astonished. "So the district attorney had the gun six or eight weeks?"

"Objection—he didn't give it to me. He doesn't know how long I had it."

Bomber smiled and didn't care that the judge said, "Sustained." "Very interesting," Bomber said, looking at Web, who started to open his mouth.

"Save your comments on the testimony for your closing argument, Mr. Hanson."

"I stand corrected. Now, Mr. Johnson, do you know what the cops did with the gun?"

"I guess they gave it to the district attorney."

"Objection—strike that—speculative."

"Yes, strike it from the record. The jury is to disregard the speculation."

"Did they *tell* you what they were going to do with it?"

"No."

"Have you seen the man who gave you the gun since he gave it to you?"

"No."

"Had you seen him before that?"

"I may have seen him around. I don't remember anything specific."

"Were you acquainted with the district attorney or anyone of his associates—anyone in his office before you came into possession of the gun?"

"Nah."

"Did you know Attorney Morely Tushman?"

"No."

"The Presidential candidate, Otto Underwood?"

He snickered, "No!"

"Zachary Roseleer—under any of his aliases?"

"Not that I know of."

The well was dry. The kid was not particularly believable, but Bomber couldn't get anything out of him. It was indicative of the whole case—lot of suspicions, no smoking gun.

Ballistics expert Van Wert was back on the stand. Web asked him a couple of questions establishing it was the gun that matched the bullet that had been dug out of Madame Anna Poritzky Claddington's skull.

Bomber, on cross-examination, asked if Van Wert could tell who fired the gun.

The expert smiled and said, "No," though it looked like he was about to say, "You know better."

When Bomber asked when Van Wert got possession of the gun he squirmed and looked at the district attorney. "Six, maybe seven weeks ago," he said.

"Maybe eight weeks ago?"

Van Wert shrugged as though it were of no consequence. "Possible," he said.

That night on my way home I heard on our classical radio station a news snippet that said Otto Underwood had slipped in the polls, putting him for the first time behind his strongest challenger.

At home above the garage, Joan and I did some Brahms duets, and it put me in mind of his lullaby, and I must have fallen asleep at the piano for all I remember.

It was a good thing too, for I wanted to be alert for the closing arguments the next morning.

THIRTY-EIGHT

THESE DAYS BOMBER SELDOM had a case that didn't sell out the house. It was by far the best free entertainment in town.

But today the room seemed fuller—more bodies per square foot—claustrophobic almost. Then I discovered why that was. Since Joan had been coming to court, my customary scanning of the audience for witnesses and surprises (or *both*) became (or so I thought) more subtle. I wouldn't say my glancing behind me while I sat at the defendant table was so much sur-reptitious as it was casual, as if the gesture of turning my head and body were an unconscious, even insouciant gesture.

Today I began my casual turn when I did a double take that would have made Keystone Kops hang up their badges. For while I had my back to the crowd and was trying to cheer up Inocencio, our client, who had slipped into the courtroom but *my mother!* And she was sitting, chatting away as though they were old friends, *with Joan!* Before I could dwell on the subterfuge that must have brought about this meeting, Bomber came hustling down the aisle a second before the judge came in. It was almost as though the latter was waiting until the former were in place to make his entrance. Or was he trying to forestall any questions about his wife cozying up to my girl-friend?

I had to force myself to concentrate on the proceedings, my mind was spinning with thoughts and speculations about dear mom and my beloved Joan. It made me wonder if some women felt their only mission in life was to reproduce

(Inocencio would say to prolong the agony) and once that was accomplished their charge was to see that every unmarried male was coupled with an unmarried female to the same end.

Bomber had been good about respecting my privacy. At first I thought it was disinterest and self-absorption on his part, but now I realize he's just giving me space.

I'm afraid I only half listened to the district attorney as he began his closing argument. I knew he was going to rehash the testimony for his side, but my mind was on how my mom brought off this meeting with Joan. Bomber *had* to have told Mom, because I didn't.

Now with them sitting together—the two most important women in my life—I could just imagine Mom prattling on about some unconscious belittling episode in my life. Something that would make me look like a klutz or a dumbo or both.

"And that's how it happened, pure and simple," the district attorney was saying in earnest to the jury. I don't know why Web's earnestness always struck a false note with me. He was a good old boy all right, but I always pictured him at the country club hoisting a cocktail with his buddies. He didn't seem so comfortable in his prosecutor's skin. He was like a guy drawn to teaching because the hours were good.

"*Three* witnesses said that was the way it happened, ladies and gentlemen, the defendant says not. Naturally. He has no desire to pay his debt to society. You should always be aware of the self-interest factor when you weigh the testimony of both sides.

"Now, it is painfully obvious defending counsel is concocting a fairy tale to try and manufacture reasonable doubt. He is a well-known trickster, and you have to be on your toes to separate the real—the *facts* I just reviewed with you—from the fanciful. Bomber's is a fantasy scenario, which I'm sure he will try to sell you again.

"Don't buy! It is bogus goods he's pushing in the hope you will say, 'Oh well, I guess there is some doubt'.

"There is *always* doubt, ladies and gentlemen. But our standards require it be *reasonable* doubt—not fanciful, not capricious.

"Doubt—doubt," Web said, "reasonable doubt. I daresay there is nothing in this world reasonable people could not doubt if they set their mind to it. Bomber Hanson, it must by now come as no news to you, is the Master of Obfuscation. It's his middle name. But don't be fooled with studies, don't be fooled with outlandish scenarios. If I understood him correctly—and I'm not at all sure I did, and I don't see how you could be either—his theory is that a dying man left his sickbed or couch, snuck outside where no one saw him, disposed of the weapon on the sand, then blithely snuck back in the house, and crawled back under the covers on the couch as though nothing happened? In the meantime the defendant is outside taking the rap?" Web lifted an eyebrow to show what he thought of that statement.

"Ladies and gentlemen, the doubt must be *reasonable*—not fanciful.

"If you put any stock in Bomber's outlandish theories, you might as well believe the moon is made of green cheese.

"Reasonable doubt, Ladies and Gentlemen, has the emphasis on the first word, not the last—as Bomber would have you believe. I can't remember a case where I've had *less* doubt. But are we being reasonable to turn our backs on all the people who were there? Yes, I'll include the chauffeur—he didn't hurt our case, as Bomber would like to have you believe. We didn't call him because he couldn't *add* anything.

"He most decidedly did not say he saw the man dying of AIDS rise up from his sickbed and make the circuitous route around the backyard to position himself just so he could take a perfect shot at Madame Claddington, without anyone seeing him, then trundle right back to the couch, crawling back under the covers. A neat trick when you think of it, ladies and gentlemen, I submit that any doubt that creates in your mind is not *reasonable,* by evidentiary standards in the courtroom.

"I don't know about you, ladies and gentlemen, but I get weary of punk kids telling us to jump off a tall bridge. Take the defendant—you saw him act out his juvenile psychosis— I'm sorry you had to be subjected to it. To me, Ladies and Gentlemen, he has guilt written all over him. His outrageous acts are a transparent cover.

"Bomber's theory of the crime is fanciful—wishful thinking. It would be nice if a fall guy stepped in and made a clean break of it. But it was not to be. The idea that Morely Tushman, a highly respected attorney from Chicago, or Otto Underwood, candidate for president, had anything to do with this murder is ludicrous. And what does Bomber theorize? He says Morely Tushman's friend did it as a favor to the attorney. Imagine! Some favor. But Bomber did have the sense to hang his crepe on a dead man. *They* tell no tales, Ladies and Gentlemen.

"It is pure and simple obfuscation. It is a red herring. Above all it is wishful thinking.

"Now the gun, Ladies and Gentlemen. Certainly we didn't make a circus out of it. We tried to research it—trace its origins. Certainly we tried to tie it to the defendant—that is our job. We were unsuccessful in making a positive link to the defendant—but that doesn't mean he didn't use it. It is the gun.

"Ladies and Gentlemen, don't let Bomber mislead you. Otto Underwood is not a radical. It serves Bomber's scenario, but that is *all* that speculation is good for. Otto Underwood is a fine, upstanding American—he's no threat to the U.S. Why, this kid at the defendant's table—this Inocencio Espinal—is

more of a threat in his insignificant way than Otto Underwood
could ever be."

I thought he identified him by name so the jurors wouldn't
think he was talking about me.

"Inocencio Espinal is the one who professes to want to
replace our economic system with communism, and Otto
Underwood is a patriot who at great personal sacrifice is
running for president of the United States. I ask you, which
would you want to control your destiny, Otto Underwood or
Inocencio Espinal? Think about it in your deliberations,
Ladies and Gentlemen. Which of them would you have lead
your country?"

Then, unhappily, my thoughts turned back to Joan and
mom, what *had* they talked about? How did they connect? So
I missed Web's winding down. I tuned in sporadically and
nothing of consequence jiggled the air. Web wasn't much of
a speaker, I'm sad to say. Not that Bomber needed more competition, but it would make things more interesting.

When Web finished his thanks-for-your-service windup I
checked the juror's faces: impassive—could I even say bored?
I had to check myself—I was getting too cocky—and nothing
sets you up for a rude shock more than getting too cocky.
Cocky I suppose comes from the chicken who is cock of the
walk, which melds nicely into the grand Australian saying:
"Rooster today, feather duster tomorrow."

Judge McCoy called a recess before the great Bomber got
his say. So I was faced with the awkward situation of introducing my girlfriend to my mother whom she had already
met. I was half hoping Bomber had some errand for me—like
he forgot something at the office he just had to have for his
speech. No such luck.

I made a large show of reading my blank tablet, paging
through it as though searching for something indispensable,
hoping that by the time I could put it off no longer, I would

turn around and they would be gone. Then it suddenly occurred to me if that *were* the case, perhaps it would be because Mom scared Joan off with some outlandish tales about me—when I got my paranoia in check I realized scaring Joan off was the last thing Mom wanted—so I bit the bullet and turned. I got half my wish. Joan was waiting for me alone. I hastened to her side, gave her a hug and said, "So you met my mom" at exactly the moment she said, "I met your mom— she's delightful."

"Phew," I said. "She didn't tell you any off-putting tales about me?"

"On the contrary," she said, "she was singing your praises. I was getting the idea I'd better stay on my toes or all these eager local women would snap you up."

"Ha! She told you that?"

"Not in so many words, maybe."

"Where *is* she?"

"Went to the ladies room. Said when you turned and saw her with me you got this crestfallen look on your face, so she thought she should make herself scarce. That's not *true,* is it, Tod?"

"Well, you've got to understand. She *never* comes to court. I don't think Bomber is comfortable with her in the audience. He never said so, it's just my sense of it. So to see her here sitting next to you—I guess she just couldn't wait to meet you—and I can't blame her for that—best day of my life when I met you."

"Oh, Tod," she said—just as the bailiff called us back to order and Bomber appeared from the back of the courtroom walking down the center aisle with his arm around Mom as though it were a wedding ceremony for crying out loud. I don't know when the last time I saw such a public display of intimacy; it was a far cry from him not wanting her in court. Then I realized the old ham was making a show for the jury, which was just being brought in. It was as if he were saying 'Webster A. Grainger III, let's see you match *this*.' I don't doubt Web would have matched it, had he any inkling that Bomber would pull such a stunt.

It was, as I thought of it, not a gesture that should build any confidence in our client. I feared that Bomber had serious qualms about his case and was grasping at peripheral straws to win points with those twelve judges.

THIRTY-NINE

"WELL, THIS IS IT, KID," Bomber said to Inocencio when he sat awaiting the judge.

McCoy came in and nodded to Bomber. When Bomber rose to begin, Inocencio put his hand on his arm, looked up at Bomber and said, "Thank you."

Bomber looked so startled, I think it put him off his feed; then realizing another opportunity, patted Inocencio's hand and winked at him, then turned to stride to one of his favorite positions—in front of the jury box, where he could connect with those twelve judges of fact, and in some cases of fiction.

"Ladies and Gentlemen, thank you for your kind attention during this trial. It is people like you who make our best of all systems work. Dedicated people from all walks of life who listen patiently to a lot of testimony—and to be sure, bickering—some of it tedious; but you listened, Ladies and Gentlemen, and I thank you for it. Now you get to sort out all the palaver and try to make sense of this bizarre case—and it is a case of a seemingly unpleasant young man and his political beliefs. He's a communist. There I said it, and you know it already. I can see us getting worked up about communists thirty, forty, fifty years ago—I got worked up myself while I proudly wore the insignia of an airforce bombardier in Korea. But today? The Berlin wall is down—they are selling chunks of it for souvenirs; Russia is in a shambles; Vietnam is a hotbed of capitalism, as is my beloved Korea.

"Today it is a big stretch to get worked up about a poor

commie. And have no fear my client is in any position to over-throw the U.S. government.

"No, this poor misguided lad was the fall guy for a big en-chilada in our capitalist society on his way to being the leader of our country. The ramblings of one old woman who probably had no thought of spilling the beans, threatened the candidate until he shook in his boots. He thought unless Madame Anna Poritzky Claddington was silenced, he would lose the election—and well he might, just from the informa-tion we have gathered for this trial."

Bomber went on and on about the glories of capitalism and the failure of communism. I thought he overdid it, but Bomber speaks without notes which lends itself to the danger of excess. Perhaps he was trying to convince the jurors just because he was defending a commie, he certainly wasn't one himself.

"Now, if you want to fry Inocencio for his beliefs, so be it. I can't stop you—Inocencio can't stop you. Only your com-passion and good sense can stop you.

"True, my client seems to have gone out of his way to ag-gravate you. And I ask you in the spirit of fairness, the spirit of justice, to put emotional considerations out of your minds and focus on the strange facts of the case, and be large enough spirits to recognize there is very reasonable doubt here. Very reasonable indeed.

"Otto Underwood in his youth, held similarly unpopular beliefs. He went so far as to make bombs to get the attention of the establishment. Now he is running for president.

"My friends—someone leaked the existence of that use-less, worthless piece of evidence, the gun, to the newspapers, and those lords and ladies of the press ran a picture of my client with the story the gun had been found. Found… yes…some two months before that story ran—but no matter—they treated it as late breaking news, which if I might speculate, probably didn't displease the district attorney.

"Six weeks! Maybe two months they hid that knowledge from us while they were frantically trying to tie it to the defendant in this case, Inocencio Espinal. And in all that time, with all the resources of the government machine, they were not able to turn over one shred of evidence connecting that vaunted gun to my client.

"Now I am bound to tell you, my client is a simple man. You heard him on the stand. You judge him. We may see naïvete, we may see unsophistication, but what we don't see, Ladies and Gentlemen, is a murderer. Nor do we see a complex, highly intelligent and cunning soul who could manage to secure a weapon that could absolutely not be traced to him. Why, if Inocencio *had* done this foul deed, I'm afraid the evidence would stare at us from every billboard on the planet. He would have bungled it, big time.

"Now, Attorney Morely Tushman is a horse of a different color. Suave, sophisticated, cunning, clever. If *he* had to, I'd have full confidence in his ability to secure an untraceable gun. Chicago is not a mob-free town. It is not too great a stretch to imagine Attorney Tushman—or someone else, Harley Holiday perhaps—would have connections that would secure an untraceable handgun for this hit.

"Is the gun Inocencio's? Of course not. Inocencio is innocent.

"Compare the motives—making a statement for economic equality by an immigrant kid, versus silencing an old woman who could cost an ambitious man the presidency. I don't know but what the accomplices might have been in for some prestigious government jobs like attorney general. Speculation, I'll grant you, but you are entitled to speculate when a man's life and liberty are at stake.

"Ah, but the district attorney is woefully misguided about

the significance of the gun and where it was found and by whom. Suppose it was not found on the beach, but in the county dump instead? Wouldn't that weaken their story that the defendant displayed a movement of his arm that was really throwing the murder weapon in the Pacific Ocean?

"So they found a gun, which, try as they did, they could not trace to the defendant. They have his fingerprints on file— every prisoner is fingerprinted. There is no evidence the defendant had gloves on when he stood in the backyard and made that defensive gesture with his arm. You can bet the ranch they tried everything to get the defendant's fingerprints from that gun—but they didn't succeed for the simple reason his prints were not on it because he didn't fire it! Doubt? Very reasonable doubt. The closest they came to nailing him with any gun was the talk of that big mountain in his pants. I leave it to you to work that out. One after the other of the puppets said they saw Inocencio throw a gun in the ocean. No one heard a splash, and no one looked for it. Strange? Damn strange in my book.

"Did Inocencio throw a gun in the ocean? Of course not! Inocencio is innocent.

"Put yourself out there on the Fourth of July with the Madame and her entourage. It is dark. The ocean surf is pounding the shoreline. Fireworks of startling magnitude are popping in the sky. So how was it, with this egregious distraction, all the flunkies were watching Inocencio, who was standing in the other direction—*away* from the fireworks?

"Now, Ladies and Gentlemen, you heard Attorney Tushman say the key notes he squirreled away in his secret safe were just doodles. If he looks like a man who acts impulsively, or carelessly, he looks different to you than he does to me.

"Madame Claddington had the goods on Otto Underwood, my friends. It gives me no pleasure to say so. Otto Underwood is running for the highest office in this great land of ours and has set himself up with a new persona as politicians so often do—a persona so perfectly drawn that his survival depends on maintaining it. The goods Madame Claddington had on Otto Underwood about the underground would have sunk his ship. And if I can believe what I read, those goods are already sinking his ship.

"Do I have a case I can prove? I have some doubt about it. The man I think did the shooting is dead, so I can't bring him before you to question him—to take his measure. Dick Funkhauser was his name. He was the companion—lover, whatever you want to call him—of Morely Tushman. He was also a crack marksman.

"Morely Tushman is in bed with Otto Underwood. Harley Holiday, their bodyguard, tried to kill my son. Zachary Roseleer tried to silence Madame Claddington but she wouldn't silence. It was not her nature.

"I submit, it was a simple matter for the gunman to escape notice when all attention was drawn to this innocent Inocencio. The trip from the living room to the ocean and back could have been accomplished in about a minute.

"I'm bound to tell you, I am as proud as a parent could be at my son's handling of the witness Avery Knapp. That expert police witness, who should know if anyone does, said an expert marksman such as Dick Funkhauser was, could do the deed in one second. So we aren't talking about a lot of time. There was no evidence presented that said Inocencio even knew how to hold a gun.

"The policeman didn't check Inocencio's hands for powder burns—but I can tell you something, if he had, he wouldn't have found any. Now, Lawyer Tushman must have known about powder burns—did he insist they check the defendant's hands? Did *he* check them himself? Of course not. Inocencio didn't shoot Madame Claddington.

"Inocencio had no powder burns on his hands. Inocencio is innocent.

"I don't mean to belittle the district attorney's argument, but this case is not about who we want to lead our country. It isn't an election, it isn't a popularity contest. I don't doubt Otto Underwood would prevail in both those tests.

"I've had a long career, Ladies and Gentlemen, and I hope you won't begrudge me a few mistakes. I hadn't wanted my client to testify. I'm frank to admit I thought he would offend you. I thought the far more sophisticated Webster A. Grainger the third would tie him in knots and throw him to the sharks.

"But I was wrong about my client, and I apologize to him for it. Inocencio fooled me, Ladies and Gentlemen. I told him he was an unpleasant person and the outbursts you saw were unforgivable and he's lucky the judge was forbearing and didn't pile contempt of court onto the burden of charges he is already bearing. But, how many of us could put ourselves in Inocencio's place? On trial for a murder we know we didn't commit, but one that looks like a slamdunk case against us. Ladies and Gentlemen, it's the worst nightmare we can imagine. I deal with people accused of crime day in and day out, and, I must tell you, I *still* can't imagine it. I'm not sure I want to—for I might just be dragged down with the horror of it all.

"But, my friends, think for a moment of this young lad on the stand struggling for life itself. No one can project innocence like the innocent—Inocencio is an innocent—he proved that yesterday. And he *is* innocent. *How* did he prove it? Not just by sitting there and saying, 'I'm innocent'—No, he did it by omission. Remember he was sitting here just as you were throughout the trial, listening to all the witnesses, and he heard as you did the theory that Dick Funkhauser, may he rest in peace, was the assassin. He was an expert marksman, he had the beginnings of a disease for which there is no known cure, he owed Lawyer Tushman big time—Tushman was Otto Underwood's Illinois lawyer, remember, and Madame Anna Claddington had threatened to blow his campaign right out of the water.

"So, armed with that intelligence, what did Inocencio do? Did he, as most of us might have been tempted to do, did he throw the blame? Did he say he saw Dick Funkhauser sneak into position and pull the trigger? Inocencio was the only one who might have seen the maneuver—not an impossible task as the district attorney would have you believe. I hope, Ladies and Gentlemen, it doesn't cost him his life and liberty to be so honest, but Inocencio refused to take that easy out. Instead he spoke truthfully when he said he was watching the fireworks and saw nothing else. And he spoke truthfully when he said he did not kill Madame Anna Poritzky Claddington!

"How could Inocencio afford to be so honest? Because, ladies and gentlemen, Inocencio is innocent.

"Now, I don't know about you, my esteemed jurors, but if I were going to shoot someone—out in the open in front of four or five witnesses, I would instantly make a run for it. The defendant is young and strong—I expect he could have outrun everyone of those oldsters—all the way to Mexico if necessary. At least he could disappear somewhere in the Fourth of July crowd with the fireworks bursting in air—*any*where!

"Did Inocencio run? Of course not. Inocencio didn't shoot her. Inocencio is innocent.

"Peter Williams, Madame's chauffeur, was the only other witness with the guts to admit the fireworks were distracting from everything else. That's why they planned it that way, don't you see? Peter Williams was not beholden to Attorney Morely Tushman—only to his conscience. He didn't see Inocencio throw any gun, and he had the guts to say so. Naturally, the prosecution didn't call him as a witness because he didn't conform to their story. *I* had to call him—and I'm glad

I did. Stack him against Attorney Morely Tushman any day of the week and that perfectly turned out, perfectly controlled fop comes out second best. And I can sympathize with his loss of his lover. But we are concerned here with the living, not the dead. Are you going to throw to the wolves this young man with his whole life ahead of him on the word of Attorney Morely Tushman and his collection of sycophants, who all seem to have the same speechwriter; or are you going to search your hearts for the preponderance of evidence that says we have *more* than *reasonable doubt* that this innocent Inocencio should *not* be locked up for the rest of his life for a crime he did not commit? Have the courage of your convictions, ladies and gentlemen. Please be strong. Return a verdict of not guilty.

"Life is sacred. Your life, my life, my client Inocencio's life…all sacred. Remember, please, ladies and gentlemen, it is your sacred duty to acquit an innocent man. And, Inocencio…" Bomber paused, "…*is* innocent.

"God bless you—do your sacred duty, and God *will* bless you."

When Bomber returned to our table, Inocencio jumped up and embraced him.

FORTY

THE DISTRICT ATTORNEY'S rebuttal did not surprise—he replayed his old themes, waving the American flag of his troops against the hammer and sickle of ours.

The judge charged the jury in his usual boring fashion. He did plug our point about no inference should be drawn from the found gun inasmuch as it could not be tied to the defendant. I like the way he said that, leaving open the possibility that it could be tied to someone else.

Inocencio was taken back into custody, I hoped for the last time. He would await the verdict in the police station jail.

When we connected with Joan and Mom—Mom preempted the conversation, and to my embarrassment said, "Oh Tod, she's *wonderful*," as though Joan weren't there. I smiled, a thin, sickly smile.

"I'm glad you like her," I said. Then I turned to Joan, "Of course, before you get too big a head over it, you should know Mom would adore Sheena of the Jungle if she thought it might result in a grandchild."

We repaired to the Mexican place over on Antonio Street—Bomber's favorite. "I like poor food," he liked to say, eschewing places that he claimed laid a stick of butter on you at each meal. "Like eating a ton of popped corn," he would say.

We settled into our cheap-o plastic chairs, after ordering at the window of the place that had been a Foster Freeze in a former mutation.

Joan asked, "How do you stand the suspense?"

"I don't," Bomber said. "Never have. You'd think you'd get used to it, take it in stride, but I'm so wound up, I can't let go until I hear the verdict."

"And that was with almost all of them being favorable," Mom said.

"Would it be bad luck if I asked if you thought you were going to win this one?" Joan asked.

Bomber smiled his most ingratiating—geez, I'd even have to say—flirty smile, "It wouldn't be bad luck to ask, but it would be for me to answer. Ask Tod what he thinks."

She turned to me—I'd kept my mouth shut so I wouldn't stutter in front of Joan. I'd told her about it, but telling and displaying were two different things, "I'm al…ways op…tim…ist…ic." I slowed my speech down so much I managed not to stammer over any of the syllables, but no one was fooled by what I was doing.

When the food came, Bomber raved about it as he always did, then turned to Joan. "You know, you weren't here to see it, but Tod made me very proud the way he handled himself when he had to step in for me in court. The district attorney made a fool of himself getting me recused on the thinnest grounds. Apparently thought Tod would fall on his face. Well, I'll tell you, he did *better* than I could have—there was enormous good feeling in the courtroom. A lot of pulling for him, you know, he'd make a great trial lawyer."

It was another opportunity for me to blush.

Joan dutifully complimented the food, and during a lull asked—

"Bomber—do you believe your scenario of the case?"

"With time, believing in anything gets more difficult. I certainly believe it more than I believe that beleaguered kid murdered that old woman. The jury has two options to engage their belief mechanisms. We will see which one they select."

"Will we ever know the truth?"

"Do we ever?" he asked. "Truth is the most elusive thing in the world. The journalists are digging into the Otto Underwood underground thing. Things are beginning to surface. So many things, I expect he'll be out of the race before you know it."

I asked Joan if she'd heard from the LA Philharmonic.

"Oh—yeah—just today. I got the audition."

I gave her a big hug and a chaste kiss on the cheek—was it in an effort to fool my mom and dad into thinking it was a platonic relationship? Pretty silly.

"How self-effacing. You didn't even mention it," Mom said.

"Well, I didn't want to detract from the big event at hand."

After we finished, we went back to the office. On the way in the Bentley Joan said, "Wouldn't it be nice if they reached a verdict already?"

"Probably not so nice," Bomber said. "An early verdict usually favors the prosecution."

"Oh—why?"

"Nobody knows for sure. But if we speculate, I'd say we start out in criminal cases believing the accused is guilty."

"Why?"

"Most of them are. The police don't often arrest the wrong person. If they do, it doesn't usually go to trial. So you have that. And prosecution cases are usually straightforward fact things. The defense requires some complex thought."

"Oh, Bomber," Mom said, "aren't you giving yourself too much credit?"

He smiled as he might not have, had Joan not been there. "Anything wrong with that?" he said. "Then too, maybe a prosecution more often has a slamdunk case, as it is known as in the parlance of the enemy."

We went to the office where Bonnie Doone was sitting by the phone to field any call to return for a verdict. The jury would be locked up overnight if they didn't reach a verdict—which was an extra impetus to return with a verdict.

It may have been my imagination, but I thought Bonnie was eyeing Joan with something akin to jealousy. I'd never ask her, because she'd never admit it.

Bonnie Doone bade us goodbye, and Bomber suggested we all go home. Mom was the only one to take him up on it. Joan wanted to stay a while longer.

Mom wasn't gone ten minutes when the phone call came to tell us the jury had reached a verdict.

Bomber sighed. Relief? Disappointment? We went to the courthouse. It was pretty empty. It was eight-fifteen at night. Web was already there.

Our party was fairly gloomy because it was, we thought, too soon to bode any good news for our side.

It all happened so fast.

"Have you reached a verdict?"

"We have, Your Honor."

"Hand it to the bailiff."

The bailiff took it and handed it to the judge. He looked at it and handed it back to the bailiff to read. Of course the judge didn't glance at either side and struggled to keep his expression passive.

The bailiff read, "We, the members of the jury in the case of the state of California versus Inocencio Espinal find the defendant Inocencio Espinal not guilty."

Inocencio jumped up and shouted, giving a two fisted salute. Judge McCoy opened his mouth to reprimand him, then closed it and smiled. I suppose he realized he might have done the same.

Hugs all around—Inocencio was free to go. We walked out together and when he got an eyeful of Bomber's red Bentley, I thought his eyeballs would roll on the sidewalk. Bomber noticed it. "Want to drive it?" he said.

"Oh, man—would you let me?"

Those were my sentiments exactly. Bomber waved to the driver's seat and handed him the keys. Bomber got in beside him—Joan and I sat in the back. What if he smashes it, I wondered. He'd had that accident when he was twelve.

Well, he did all right, but I was so consumed with jealousy when we left Inocencio off at his Uncle's house, I could not contain my feelings.

"Bomber," I said, "how c-come you l-let Inocencio drive your car and I n-never did?"

Bomber thought a moment, "I guess I never thought I had to sell you on the joys and benefits of capitalism."

"Sell me," I said.

"Okay," he said. "You did such a good job on this one—I think you, and Joan of course—are why we won this case— come on up," he said, pulling over to the curb, getting out and hopping in the back seat with Joan.

And I drove the Chinese red Bentley for the first time in my life.